Charlie Williams was born in
He went to Swansea University, and then worked in
London for several years. He now lives in
Worcestershire with his wife and children. His first
novel, *Deadfolk*, was published by Serpent's Tail in
2004. *Fags and Lager* takes up life in Mangel once
again.

Praise for *Deadfolk*

'Charlie Williams has come up trumps ... the more
politically correct among you can read this as social
comment, the rest can just enjoy the ride' *Guardian*

'There is a dark heart to England, a claustrophobic
core of oddity and violence. *Deadfolk* comes straight
from this English heart, and even through all of its
offbeat humour, there is no mistaking the earnestness
of a writer who has something to say' Nicholas
Blincoe

'Cross James Ellroy's unblinking eye for vicious gang-
land enforcement with Bill James's gut-feeling for
Britain's meaner streets and you would end up in a
trashcan alley somewhere near Mangel ... I can't wait
for the next instalment' *Western Daily Press*

'Plenty of memorably grim moments along the way'
Big Issue in the North

'Carnage, chaos and a chainsaw called Susan add to
his remarkable debut, which marks the appearance of
a totally new voice in British fiction' *Buzz*

fags and lager

charlie williams

A complete catalogue record for this book can be
obtained from the British Library on request

The right of Charlie Williams to be identified as the
author of this work has been asserted by him in
accordance with the Copyright, Designs and Patents Act
1988

First published in 2005
by Serpent's Tail,
4 Blackstock Mews, London N4 2BT

website: www.serpentstail.com

Printed by Mackays of Chatham, plc

10 9 8 7 6 5 4 3 2 1

For Mum

1

ONE NIGHT, FIVE BURGLARIES
Steve Dowie, Crime Editor

The recent spate of burglaries came to a head yesterday as five households were reported broken into. None of the perpetrators was apprehended, although Mrs G. Fulley of Grape Lane disturbed two youths in her bedroom.

'Just lads they was, dressed in them silly big clothes they all started wearing just now,' she said from her doorstep last night. 'There were summat odd about them, mind, summat in their eyes. I ain't ever seen such a look before. It were like ...'

Mrs Fulley gazed into the overcast sky, searching for the word. Then the dark clouds seemed to enter her mind and she stepped inside. 'I ain't saying no more,' she said, closing the door. 'They're still out there somewhere, ain't they.'

I had me eye on her the minute she stepped around the corner up yonder and began wending her way Blakeward. She'd taken a fair old stretch of time to get as close as she were now, I can tell you, but she'd made it and now I were honour-bound to give her summat for her efforts. Namely letting her into Hoppers.

But I never.

Like I says, she were up close. Close enough so I could kiss her without shifting on me feet, though she were a foot shorter than meself and not my type anyhow, what with that skinny arse and all them freckles across her nose. But I couldn't smell nothing on her breath. And by rights I ought to be whiffing the pop fumes from a couple of yard off going by her unsteady gait and that. So if she weren't pissed there were only one thing she could be. And we don't let them sort in.

'Not tonight, love,' I says, blocking her way. I thought about adding 'No mongs in here' by way of explanation. But to be honest she didn't look capable of taking it in.

She pushed on anyhow, not caring that her tits was squashed up against my outstretched arm. She gave us a look and all and I didn't much care for it. There's two kinds of looks I'm used to getting from birds: special, and aggro. Most birds will go for the former, and I can't say I blames em. I'm Royston Blake, Mangel's top doorman. I got class and I carries meself well, and the birds knows it and appreciates it. But you can't keep em all happy, can you. There's always one or two don't like being loved and left. That's where your aggro look comes in. But this one here weren't even giving us the aggro. She were peering up close with a little smirk on her chops, like I were a ladybird crawling up her arm or summat.

And like I says, I took umbrage to it.

'Deaf or summat?' I says, politely pushing her back.

She went roadward a bit faster than I'd intended. Arse over tit to be precise. I checked left and right to see if anyone'd clocked us. A doorman's gotta do what he's got to, which sometimes can entail a spot of light physical. But it never looks good when a bird's involved. No matter how much grief she's doling.

But no one spotted it, so I were alright.

I trotted up to her and offered me hand. I might be a cunt now and then but if I knocks a bird down I'll always help her up again. 'Blip,' she says.

I waggled my ear with me free hand, reckoning quite reasonably that I'd heard her wrong. 'You what?'

'Blip.'

I pulled back the other hand, which she hadn't wanted anyhow. Some folks was coming out of Hoppers behind us. A feller and a bird as it turned out. I went to salute em on their way but they was tonguing each other ragged and beyond saluting. I turned back to the girl on her arse, scratching my head. 'I reckons you just said "blip", or summat,' I says. 'That right?'

'Blop.'

I scratched my head again, looking northwards at the corner she'd walked around not but three minutes prior. I were in a bit of a quandary, see. By rights I ought to leave her be and piss off back to my door, me being Head Doorman and Manager of Hoppers, and a doorman's job being to keep door at all times and never ever leave it, and that. Unless there's a spot of nearby argy-bargy that needs sorting, course. But there weren't no argy-bargy. There were a right odd bird sat atop the hard stuff and fuck all else besides.

Like I says, I were looking up yonder, scratching me swede, when a feller comes haring round the corner like a cat with a banger up his arse. I stood up tall, sensing aggro in the air. No one hares that way in Mangel unless bother's up. And a finely tuned doorman such as meself can sniff bother from three furlongs off.

When he clocked us he slowed up and started walking all casual like, setting his floppy hair to rights and pulling his top straight. He were about twenty-five, I reckon, with lank blond hair hanging over his ears like a pair of old curtains. Going by his physique he didn't seem one for big eating nor heavy lifting. At about shoulder-high to meself he weren't a tall feller neither. Bit of a streak of piss all in all. And he were dressed like a cunt: jeans and hooded jogging top, the both about eight sizes too big for him.

He stopped five yard off and spread his arms wide, like he were showing us how long a yard were. He had a big smile across his chops and all, and I didn't much care for it.

'Who the fuck do you reckon you is?' I says, looking him up and down. I had a good mind to smack him, acting like he were somebody when any cunt could see he were fuck all. I'd never clocked the bastard before in me life, had I. And that ain't summat you'll often see in Mangel – a face you ain't seen fifty times already. If you really wants to know –

and I reckon you does else you'd have fucked off by now – the feller looked like an outsider. Weren't just his togs neither. Everything about him gave it away, right down to the way he walked. Sounded like an outsider and all:

'Well,' he says.

See what I mean? Pure big city. Bit posh and all. Here's a bit more:

'Well, I'm not sayin'—'

'Ain't sayin' much, is you,' I says. 'I was you I'd keep it that way and all.' Cos if there's one thing I hates it's a cocky outsider.

His face fell like a pissed-up blind feller near a cliff edge. But he had it up and running again sharpish. Bit too sharpish for my liking. Not so cocky now, mind.

'Nah, man,' he says, putting his hands up. I don't like folks who puts their hands up when I ain't even threatened em yet. Presumptuous it is. 'I'm no one special. Just looking for my girl here. She ran away back there. But, you know, girls do that sometimes, don't they? Attention seeking, yeah?' He winked at us.

There's another thing I don't like and it's a feller winking at us. So when I piped up again there might well have been a touch of the narky in me voice. 'So this un's with you, is it?' I says, nodding at the bird. 'Gonna say woss up with her, then?'

'There's nothing wrong with her, man. Honest. Just the drink.'

'Blip,' she says, staring into the black sky.

I looked up. No blips up there far as I could see. 'This bird ain't been drinkin',' I says with the confidence of one who's spent his working life sifting the bladdered from the borderline.

'She has, man. Honest. Tequila. You can't smell tequila on breath.'

'Tequila? Who the fuck drinks tequila round here?'

'Oh, you'd be surprised. You can get it. Listen, I'm gonna take her now, alright?' He leaned over to haul her up, never taking his eyes from off us.

'No you ain't.' I pushed him back with the tip of me boot. 'I ain't satisfied yet. How does I know you ain't a stranger aimin' to have away with her, poor and helpless like she is?'

'Look, I'm alright. I'm not gonna hurt her.' He held his hands up again like I were meant to read his palms or summat. Now he were up close and I could get a good gander of him I reckoned he were a bit older than I'd first adjudged him to be. His face were quite smooth, but there was a few lines here and there and the odd bust vein. It were hard to put me pointer on how old he were but I'd say somewhere between twenty-five and fifty. 'I just need to get her home. She'll be ill.'

'Well, she'll go sick, then, won't she. Cos I ain't lettin' you have her.'

He stood up and stuck hands in pockets. 'OK, what am I supposed to do to convince you?'

I folded my arms and kept me gob shut. You ain't meant to talk of such matters in the open, after all, are you. There's certain signs you can give that gets the job done for you. Hand signals and that. I rubbed thumb and pointer of my right hand together.

'Oh, I get it,' he says, reaching into his pocket like

a good boy. He counted out a few sheets, shaking his head and smirking down at his wallet.

'Got summat to say, have you?' I says. Like most folks in Mangel I'll tolerate an outsider. But I won't stand for cheek from no streak of piss. If he's giving us lip I don't give a shite where he's from – I'll fucking have him.

'Just chill, man,' he says, proffering three notes and a nervous smirk.

I unclenched me paws and took the notes, staring him down until the moment came to count em. They was fivers, which were a bit of a blow. But fifteen pound weren't bad for a spot of freelance. 'Go on then,' I says, turning me back and filing the sheets in me pocket. 'She's all yours.'

The rest of the night were piss easy, Mondays being quiet by tradition and the damp autumn air putting an early stopper on any thoughts of aggro folks might have been harbouring. I sank a pint of lager, chatted to Rache for a few minutes while sipping on another un, knocked back another couple for the road, says goodbye to Rache, taxed a bottle of whisky from behind the bar, pulled meself another pint cos it were the end of the barrel, locked up, had one for the road, and got in me car.

Seemed like only a couple of minutes later I were pulling up in front of my house. You can put that down to the superior engineering of your Capri 2.8i. Running like a thoroughbred them days she were. I had the power steering sorted and everything. Stuck sometimes when you wrenched her too far to the right but anyone bar women and children could haul her straight with a bit of elbow. And your 2.8i ain't meant for birds and younguns anyhow.

When I got in I loosened me dicky bow, kicked off me boots, and plonked my arse down on the good kitchen chair, the others all being a bit shaky. I'd forgot to get meself a glass, knackered as I surely were, so I opened the whisky bottle and stuck him to me lips. I held him there for a goodly while and it were a sweet moment while it lasted. I were a hard grafting feller and I'd come to the end of another working day. But sweet moments never last long. Not in Mangel anyhow.

'Alright, Blakey.'

I reckon you knows all about Finney. I'll not be trotting out all the old stories about him so don't fret. Suffice to say, he were a useless cunt.

'Alright, Fin,' I says, politeness being the rule in my house.

'Sally called for you again,' he says, wheeling himself over to the table. He poured some whisky into a dirty mug without so much as a glance at us, then sat there slurping, sloshing it round his mouth and between his teeth. Then he says: 'What you been up to, then?'

I tapped me finger on the table for a bit, wondering whether to have a smoke or no. I'd been thinking about giving up of late. Fags just wasn't same as they used to be. The baccy was all dry and manky and the filters seemed to hold onto half the goodness, no matter how hard you sucked on em. Aye, I were wondering if it weren't time to pack em in and move up to cigars full-time. 'What have I been up to?' But I only had smokes on us right then so I lit one up. 'What the fuck have I been up to?'

'Alright Blakey, don't start on us. I were just—'

'"Alright Blakey", is it? I'll tell you woss alright Blakey. It's alright Blakey for you to sit on yer arse all day watchin' my fuckin' telly, eatin' my fuckin' scran, smokin' my fuckin' smokes and swillin' yer fuckin' gob out with my bastard whisky. Thass alright Blakey, ennit.'

We stayed like so for a bit, drinking and smoking and trembling and fuming and not talking. After a while I couldn't stand it no longer. 'Alright,' I says, going to the sink. I stood there for a bit with me back to Fin, then says: 'I didn't mean it like that. You knows I fuckin' never.'

He said nothing to that. The cunt. I'd apologised, hadn't I? He could at least say summat. I counted the dirty mugs in the sink and waited. There was eight of em. 'Look, I've had hard day. Aggro all night long at Hoppers there has been. One ruck after another, me expected to wade in and win every one of em. Poor knuckles is hurtin' us chronic they is. So you can't blame us for havin' a little go, like. Alright?'

Still the cunt said nothing. I wanted to turn about and see what kind of a look were on his face, but I couldn't. Not until he made his move. But no such move looked to be coming. He were silent as a kitten in a freezer. I couldn't even hear the whisky sloshing through his teeth no more.

'Fuck sake, Fin. I'm fuckin' *sorry*, alright? Happy now?'

There was about ten plates in that sink besides the

mugs. And a half-empty tin of beans. And a dozen or so old teabags. And some eggshells. He started talking just as I got to counting the cutlery.

'I knows how it is, Blakey,' he says, not sounding much like himself.

Now he'd made his move, I could turn about. So I did. He were looking into his mug, a frown on his face like a downturned horseshoe. Anyone'd think he were homeless, destitute and friendless, rather than living keep-free under his mate's roof. I had a good mind to slap him around a bit and make him see how good he had it. But hitting Fin hadn't seemed right ever since he'd come out of hospital a couple of year back. And it were no different now.

'Yer a young man compared to some,' he were saying. 'Whole life ahead of you, ennit. Got a good job. Birds flockin' round you. You got a strong body and you knows how to use it. Last thing you wants is a cripple hangin' about.'

Finney were more than a useless cunt. He were a fucking bastard. 'Fin . . .'

'I wouldn't wanna be lumbered with meself neither if I was you. Ain't just the wheelchair getting in the way, is it. Who'd want to see my fucked face every time they gets up or comes home from work? Can't even bear to look in the mirror meself. Not even if I could stand up to see in it, which I can't.'

'Fin, come on . . .'

'No, I've said it once and I'll say him again: don't go blamin' yerself for my ills. Can't be helped now, they can't. An' it weren't like it were your fault. No it fuckin' were not. Not even if folks says it was . . .'

'Who—?'

'Don't matter who says. Matters is it ain't true. You knows it and I knows it. I'll always know it, Blakey, wherever I ends up.' He plonked his mug down and backed away from the table, then wheeled himself into the hall. Couple of seconds later the door shut on the front room, which were the one he dossed in, being as he couldn't get up the stair. I sat at the table and got back on the whisky and fags. Long as I had me smokes and pop I knew I'd be alright. Alright as I had right to hope for anyhow, I reckoned.

I were still alright when the front door slammed a bit later. Weren't sure how much later, cos, well, I might have dropped off there a moment or two. Anyhow, I righted the nigh-empty bottle and brushed the fag ash off me shirt front, then went for a gander.

Fin always had trouble with that bumpy pavement outside my house. Once he were on tarmac he were alright, but until then he struggled. 'Hoy,' I says between a whisper and a holler. 'Where the fuck is you off to?'

He slowed and sort of looked sideways. Then he pressed on, grunting with the effort of it all.

'I says hoy,' I says, catching up and holding the back of his chair. 'Hoy means stop. It don't mean slow down a bit then piss off again.'

'Leave it, Blake. T'ain't worth it.'

'What ain't worth what?'

'Just let us go. For the best, ennit.'

'Woss for the best? Where you off?'

'Don't matter. I'll find somewhere.'

'Somewhere for what?'

'Blake,' he says, stopping his struggling but turning his face from us. 'I'm grateful for you lettin' us stay in yer house and that. Surely I am. An' I dunno what I'd of done if you hadn't of done. But I knows when me time is up. Just let us go, Blake. Let us *go*.'

I thought about it for a bit, the words he were saying and the situation we was finding ourselves in out here in the street at fuck knew what time in the smalls. I actually did think about it. Then I shook me head and started to turn the chair about. Only it didn't turn proper. Nothing ever turned proper with Finney. He started pushing the wheels the other way, didn't he. So what you had, right, were him versus meself in a battle of wills at dead of night, outside my house and a few yard up the way.

Now, it's a well-known fact that Finney, despite his skinny arse and that, were not short on elbow. Legend down at the slaughtering yard had it that he could haul the better part of a cow over his head when such were called for. But then he'd gone lame and his strength soon went to shite. You might reckon that him being in a cripple chair would make his arms even stronger, what with all that pushing up hills and that. Only Finney didn't do much of that. Longest trek he done of a typical day were from the front room to the outside crapper, for which I'd put down some bits of wood to help him up the step. Now and then he'd drag himself along to the bus stop and head into town for his cripple money, but nothing else could get him out the door. Not even a night out at the Paul Pry tempted him. And that's with me driving him down there in my Capri. So

when it came to him against the rockest doorman in
Mangel in a struggle over the direction of his wheelchair . . . What do you reckon?

Only you'd be reckoning wrong, wouldn't you.

See, he fucking put the brake on, didn't he, tipping
the cart and sending him onto the hard stuff, swede-
first, arse-second.

I scratched my head for a bit, then stopped that,
remembering how sparse things was getting up
there. Upstairs lights was coming on up and down
the street, and I knew I were none too popular
among the neighbours on account of the shame I'd
brung em in the past, what with my address being
printed in them articles about us in the paper and
that. So I squatted down to get a good grip under
Finney's rank armpits.

He were light as your proverbial and I had him
stretched out on the floor of the front room without
too much fucking about. I went back out and got the
chair in before the curtain-twitching started for
proper. I went to kick the door shut behind us but
me leg froze.

There were a motor out there.

For surely there were. I'd clocked summat turning
into our street as I were dragging the chair in, but in
all the fuss it hadn't hit home to us how it were such
a rude hour, folks tending not to come up this street
at unsociable times besides meself. And here she
were now, pulling up right outside me door and
turning herself off.

I stayed like so, leg out, while I thought about
how that engine hadn't sounded like one you'd likely hear in the Mangel area. Then I got cramp in me

leg and had to put it down and hop around for a bit. When I were alright again I poked me swede out the door.

I were right about the motor. She weren't from local. Shiny and new she were, and about as pretty as a bulldog in a bonnet. Had none of the style and panache that made your Capri the work of art she surely is, lacked the sumptuous lines of your Mk III Cortina, and even made the Avenger across the way come across all erotic. To be frank with you it were a shite motor and I got a queasy ache in me gut just looking at her. But look at her I did, for a bit longer at least, wanting to know as I did who the fuck were behind the wheel.

It were hard to see at first, our street boasting only the one street lamp between the lot of us. But when me peepers adjusted I got a good look at him. And he clocked us and all, perhaps even nodded at us a tad. But it were only after he'd pulled away and slipped into the main road that I recognised him.

Feller from outside Hoppers, wernit. The one who'd bunged us fifteen pound just now.

2

OLD LADY MUGGED
Steve Dowie, Crime Editor

Mrs J. P. R. Plugham of the Muckfield district was attacked yesterday by a youth as she pushed her shopping trolley home from the town centre. The unidentified youth got away with a purse containing four pounds and change. 71-year-old Mrs Plugham got away with her life. Just.

'It's me ticker, see,' she told me from her hospital bed yesterday evening. 'You gets to my age you just can't take a shock like that. Frightened the life out of us it did. I fell right on my backside.'

At this point a nurse came to mop Mrs Plugham's fevered brow. When she had recovered I asked her what the world is coming to, that an elderly woman cannot leave her home without risk of violence. 'Coming to? World ain't coming to nothing that it ain't been already long enough. I been getting mugged far back as I recalls. Aye, fifty year ago it were when that feller there ... What were his name? Anyhow, he ... er ...'

But what of the fear, I asked her. What of the terror that pushed her old heart to its limits and left her wired to a drip in Mangel Infirmary? 'Oh, it weren't that he were mugging us. To be fair on him he didn't so much as touch us. Just handed me goods over, I did, same as always. No, it were summat else had us quaking. Summat about his eyes, like ...'

Her eyelids flickered, her breathing faltered. Soon the nurse came back and the curtains were drawn. It was dark and wet outside on the streets of Mangel.

This reporter went to file a story.

Well, I were as surprised as you would be to see the feller there in his motor. What he were doing up my way were a source of great concern to us at that minute, me having not so long back lightened him of fifteen pound and all. Feller collects his dues off another feller, he don't want to hear no more about it. And if he'd gone to the trouble of finding out where I lived and coming along at such a filthy hour to have a gander – what the fuck for?

I made a note in me swede to have him up about it next time I seen him, slap him about a bit and put the shite up him proper. I didn't give a toss if he were an outsider. I'm Royston fucking Blake, and every cunt knows where I stands on outsiders. They don't scare us and I ain't fooled by their ways.

Anyhow, I put it out me mind soon as the door were shut and the cruel world were safely t'other side of it. I went into the front room.

Finney were lying where I'd left him, fast akip. I knew just how he felt. I were dog arse tired meself and wanted nothing more than the comfort of clean sheets and a firm mattress, though I hadn't changed me bed linen in fuck knew how many weeks, and the mattress were about fifty year old and as firm as an old man's tadger.

I knew it weren't easy for Fin being the way he were. Kip were the best place for him like as not. He'd be able to walk and run in his dreams. He'd look in a dream mirror and see a face like it used to be, before it had got scarred to fuck by a chainsaw. He might even tap off with a bird if he were lucky. But that were stretching it a bit, seeing as he couldn't even do that before the accident.

I fished a fiver out me wallet and set it beside him. Then I set another atop that one. Then I went upstairs to me pit.

I got up next morning at one in the afternoon, guts fairly raging with hunger. Downstairs I put the blower back on the hook, wondering how many times Sal had rung us but not really giving a toss either way, to be honest. I opened the fridge door and cursed my bastard luck aloud. There were fuck all inside but an inch of cheesy milk, an old bag of sprouts, and one can of lager.

I cracked open the can and sat at the table, wondering what to do for the best. I needed scran. All working men needs scran of a morn. And I couldn't be arsed to trek to Butcher Fred's in town. So the answer were clear:

Finney could pop to Doug's corner shop.

Do him good to get some exercise. Building up his strength's what he needed, none of this lying on the floor wailing your eyes out. But when it came to knocking on his door I didn't have the heart. Let him kip, poor old cunt. Life couldn't be easy in a wheelchair, even if he did have a fucking slave to wipe his arse for him. Not that I truly wiped his arse, course. Royston Blake don't wipe arses for no fucker. I'm just being meta . . . You know, meta . . . I'm just saying, like.

A rumbling in me belly reminded us how urgent matters was getting. I emptied the lager down me neck and went up the stair.

I were turning them matters over as I pulled me togs on. I didn't reckon as I'd last if I went into town. Perhaps I could lend summat off a neighbour. Not likely, mind. Them days I were lucky if one of em walked on the same side of the street as us. It were time to face facts.

I had to pay a visit to the corner shop.

Feller's belly comes before his dignity, after all. Don't it.

I walked slowly down the road, wishing it hadn't come to this. Been a cunt to me, Doug had. Stopped me credit and told us to piss off last time I'd been in there, after which I'd vowed never again to give him my custom. But that had been fucking ages ago and the world moves on. Aye, it were time to forget grudges and concentrate on the important things in life, like sausages and eggs and bacon and mushies. And black pudding. And fried tommies and baked beans.

And lard.

The bell started tinkling as I pushed the door open. I cursed it under me breath and strode in with my head held high, ready to meet whatever confrontation Doug had in mind. He weren't behind his counter, which were the first thing to throw us. Always behind that counter were Doug the shop- keeper. Counting coinage or scratching arse or doing what I dunno – but he were always there, ready to meet a punter with a smile or a scowl or whatever befitted em.

The other thing to throw us were the state of the shelves. They was half empty. I'd never seen Doug's shelves nothing shy of fully stocked.

I stayed put, not making a sound. You never knew, did you. I played me cards right and I could get what I needed plus a bit besides and have away unnoticed, thereby preserving my dignity and saving on much- required wedge, which only amounted to a fiver anyhow.

I started tippy-toeing around, picking up a packet of this and a tin of that. There were no bacon so I got twice as many bangers instead. And there was only half a dozen eggs in the shop, which were a few short of what I had in mind. To make up for that I filled me coat pockets with as many cans of lager as I could fit in em, then slipped behind the counter for some fags. There weren't much room left on us so I sucked me gut in and stuffed the last few packs of Number One down me trolleys. It weren't right comfortable but a bit of hardship were worth it for all them smokes. I went to the door, enjoying the warm feel- ing inside you gets from finding a bargain.

'Afternoon, sir,' comes a voice behind us just as I were reaching for the door. It were alright, mind – you could tell he hadn't clocked us robbing. But he'd like as not suss if I just walked on out.

I turned. 'Alright,' I says. 'Doug.'

'Ah,' he says, pulling his white coat tight around his skinny middle, which along with his faded brown working trousers left him looking a bit like a filter-tipped smoke. 'If it ain't Royston Blake.'

'Aye?' I says, feeling a few hackles rising. It fucking weren't on, him using that tone of voice after I'd swallowed all that pride by coming in. 'Thass me name, ennit. What of it?'

He kept on with his granite eyes and arsehole mouth, then smiled. Aye, Doug fucking smiled at us – a sight I'd not seen in fuck knew how many years' patronage of his shop. You'd not have even thought his mouth fit for it, all tight and pinched like it were. But he managed it somehow, pulling up the corners with cheek muscles that couldn't have ever seen usage before. They must have started cramping up on him cos the next minute the smile were gone and he says: 'Been wantin' a word with you.'

'Oh aye? What about?' I shuffled a bit in me boots, feeling the corner of a fag packet pressing on me left knacker. I wanted to adjust meself down there but I couldn't hardly do that with him looking on. So I sort of shifted my weight into me left leg, taking care not to clink the tinnies. 'Ain't seen you in yonks,' I says, 'and now you wants a word with us of a sudden?'

'Thass right, thass right. Will you come out back, please? Bit personal, like.'

There was stories about Doug the shopkeeper. Come to think on it there ain't a soul in Mangel who ain't got stories floating around about him or her. But the ones about Doug was what you might call nasty. You might have heard some of em, you with your big ears and all. You might have even heard the one about the sausages. Well, let me tell you summat about the one about the sausages:

It's true.

How does I know it's true, you says? Who the fuck's you to ask how I knows? But since I'm in a chatty mood I'll tell you how I knows:

I were there.

That's right – I were one of the younguns lifting joes in his shop that day many a moon back. We'd crept in nice and quiet and reckoned we'd got away with it, see. Joes was them sweets he had in that little trough under the counter, and if you stayed low and didn't make a noise coming in you was alright to swipe em usually. Not this time, mind. Doug popped up behind the counter like he'd known all along. We all pegged it, dropping joes everywhere and fighting to get out that door. All of us made it except this one lad. What were his name . . . ? No matter – come to us in a minute it will. Anyhow, the reckoning later on were that he'd slipped on the joes, hard little round fuckers as they was. The rest of us had away up the road and then crept back, nosiness getting the better of caution. We spied through the window, wondering what were coming to pass with our sad little comrade whose name I can't recall and don't matter anyhow, seeing as this here's a story about Doug and not the youngun.

Anyhow, we couldn't see neither of em. Doug had him out back like as not, telling him off or slapping his wrist or summat. Or so you'd reckon. Ages we waited out front, watching punters go in and Doug come out and then disappear again. Time came when all the mams came out shouting for sprogs to come in for tea, so off we all pissed, still scratching swedes over our missing mate.

Sammy his name were. That's it – Sammy Johnson. Told you it'd come to us. Always do if you asks yourself the right way. Aye, Sammy the Sausage Boy, as he came to be referred about in hushed tones. But I ain't told you what came of him yet, have I.

It were me found out. Next morning, off on me way to school. I stopped to spark one of me old man's fags up and noticed someone across the way. It were Doug himself putting up a bit o' paper in his shop window. He winked at us without smiling, then disappeared. Fag had gone out so I sparked him up again and went over for a gander. *THIS WEEKS SPECIAL*, it said along the top in slanty writing. And under it, in big letters: SAUSAGES.

How does I know them bangers was little Sammy, you says? I'll fucking tell you why: he were never seen again. Not at school, not in the street, not nowhere. Unless you went into Doug's that week and bought some bangers. Then you'd have seen him on your plate.

'Summat the matter, Royston?' says Doug back in the here and now, hovering in the dark passage behind the counter that led no one knew quite where.

'Course not, Doug,' I says. 'Only I'm in a bit of a hurry, like. So—'

'Well, I'm sure we can sort you out for groceries,' he says, squeezing out that constipated smile again. 'Then you can be on yer way.'

I grinned back. But not in a constipated way like Doug. Quite the other, in fact. I didn't want to move, specially not in his direction. Sussed the goods I'd stowed on me personage, hadn't he. That's why he wanted us out back. And now that hadn't worked out for him he wanted to trap us some other way. Aye, that's what his smiling were for. He'd always hated us and now he had us on a rope. Or so he reckoned.

I looked around the shelves and says: 'I were after some rashers, actually. Only it looks you ain't got none. So ...' I reached for the door handle.

He came out from behind the counter. Me heart started thumping hard, rattling against three tins of beans and some chopped tommies. He walked towards us slow, shoulders hunched and elbows bent like a spider's legs. I wanted to pull the door but I couldn't. He had us in his web, just like he'd had Sammy back then. He stopped a yard from us and cracked his fingers. If I pulled the door the bell would go and ... and ...

'Been thinkin' on you, Royston,' he says. 'Been thinking on reinstatin' yer credit.'

I wanted to scratch me swede, naturally. But if I did I'd lose the eggs and lard. 'Me credit?' I says. 'But ...'

'I know, I know,' he says, showing us the palms of his birdy hands. 'But life's a long and arduous undertakin', so it is, and grudge-bearin' only renders it more so. Don't you reckon?'

'Aye, course. Er ... nice one, Doug. I'll be along regular again like, then. But I gotta—'

'Ah, but Royston, there's summat else. I got a problem.'

'I'm a bit rushed, mate.'

'It's about my Mona.'

I let go of the door handle. 'Who?'

'Mona. My little girl.'

Not many folks knew Doug had a wife and youngun. Kept em shut up, he did, in the flat above the shop. Never needed to go shopping, course, being as they was in a shop already. And the little girl got her schooling off her mam, so everyone thought. I'd clocked the youngun once or twice in me time, all wrapped up and off somewhere that can't be avoided. Plain little thing in thick-rimmed glasses and a ginger fringe that half hid em. 'Ah,' I says. 'Mona, eh?'

'Aye. My little girl.'

'She must be . . . what . . . ?'

'Fourteen.'

'Fourteen, eh?' I were interested for a moment, then remembered the little speccy ginger bint. 'So what do you want us for?'

'I'll be comin' to that. Will you come on through?'

'I'm alright here, ta.' I were far from alright if you must know. You would be and all if you had to stand for fucking yonks with your trolleys full of fag packets.

'I'll put the kettle on.'

'No, ta. Er . . . I just had one.'

'Oh well, if you're sure . . .'

'I am.'

'Well,' he says, 'it's a bit . . .' He reached past us and put the CLOSED sign up, then pulled down the blind. 'She's started goin' out. On the town, like. I can't control her, Royston. Are you sure I can't get you some tea?'

'Yer alright.'

'I'm lucky if I sees her at all most days. Well, that ain't rightly true. It ain't lucky to have yer own daughter hold you to ransom, is it. Always after a fiver here and a tenner there. She's bleedin' us dry. Liftin' off the shelves an' all she is. Look around you. Stock ain't been low as this since the day this shop opened. She's till-liftin' and all. I'm losing me grip. She's ruinin' us, Royston.'

I weren't used to being called by me given name so many times in so short a space. I wanted to tell him to call us Blake like the rest of Mangel do and did and always will, only there were summat of a more pressing nature to sound him about first. 'But Doug,' I says. 'That ain't good about yer daughter and all, but I don't see where I comes in.'

'I were coming to that, Royston. I needs your help. God knows I needs somebody's help. And you're the best man, as I sees it.'

That were funny, I were thinking. Last time we'd spoke he'd told us different. Going by what he'd said back then you'd think us fit for fuck all. Unless summat nasty needs doing, course.

'See, I needs summat doing. Of a specific nature, like.'

'Oh?'

'Aye.'

'And that'll be ...?'

He looked behind him. He pulled the blind aside

and checked out there and all. Then he looked behind him again. 'I needs a feller sortin' out.'

'Sortin' out?'

'Aye. Seen to.'

'Seen to?'

'You know, done over.'

3

CRIME WAVE CONTINUES
Steve Dowie, Crime Editor

Yesterday saw seven domestic burglaries, eleven car thefts, six muggings and two armed robberies as the current spate of petty misdemeanours went on. All witnesses described youths alone or in pairs, with one armed robbery gang of four.

I spoke to Bob Gromer, proprietor of Gromer Wines & Tobacco in Cutler Road. 'Aye,' he said, rubbing his shiny pate. 'Younguns they was. Four of em, all wearing balaclavas. Tall one were pointing a sawn-off shotgun at us. Reminded us of the old days it did, when that Tommy Munton were up to his tricks.'

I asked him if he had noticed anything strange about the robbers. 'Summat odd? What sort o' question is that? Who'd you say you was again?'

I showed him my credentials and repeated the question. Something in their eyes perhaps?

'Never mind that. What I want to know is how lads aged thirteen or so gets their paws on a shotgun. Mangel

ain't the sort o' town to have guns and the like. Your typ-
ical robber will come in this here shop with a stocking
over his head and a lot of shouting. I can handle that. I
ain't been standing behind this here counter these past
thirty years without knowing how to handle a thug and
his shouting. Spanks em with this I does . . .'

Mr Gromer reached under the counter and produced
what looked like a cricket bat with ten or twelve four-inch
nails driven through it. A nail at the end pointed out-
wards like a bayonet. He swung the bat through the air,
the end nail coming within an inch of my nose. 'Oh aye,
I've had all kinds try it on in here. Let em come, I says.
Let em come and meet my Betty.' He thrust the bat at my
leg. I cried out as the end nail pierced the polyester knit of
my trouser. 'Fancy yourself, does you, you there with your
pen and your bits of paper? Come on, here's me till. Try
and get past us. Try and get past me and Betty.'

This reporter made his excuses and left, wondering
when was the last time he had had a tetanus jab.

At the infirmary I signed in and took a seat in the
waiting area. I turned to the elderly gentleman on my
right and asked him what he thought of the crime epi-
demic ravaging our town. Maybe he had been burgled
himself? Or robbed in broad daylight by cowardly youths?

*'**** off and mind your own business,' he said.*

I turned to the fellow on my left, a young man of no
more than sixteen summers. Perhaps he could tell me of
the pressures facing a young person today, that they
should turn to crime? Perhaps he himself was a criminal?

He raised his ashen face out of his hands and looked at
me. His eyes sparkled weakly like dusty light bulbs in the
upper rooms of a condemned house. I searched them for
something, the thing that the two ladies had seen but

failed to name. But there was nothing there. Nothing at all.

'I been pissin' blood,' he said, grinning. Then frowning. 'Crash us a tenner, eh?'

Doug had got that bit right. If there were one thing I were good at it were doing fellers over. Alright, alright. It were true – I'd gone through a rough patch a while back whereby a couple of bastards had got the better of us. But they'd had guns and chainsaws and that, which ain't playing fair in my book.

You what? Forget it, pal. I ain't telling that story no more. I've told it enough times already – specially to the coppers – and I'm sick of it. You wants to know about the guns and chainsaws, go ask someone else. Everyone knows round here. Anyhow, where the fuck were I?

Oh aye, that's it. I were good at doing fellers over. Fucking good. I'd been getting meself down the gym a bit more regular of late and now I were nigh on perfect – twenty-odd stone of pure rock.

'What makes you reckon I'll do a feller over for you?' I says to Doug. 'Sayin' I'm a thug or summat, is you?'

He went to say summat, then stopped. You could see him thinking for a little while. Then he goes: 'I'll not call you a thug nor any other such thing. All I knows is you're a big feller who can mix it a bit. I've said it before, Royston, and I'll say it again: you can't hide what you are in a place like Mangel. No one can. A man crawls from cradle to . . . Anyhow, I won't bore you with that. I knows you can help us if you so chooses. Question is, will you?'

There was all kinds of gestures me arms and legs was gagging to make. But I couldn't do none of em, burdened as I were with Doug's groceries. So I had to put it all across with me voice. 'Perhaps.'

'"Perhaps" meanin' you will if suitably induced, am I right in thinkin'?'

'You what?'

'Here, I'll show you. Come on now.' He trotted off out back. I took a deep one and followed, but not trotting.

Weren't so creepy as you might imagine back there. Not once he'd turned the light on anyhow. We was in a stockroom, though stock was mostly empty boxes. Next to a tatty armchair in the corner were a little table. A portable telly atop it were on but the sound turned down. Looked like the war were on, though you couldn't ever be sure them days. In the middle of the floor were a pile of summat or other with a scummy sheet draped over it. 'Here we are,' he says, pulling the sheet off.

It were summat to see, I can tell you. I dunno how many tinnies was there but they'd keep a man in lager for a goodly length of time for surely. 'There's four hundred here,' he says, doing me sums for us. He stood back and folded his birdy arms.

I picked up a four-pack and had a gander. I dunno what I were on the lookout for but it's a foolish man who don't go through the motions. And it were lucky I did. 'Woss this?' I says, pointing at the bottom of a can. 'Past the sell-by this is.'

'Only by four days. Makes no odds.'

'Still past it, fuck sake. Tryin' to pull one on us, is you?'

'Last another six month at least. Tastes just same, Royston. Better, in fact – improves with age this particular one do.'

'Bollocks.'

'Don't want it?'

I cracked it open and emptied half of it down me neck, trying not to lift my elbow too high. 'Never said that,' I says. 'Just don't reckon iss quite enough is all, for what the job is.' I sucked the rest off then let out a belch that had the light bulb swaying. 'I mean, feller can't drink without a smoke, can he.'

Doug glared at us a while. I opened another. Alright it were. Maybe he were bang on about improving with age. I were, after all. So perhaps the lager were and all? I were looking forward to putting it to the test, if I could drag out four hundred cans long enough to age em a bit.

'Thass yer lot,' he says, plonking two trade boxes of bennies atop the beer stack, which made four hundred fags.

I shook me swede. 'Don't care for Bennies. Smokes Number One, don't I.'

'I seem to be out of Embassy Number One of a sudden. Iss Bensons or nuthin'. I got some Consulate somewhere if you wants them.'

I shook me swede again. Consulates is for birds. I'd made do with Bennies in the past and I'd just have to do it again. Mind you, four hundred weren't so many. 'That'll only last us ten days,' I says. 'I'll need more.' I tossed the two empty tins in the bin. 'Nice pop, mind.'

He looked at us a while, chewing his lip. I got started on another tin. No point wasting time, is there. 'You'll take what I'm offering,' he says of a sudden.

I stopped mid-gulp and turned me eyes on him, not caring much for the edge in his voice.

'You'll take it,' he went on, 'and you'll do the job for us. T'ain't a hard job, after all. Mangel ain't a place a man can hide in. All you has to do is foller my Mona into town and see who she consorts with. And when you finds him, I know you'll prosecute him thoroughly.'

I belched and opened me gob.

'No,' he says, cutting us dead. 'Four hundred beer cans and four hundred cigarettes is what you'll get. Plus the sundry items stowed away there under yer overcoat. We has a deal, Royston, don't us.'

I shrugged but couldn't look him in the eye. Bastard. Fancy stringing us along like that about the sundry items. Trapped us he fairly had. Hauled us out the water like a twenty-pound barbel. I ought to break his fucking face. Cheeky cunt. He can stow his rotten lager and ten days' worth of fags up his backside. I turned and trudged out, rattling a bit now but not caring.

'You can come back for this once you've dropped yer vittles off,' he says, draping the sheet back over my gear. 'Only half now, mind.'

'You what?'

'Half on completion. Fair, ennit?'

I shrugged again. It were fair as anything else I could compare it to. I trudged out onto the street, the bell tinkling and the door creeping shut behind us. Weren't such a bad little job when you looked at it in the cold light of an overcast day in Mangel. I got stocked up with essentials and all I had to do were a bit of thorough prosecution, as Doug had put it just now. See, I knew who this feller were he wanted slapping. It were the outsider from last night, wernit. And Mona were the bird talking shite outside Hoppers. She'd took her glasses off and tarted herself up a bit is all. I'd thought her familiar at the time. And him there last night in his motor, driving up and down our street – that's the feller dropping her off at home, ennit.

Aye, this were a piss job. Doug might have shoved us a bit but I'd have said aye anyhow. All them smokes and tinnies? How can a man not bow under that kind of pressure?

Tell you summat, mind. I wish I had have said no.

'Alright, Rache,' I says.

'Hiya, Blake.' She were standing behind the bar doing her nails. 'Sal called for you again. Gonna call her or—'

'Giz a fuckin' pint,' I says. The good bit about being Manager and Head Doorman of Hoppers were that I could give orders to the staff. I could order Rache to get us a fucking pint.

'You what?' she says.

'Come on, don't fuck about.'

'I ain't fuckin' about,' she says, pointing her nail file at us. 'You knows how to ask for summat and that ain't the way.' She turned back to her nails.

'Alright, alright, just giz a pint, please. Alright?'

She pulled us one and plonked it in front of us. I sat a while, supping and thinking. Now that I were in Hoppers the idea of chasing some tosser for a few

tinnies and some fags seemed a mite unseemly. I
mean, I were boss of Mangel's premier piss house
and therefore a prominent figure in the community.
I wore a smart DJ and a nice big sovereign on me
finger. I ought to be hiring donkeys to do donkey
work, not doing it meself. But here I were, hench-
man to a shopkeeper. It weren't right. But if there's
one thing you ought to know about Royston Blake
it's he keeps his word. Always. You can have his
knackers on a string else.

'Rache,' I says. 'Watch the door for a bit, mate.'

'Watch the door? I'm a barmaid, not a blinkin'
doorman. Watch it yerself.'

'I'm off out for five minutes.'

'Blake, come back here. You can't . . .'

I went for a slash before going in, as were my habit.
The Paul Pry were a place for swilling, not getting up
every half-hour to splash your boots. I slashed for
about a minute, eyes wandering over the scribblings
on the tiles above the piss wall. The stuff about
meself never bothered us no more. There'd been a
time not so long back when a Blake-related scrawl-
ing would have us either punching walls or crying
into me lager, depending on the weather. But them
dark days was long gone. I'd come to realise that,
being a local legend, I had to expect a certain
amount of coverage on the walls and doors of bogs
all over town. To be honest with you I'd come to
like it. I didn't even mind the bollocks about me
being an arse bandit, though it were about as far
from the truth as the moon is from the sun. But
these ones here in the Paul Pry was all phrased with

a certain respect, the Pry being well known as my local. And they was as familiar to us as the smell of my own gas. Except a new one, slap bang in front of me face:

> WANNA GET JOEYD?
> SEE THE J-MAN.
> DOWN THE ARKY

'Who the fuck is the J-Man?' I says to Nathan the barman.

He started pulling us one, thinking about it. That alone were a sure sign he didn't know the answer. 'Can't say as I've heard of him, Blakey. And mind yer language, ladies bein' present. Entertainer, is he?'

I got started on the pint. 'Who?'

'Jim Wossname.'

'Oh, the J-Man? Dunno.'

'Well, who is he, then?'

'Dunno, I were askin' you.'

'How ought I to know?'

'Come on, Nathan. Knows everythin', you does. Feller can't fart—'

'Aye, I've heard it before, Blakey. It made no sense that time and even less now. And I've gat summat else to say to you, before you answers back. Why ain't you at Hoppers?'

'Early, ennit. No trouble happens before eight on a weekday.'

'And who's on the door?'

'Rache.'

'Rache?'

'Aye. Barmaid. Big tits.'

'Thass no way to refer to a woman, Blake.'

'But she has got big tits.'

'That may be so, but there's a way to refer to a woman and that ain't it. Here's a tip fer you, Blakey: treat a woman well and the world will unfold before you. Heared it before? Didn't reckon so.'

'I has, actually.'

'I doubt that, Blakey.'

'My old man used to say it.'

'Your old man? That old sot killed his missus, your mam. That ain't treatin' no woman right, now, is it?'

'He fuckin' never, Nathan.'

'Easy on that pint glass there. You'll crack him.'

'Well, iss a fuckin' lie. You oughta know better.'

'Oh aye? Why'd you kill him, then?'

'Thass bollocks an' all. Who telled you that, you fucker?'

He didn't reply to this at first, which weren't a complete surprise to us. Nathan weren't hard nor nothing but you didn't want to tangle with him, for one or two reasons. The first being that he were my boss. Sort of. So I thought it best to change the subject, being as he were right about me dad anyhow. 'Anyhow,' I says, 'I'll be back on the door in a minute. Just came down here to ask you summat. Other than that thing about Jim Wossname.'

'The J-Man.'

''S what I says, ennit?'

'No, you says "Jim Wossname".'

I plonked my glass down. 'It were you says "Jim Wossname".'

He shook his head and picked up my empty. 'This is yer last one,' he says. 'I want you back on that Hoppers door sharpish. I didn't acquire that concern to have it run into the ground by absent door staff.'

'I ain't runnin' her into no ground. Fuckin' hell, Nathan, go easy on us, will yer? Got that place tickin' like a carriage clock, I has. Premier piss house in Mangel she is these days.'

'Premier piss house, you calls it? That might well be, if premier piss house means folks goes there for a piss. But premier drinkin' house it surely ain't.'

'Woss you on about? Packed nigh on every night she is. Weekends you can't see the floor for folks standin' on it.'

'I don't doubt that, Blake. In fact I knows it. But just cos they're standin' there don't foller they're spendin'. They ain't, Blake. Not at my bar anyhow.'

I noticed the fresh pint under me nose and picked it up. Not cos I were thirsty nor nothing but I wanted a minute to think.

Not spending at the bar? Alright, your typical punter in there were a bit younger these days and young means skint in most cases, but hadn't I been throwing my weight around more than ever of late, fighting the civic menace of public drunkenness? And how could they get pissed if they wasn't buying?

'Gat summat to say about that, have you?' Nathan were saying. 'I'm bankin' half as much a week as I did last year. Explain that to us, can you?' He let us stew for a bit then says: 'And don't fret, I knows it ain't down to fingers in tills. Stock ain't goin' down, Blake. Folks ain't drinkin'. Or if they is it ain't my beer.'

'You know what, Nathan,' I says, licking froth off me tash. 'I honestly don't know—'

'Calls yerself Manager you does. And don't say you don't cos I knows you does. There's more to runnin' a place like Hoppers than standin' at the door, Blake. A blind dog can stand at the door. Takes a business brain to keep the till movin'.'

'Alright, alright,' I says, glancing sideways. There weren't more than four or five other punters in the place and they was talking shite of their own. But it were the principle, wernit – a boss oughtn't to be talking to his staff like Nathan were doing here. 'Can we stop talkin' about all that?'

'Never mind that. I gat a plan to get Hoppers back the way she ought to be. Tomorrer night I wants that place runnin' like tick-tock, like you claims to have it runnin' already. I wants no brawlin' and no public displays of indecency, such as I been hearin' about.'

'That were—'

'I don't care. I want none of it the morrer. And I wants no slackin' staff neither. Tell wossname to leave her nails alone and put her heart into the job fer once.'

'Aye.' I nodded. 'I were tellin' her that just—'

'But don't scare folks off. Most of all, the morrer night, I want folks to relax. Get em relaxed and watch that till slammin' in and out like a stallion on a brood mare.'

I were nodding away. See, I had this question for him. But it still weren't the right moment. I weren't in the right frame of head. Flummoxed us he had with all this talk. 'Nathan,' I says. 'Nathan, woss goin' on the morrer night?' Cos it weren't normal, see. Hoppers ran herself the way Hoppers wanted to. You couldn't tinker with her. Whatever came to pass of an evening, it were all part of the rich tapestry of a night at Hoppers.

'Well, Blakey,' he says. I fucking hated it when he said that. 'Thass fer me to know and you to keep yer job over.' He winked at us and started moving off. 'And oh,' he says, stopping, 'keep the stage area clear.'

'What fuckin' stage area?'

'Come on, Blakey. Worked in that place all yer workin' life you has. You knows where the stage is.'

'Aye, but it ain't a stage no more. Raised drinkin' area, ennit.'

'Call it what you will – the morrer iss a stage again. So stop arguin' and keep him cleared, will you? Gat summat planned, ain't I.' He winked at us again and went to serve a punter. After that he picked up the blower, which were ringing. 'Oh, alright, doll,' he says into it, then turned away and started mumbling.

I nursed me pint, watching the bubbles rising and savouring the unique taste you got in the Pry. Sometimes it's better concentrating on such things than bogging yerself down with all the bollocks life throws up.

I were reflecting on the ripe-corn hue of the lager in the subdued light of the Paul Pry when Nathan stuck the blower out to us. 'Fer you,' he says. 'Your Sal.'

I shook me swede, mouthing, 'I fuckin' ain't here.'

He shook his and gave her the news, then went to serve another punter.

When he came past again I put me empty down quiet and raised an eyebrow at him. 'One other thing,' I says, glancing left and right to let him know it were summat of the highest import. He leaned in, bushy eyebrows reaching out like feelers. 'You heared about a new motor goin' about town?'

'Sorta new motor?'

'New un, ennit. Big and shiny. Ugly.'

He turned down the corners of his gob and shook his head once, firm. 'Can't say as I has.'

It were already palmed in me right, see. The fiver. My last fucking fiver. I moved me hand forward and showed him the blue edge.

He leaned in closer. 'Wanna get those ears of yours testin' you does, Blakey. Says I ain't seen no shiny new motor, didn't I. And if you'll take my counsel you'll keep clear o' shiny new motors cos shiny new motors ain't your concern. Your concern, Blake, is keepin' door at Hoppers.'

I went out to the car park, quietly calling Nathan a wanker and a cunt and a few words that don't bear repeating here. He knew full well I were Manager as well as Head Doorman. He were aiming to knock us down a notch by leaving that one out. And he did know everything, despite his saying different. If he weren't bleating about the motor, not even for a fiver, it were cos he had a good reason not to.

And I didn't like the sound of that.

4

DRINK MORE, SEE MORE

The Management is proud to announce, after a long absence, the return of **STRIPPERS** to Hoppers. From now on the most beautiful young ladies in the Mangel area will be paraded before you every night of the week **STARTING TOMORROW.** Get yourself down there early if you want a good eyeful.

And that's not all . . .

We all know how frustrating it can be when you're sat there rubbing your hands only to find she don't take enough clothing off. Well, these ones are the genuine article. Our girls know **NO LIMITS.** But here's the catch . . .

The more drink sold at the bar,
THE MORE KIT SHE'LL TAKE OFF.

What? Still not happy? Alright, then . . .
To mark this historic occasion – for one night only –
all **DRAUGHT BEER** will be **HALF PRICE** for the whole evening.

So do yourself a favour –
get down the Hoppers tomorrow night.

HOPPERS
FRIAR STREET
MANGEL

What followed, after I'd jumped in me Capri and coaxed her across town, were plain and simple one of me greatest ever nights on the door. And what makes a great night, you might well ask. Well, ask you might. And I'll tell you.

But not before I've telled you summat else. Alright?

On me way over, gently slipping her fourth to fifth up the Wall Road, who should pass us but Mr Big Shiny New Motor himself: the feller Doug had hired us to sort out. I clocked him a mile off in me rear-view, cruising along in the fast lane a shade quicker than meself. You couldn't hardly miss the fucker, that great cow's arse of a bonnet coming up behind you.

Nice one, I thinks. Saves us waiting around for him to show up. Or following young Mona into town like Doug had suggested. I ain't in the habit of following young girls around. Nor older girls neither. Don't have to, see. Birds comes to us. Perk of being Head Doorman that is. So I lagged back a bit and shoed it when the feller turned left at the lights.

I followed him westward and over the river, which had me guts going a mite queasy for some reason. A short while later the reason turned clear: we was headed for Norbert Green.

I didn't enjoy Norbert Green. Besides them who lived there already, no folks in Mangel got much pleasure from that district. But you already knows that like as not. There can't be many folks who ain't heard the name Norbert Green and the stories what went with it.

Over the years I hadn't had much luck in Norbert
Green (unless you counts the bad variety, in which
case I'd had fucking plenty). And as a rule I didn't
venture there. Not that I were scaredy of it, mind. I
ain't fucking scaredy of nothing, me. And anyone
tells you different can fuck right off. No, it were Fin
who were afraid of the place. And you couldn't
blame the poor cunt. Not with the shite he'd been
through out there not so long back, shite that had
condemned him to a life of sitting on his arse, reliant
on others. So no, *I* weren't afraid of the place. We're
all straight on that. But I'll tell you what.

I cacked me strides when he pulled up outside the
Bee Hive.

Norbert Green is one thing, but the fucking Bee
Hive? Come on. Aye, Norbert Green's a bad place.
But all its badness came from that one pub, so they
says. The Bee Hive just weren't the sort of place nice
folks went. Know what I mean? Alright, I ain't nice
folk and never have been nor never will be. But bad
folk never even went there neither. Unless they came
from Norbert Green, course, which opens up a
whole new grade of bad folk. So where Mr Outsider
here in his shiny new motor fitted in ... Well, I'd be
scratching me head til I got bits of brain under me
fingernails and I still wouldn't know.

I were up the far end with the engine ticking. I
weren't even driving past that place if I didn't have
to. As I let the handbrake off I watched him climb
out. He were dressed much same as when I'd met
him outside Hoppers: hooded jogging top, baggy
jeans, odd-looking trainers. If he only knew what a
cunt he looked. No one wore baggy jeans like that.

And as for the fucking hood – that ain't gonna help him much if it starts pissing down, is it. The door of the Bee Hive opened and two fellers came out to meet him:

Nobby and Cosh.

Been yonks since I'd seen them two cunts. And I don't use that word lightly here. Put quite simply Nobby and Cosh was the biggest pair of cunts Mangel had ever thrown up, which is saying summat considering the competition. I knew they must have been hiding out somewhere in the Norbert Green area on account of the bad reputation they had, to put it mild. They could handle emselves like the best of em but there ain't much you can do against a ton-strong lynch mob, which is what they'd get if they showed up in town. I'd tell you why they was so hated but I can't bring meself to just now. Later perhaps, if I remembers to.

They chatted for about half a minute, then Wossname handed one of em summat and went inside, leaving em to walk across the road to where a few motors was lined up.

I pissed off sharpish.

Alright, so that's what I were wanting to tell you prior to describing this top night of bouncing I went on to have. Weren't so painful, were it? Course not. And now let us ask *you* summat:

What is a top night of bouncing?

It's one of them question that bothers us all from time to time. Like 'why don't folks have tails, like cats and monkeys does?' Or 'why do fellers have nipples?' Well, I'll tell you then. (About the bouncing, that is. I can't account for tails nor nips.)

Action, mate.

I've heard all that about a bouncer's job being to keep the peace and make sure nothing kicks off, and a good doorman being one who gets folks to leave their aggro by the door when they goes in. You know what I says to that?

Bollocks.

There's only one reason a feller takes to door work and that's cos he likes a rumble. The more of it the better. But you got to deal with em right. No point getting ten bouts of an evening and having the shite knocked out of you. Should be you doing that to them. Most of em anyhow. And tonight, well, I were using boot, paw and swede all night and I won every time. Every fucking time.

How's that for percentages?

And it were good, see, cos Nathan had wanted the next night to be a nice one, like you gets in places you might take a bird to. And the best way to get your punters behaving is to knock the shite out of em the night prior. Then they'll behave alright. Be too knackered to do otherwise. And the ones who ain't knackered won't be keen on starting nothing, memories of my bouncing prowess being so fresh and that. So by the time I'd kicked the last cunt out I were in a right jolly old state of head.

I sat meself at the bar right opposite Rache. Looking fine tonight she were. Tight-fitting skirt showing off her arse, nice bit of squeezable out front. What more could a manager want from his bar staff? 'Giz a pint, eh,' I says, a mite narked that I even had to ask.

She tutted and did like she were told.

I sank it in one and demanded another, glaring at her.

She carried on wiping the bartop or whatever she were doing. I had to wait nearly a full minute before she got round to my beverage. Night like I'd had, birds ought to be swarming to us like flies to shit. So what were up with Rache here I truly did not know. I didn't like it neither. I were so put out I necked the new pint in two second flat.

And demanded another.

She tried to carry on ignoring us for a bit. It were plain as my head that she were putting it on. She knew I were there and what I wanted. I opened me gob to tell her as much, then shut it.

See, I'm clever. They wants you to bite, don't they, birds. Like the old honey trap, ennit, but with shite instead of honey. They puts summat manky under your nose and waits for you to bawl about it. Then, soon as you does, they lets rip on you. And if there's one thing a bird does better than a feller it's letting rip on you.

So forget it. I weren't playing that game. I'd had enough of it with Beth, me first and only dearly betrothed, God rest her charred remains.

I reached over the bartop and pulled one meself.

She whacked us across the knuckles with a damp cloth and started shrieking about her doing her job and me doing mine and the day she walks round the bar and starts beating up poor innocent younguns, that's when I can start pulling meself pints.

We went quiet for a bit, her returning to her wiping, me to my smoking. And it were hard sitting in

front of all that booze and not having a drop of it to
call me own. So hard, as it happens, that after a bit I
shrugged and picked me fags up. It were alright
watching Rache's arse wiggle about as she went at
her polishing, but there's no point dying of thirst for
it, is there? Not with all them tinnies waiting at
home.

Aye, bet you'd forgot about them.

Well, I fucking hadn't. Been on my mind all day
they had. Four hundred tinnies and four hundred
smokes. Half now, half later. Stingy fucker, weren't
he. Couldn't blame him, mind. And he had restored
me credit, which were a bonus. 'Well, Rache,' I says.
'Nice chattin' an' all, but—'

'I just don't understand,' she blurts, as if I'd
missed half a conversation. 'What's happened to you,
Blake? You used to be such a . . . such a . . . I dunno,
but you weren't nuthin' like what you are now.'

'Oh aye?' I lit another one up and sat back down.
'And what am I like now, eh?'

'You knows what you're like. You seem to love it so
much.'

'Love what, eh? Come on, I'm interested. I'm all
ears, ennit. Look at us, a big pair of ears and fuck all
besides, waitin' for you to—'

'Ears? How about a big pair of fists, a big pair of
boots, a big nasty mind and a big beer belly.'

'You what?'

'You heard.'

'No, go on. That last bit . . .'

'You heard. All ears you said, and I agreed.'

'I fuckin' ain't got no beer belly, alright?'

She turned away. There might have been a little

smirk on her chops. I ain't sure. Fucking better not have been, though.

'I said I fuckin'—'

'I heard you,' she says. 'Half of Mangel heard you.'

'Well . . . Well, how's this a beer belly? Look . . .' I slammed my right fist hard into me gut. It weren't too bad. I did it again and again, harder each time. It hurt a bit, that last one. Not that I'd winded meself nor nothing. My guts was rock hard. Just felt like I'd bruised that soft bit atop em.

'Well, Blake,' she says, picking up her coat. 'You're right, I'm wrong. See you tomorrow.'

I locked the door after her then went back in and pulled meself a pint of lager. I were manager, see. Managers can do what the fuck they likes.

Next morning I got up a bit late. It were half two when I looked at a clock, which were after I'd had a piss and near sucked the tap dry. I went downstairs and fried up what were left in the fridge from yesterday, ignoring the ringing phone. I had a few smokes and a couple of tinnies while I tried recalling what day it were. But you can't do that all day, sitting in your trolleys in the kitchen thinking about stuff. I stood up. Me arms and shoulders was aching from all that bouncing I'd put in last night. I didn't feel like getting dressed so I put me coat on, picked up a couple of four-packs, and went downstairs to rest me poor working man's limbs and watch a bit of telly down the cellar.

There were fuck all on. Nothing but the war, which had been going on for so long it didn't quali-fy as news no more, though folks had no better an

idea of what it were all about than when it had started. It were just summat that went on out there on the
outside, same as all them other bad things you saw
on telly. None of it happened in Mangel so I dunno
why they bothered showing it us. Might matter to
folks in the big city, mind. All kinds of shite happens
there, I hears, and none of it's nice. But they're all
barmy there, ain't they. They don't bring their younguns up proper, so the younguns dunno woss what
and ends up knifing some old dear so they can buy
drugs, or whatever they calls em. But Mangel
weren't like that. Alright, so Mangel folk were a bit
barmy. But they weren't thick. They knew woss good
for em and how to get along alright.

I flicked around for a bit then turned the fucker
off. There were never nothing on worth watching
that time of day anyhow. You wanted tits or a good
film you had to wait til late or watch it on the vid.
And I had plenty on vid, I can tell you. But you know
what? I weren't interested. The world sits on his arse
for no man, and it's the early chicken who counts his
worms, or summat. I kicked the four empties in the
corner, picked up the other four-pack, and went
upstairs to get dressed.

After that I came downstairs again and bumped
into Fin. Well, I weren't expecting him to be there,
were I, sitting there in the hall in his chair. I didn't
clock him til too late, and while me legs was stop-
pered by the back of his chair the rest of us sort of
ploughed on. I toppled over him and went arse up,
knocking the chair over and bringing it down atop
us.

A cripple chair ain't a nice thing to tangle with, I

can tell you. My ankle jammed under a wheel and got scraped to fuck, and one of the handles lodged himself right between me knackers, which were a lucky thing in a way but didn't feel it at the time. I cursed that dozy twat Finney, crawled clear of the chair, and nursed me nethers for a bit. Then I had a gander to see how Finney were. He were lying on his back by the front door, eyes shut.

Knocked the fucker out cold, hadn't I.

Which don't look good when it's a cripple. Not even one who were a cunt like our Fin.

'Fin,' I says, bending over him and slapping his chops. Getting no joy from that I picked him up by the pits and lugged him round the house a bit. He were still limp as a wet jumper, but I could feel his little heart going so I weren't fretting too much just yet. I set him down on the kitchen floor and had a think.

I'd been in a pickle not unlike this one a while back. In the Paul Pry it were, me demonstrating my headbutting skills on an old mate of mine and going a bit far, knocking him cold. I'd brung him to by tipping a pint in his gob, and I saw no reason why such a remedy shouldn't do for our Fin and all. Only I couldn't remember what the pint were of. It were either lager or water. I couldn't see water doing much good for a man in Fin's condition so I cracked a can of Doug's lager and started pouring it into his cake hole.

Nothing happened at first. Then he gargled a bit and went all quiet. Just when I were thinking I should have gone for water he started spluttering and thrashing his arms. I helped him onto his arse

and punched his back a few times to clear him. Then
I got his chair and put him in it.

He didn't half look a sorry state. 'What the fuck
was you doin' there in the hall?' I says, bending down
so my face were by his. Having trouble focusing on
us he were so I slapped him a few more times. 'Come
on, you cunt,' I shouts in his ear. Then: 'Coppers at
the door for you.'

That done it alright. He threw himself out of his
chair, ignoring the fact that he had no working legs.
I picked him up again and plonked him back in it.
He were a bit more alert now, eyes flitting all over the
shop in search of the pork boys.

I had to laugh at him. 'What the fuck for was you
in the hall?' I says again. Cos I won't have folks clut-
tering up my hall like that, cripples or no. Fire haz-
ard, ennit.

He rubbed his eyes and says summat like: 'Ah . . .
soz, Blake.' Alright, it didn't sound nothing like that.
But I couldn't make out what the fuck it were he
were saying so I'm filling in for him there. It were
plain as a crap on your doorstep that he were out of
it. I wheeled him into the front room, drew the curtains, and left him to it. I couldn't hang about looking after mongs all day, could I. I were a fucking busy
man, though I couldn't recall at that exact minute
what I were meant to be doing. I were togged and
shod, mind, so it must have been summat important.

I went out the front door hoping the fresh air
would help. Memory were sure to come back before
I reached town anyhow. But as it turned out I didn't
need to wait that long. I didn't even have the key in
the Capri when I clocked her. She were down the

end of the street, heading townward, tarted up to the armpits and disappearing round the corner.

Doug's youngun, wernit.

Mona.

5

TWO HELD FOR CRIMES
Robbie Sleeter, Junior Reporter

*Mangel Police arrested two youths yesterday in connec-
tion with the recent gunpoint robbery of Gromer Wines in
Cutler Road. At present the pair are being held for questioning, but charges are expected shortly.*

*A police source has revealed that the arrest came about
when an off-duty policeman, reposing on a bench in
Vomage Park, was approached by a gang of youngsters.
Mistaking him for a vagrant, they offered him alcohol for
sale. The quick-thinking lawman accepted and agreed to
meet them later on in town, where he was to pay them.
Only two of the gang turned up and were promptly
arrested.*

*Goods from Gromer Wines were found in their posses-
sion, along with several unidentified confectionery items.
The police source reports that on arrest the youths
attempted to throw away the sweets, later offering no
explanation for this action. The sweets have been sent to
labs for analysis.*

A police statement is expected in due course.

It were a toss-up between pegging after Mona and arriving all sweaty and out of puff, or climbing in my Capri and cruising up alongside her, looking all calm and classy. I knew teenagers, see. When I were one meself I'd noticed the way birds preferred your mature feller who holds himself well. And being on the door at Hoppers I'd learned it first hand, so to speak.

I climbed in.

But when I turned the corner, already starting to wind down the passenger window, she were gone. She weren't on the pavement anyhow. She weren't nowhere that she might reasonably have been, unless she'd hitched up her skirt and hopped over a wall. Or unless she were in that big shiny new motor headed townward down there.

I followed.

Course, I were fretting a tad that they'd drag us over the Bee Hive again. Not that I'm scared of Norbert Green nor nothing. Already told you that, didn't I. Just couldn't go in the Bee Hive is all. For ... For personal reasons, alright? So just shut it and let us get on, will you? Fucking hell.

Well, they didn't end up heading west so I were worrying over nothing there. The car went right at the roundabout up by the Forager's Arms and headed down the High Street. Halfway down there she swung a left into Frotfield Way and pulled up outside the arcade. I thought that a bit odd, being as you couldn't park there by rights and there were a copper slouching his way up t'other side of the road, picking his nose. Be a bit of a give-away if I pulled in and watched so I drove on, slow as I could.

I looked in as I went past and clocked her leaning into him, like they was snogging. A few yard up I looked in me rear-view. She got out and blew him a kiss.

A bit odd, that. The fucking arcade on her tod? Not the makings of the romantic afternoon I'd been expecting. But it did explain what she were doing with all Doug's money. Slotting it into them fucking fruities, weren't she.

Silly tart.

Her feller's motor were pulling away so I sped up and turned right. He carried on west, heading for the bridge. I went round the block and parked on the High Street. 'Can't park here,' says someone behind us.

It were the copper from just now. 'Well, fuck me,' I says, clocking him close up. 'PC Plim, ennit.'

'PC Palmer to you, Royston.'

'Who says you can call us Royston?'

'Come on . . .'

'No, *you* come on,' I says squaring up to him. I fucking hate coppers.

'Alright, have it yours. But you ain't parkin' here.'

'Oh aye? Gonna stop us, is you?'

'I can't stop you leavin' yer car here, but I can have her towed away alright. And you'll be payin' to get her back, I can tell you.'

'Oh, you can tell us, can you?'

'Aye, and I will.'

'Go on then.'

'I just did.'

'I didn't hear nuthin'.'

'Blake . . .' he says. He'd been backing off, but now

I had him up against the wall. Hadn't touched him, though. Knows the law, don't I. 'Blake, just think a minute.'

'Alright,' I says. 'I just thought a minute. I thought how much I fuckin' hates coppers.'

'But . . .' He were looking side to side now and pushing back, sort of aiming to slip through the wall. Couple of young lads had stopped to watch across the way. I hadn't seen em but I could sense em. Always sensed an audience, I did. 'Please, Blake . . .'

'Please what?'

'Please . . .'

'Go on,' I says, raising me voice of a sudden. He jumped about a foot in the air. I reckon the two lads did and all.

'Please let us go.'

'Let you go? For what?'

'For . . . Cos I'm a copper.'

'But I fuckin' hates coppers. Didn't I tell you that?'

Every word I said had him blinking. It were fucking hilarious, though no one were laughing. 'Let us go an' . . . an' you can park here.'

I were laughing now. I laughed like he'd said summat funny instead of the usual shite and bollocks him and his ilk came out with, which were all they had in em. But he hadn't said summat funny. There were fuck all funny. I laughed cos it were one of them rare moments, times when you could see Mangel for what she were and not what you wanted or reckoned her to be. You had em once in a while, when the stars lined up right and the wind turned arse. Well, maybe *you* didn't, but I fucking did. And when I did, laughing were the only thing I were fit for.

But it weren't funny.

'Alright,' I says, turning serious just when PC Plim were thinking about having a chuckle himself. 'Fuck off then.'

He thought for a second, weighing up his choices. Then he slid sideways, never taking his pig eyes off us. He backed away, getting faster and faster as he went, stumbling and winging lamp-posts but still looking at us. When he were round the corner and pegging it off I faced the younguns across the way. 'Knows who I is, does you?' I says.

'Aye,' says the one who weren't goofy. 'Royston Blake, ennit.'

'Aye, but does you *know* who I *is*?'

The one who'd spoke were turning a bit chalky, so his goofy mate says: 'Doorman at Hoppers, ennit?'

'Right,' I says. '*Head* Doorman, by the way. And Manager. But that still don't tell us much, do it, when you thinks about it. I mean, what if Hoppers shut up shop tomorrer? Who would I be then?'

They slied a gander at each other, looking a mite less white but no less worried. 'Royston Blake?' shrugs Goofy.

'I fuckin' knows that. But who the fuck is Royston Blake? I mean, what the fuck *am* I other than a name and a job? Eh? Come on, cos I fuckin' wanna know here.'

The other one were looking at his boots, leaving Goofy to fight on alone. Which were alright as it happened cos Goofy turned out to be a smart little fucker once he got going. Often happens that way with goofy cunts – looks like a gimp but turns out clever. 'Well,' he says, one hand in his trouser pocket, other scratching his ribs. 'Feller's from Mangel, right, he don't need to be no one, do he. Bein' from Mangel's enough.' He were nodding at himself now, stepping side to side. 'An' . . . an' searchin' for summat past that don't pay him. It ain't right, see. Cos, right, folks from Mangel is all leaves on the same tree an—'

'An' a leaf who falls off withers an' dies,' says his mate.

'Aye,' says Goofy. 'But what I were gettin' at were, like, all leaves on a tree is same as each other. Right? So if you wants to know who you is an' that . . . Well, look at the feller next to you.'

To be honest I weren't sure what to make of this. On the one side it were a straight answer. But on the other they sounded a bit like cocky cunts. So I gave em the benefit and only cuffed the one of em. Not the goofy one, mind. I didn't fancy snagging me knuckles on them jaggedy gnashers of his.

I hadn't been in that arky for fucking donkeys. It ain't a place growed-up fellers goes unless there's summat wrong with em. But when you're still a youngun, and it's time to see how much bollocks you got, the arky's your place.

A first visit through them peeling arches is a matter of seeing how long you can hold onto your coinage and fags without having an eye blacked or a rib cracked. But them who survives and comes back for more is set up for life. There's a hardness bred in the arky that you don't get nowhere else, not even

the shops down at Norbert Green. On his lucky day
a stranger can go down them shops, buy a pack of
fags and be off on his merry way. But he's meat in
the arky. And all his lucky day will get him is a broke
nose instead of a blade in the leg.

Course, birds is welcome there at all times.
Specially ones who'll flog their gob for tuppence. But
even if you're a bird and you're short a few bob you
won't want to go there. Not unless you don't mind
what folks says. And folks can be a bit nasty in
Mangel, things they says.

'Hoy, fuck off out of here, you little cunt.'

But not every bird in the arky were there to sell
summat or hang off a feller's arm. You'd not be wanting Fat Sandra hanging off your arm. Or any other
bit of you. 'Alright, San,' I says, stopping by her
booth. 'Long time no—'

'Deaf or summat, is you? I says fuck off. Now go
on – hop it.'

Now, I hears all sorts on the door at Hoppers. I've
been told to fuck off in as many ways as there is to
cook an egg. And I'll tell you – none of em works on
us. Course, the fellers and birds who says it finds
emselves out on the street sharpish, but that's only
us doing me job. Underneath it all I don't give a shite
what they says to us. But this Fat Sandra here sitting
behind the oily glass of her little change kiosk – she
had a way of phrasing it that had your knackers
shrivelling.

'Now San,' I says, leaning on the till, 'is that any
way to—'

'Aaahh,' she says, coming across all sympathetic of
a sudden. Or so I thought for as long as it takes a fly

to shit. Bollocks were she sympathetic. Fat Sandra
could have eight fucking trillion bones in her fat bag
of a body and not one of em would be sympathetic.
'Here's me talkin' all rough and I'm forgettin' how
Blakey's gone soft in the head since I last seen him.
Someone I can call to come and collect you, is there,
poor Blakey?'

I'd had it up past me eyeballs with all that bollocks.
Everyone else knew it had just been a cock-up, and
that while a feller might have his head examined it
don't follow he's a mong. That's what I'd been
working so hard to show the world, see, by getting
back on the Hoppers door so quick and establishing
meself once again as the hardest pound for pound
doorman in Mangel. 'Don't get out much, does you,
San,' I says. 'Else you'd know woss what, and that
I'm—'

'Aye, banned. Now *fuck off*.' She were stood up
now, pointing a saggy white arm to where a bit of
light were spilling through from the street.

'Banned? You what?'

'Aye. Banned. Now for the fifteen fuckin' hun-
dredth—'

'Hang on, hang on. What for is I banned? I ain't
been in here in . . .'

But she were right, you know. Getting banned had
happened same time as I started getting sick of the
arky anyhow, so I'd took it in me stride and forgot
about it. 'Oh, that,' I says. 'I ain't still banned for
that, is I?'

'Nah, course you ain't, Blake. Juss been tellin' you
to fuck off the past five minutes for a laugh, ain't I.
Once yer banned,' she says, voice going so loud of a

sudden I had to take a step back for fear her kiosk might shatter, 'yer *banned*.'

'Come on, San. Me an' Legs and Fin, we ... Heh heh ... We ...' It were all coming back to us now.

'Turned over a pinball table. Aye, I fuckin' knows it.'

'But we was bladdered. You can't blame—'

'Don't I knows it. There were sick all over the carpet over there. Now—'

'An' it weren't me honked anyhow, as I recall. That were—'

'Oh, here we goes – gonna blame it on a dead man now? Convenient for you, ennit.'

'Eh? No, I were—'

'Aye, now shut it before I starts cryin'. Far as I cares it were you. An' it were you done the rest of it an' all. Now fuck off cos yer banned.'

That just weren't fair. As it happened it were Fin who done all three. He always went a bit barmy on the pop in them days, which were fair play bearing in mind we was only younguns. But mates sticks together, even if one of em's a twat and the other turns out to be a cunt. So all three of us got banned at once, like. But I couldn't be arsed to trot it all out to Fat Sandra now. I pulled out me wallet instead and started fingering through it, hiding it from her. 'How much?' I says, slying a gander at her.

She were eyeing me wallet and licking her lips. 'How much you got?' she says, no edge to her voice of a sudden.

The answer were six old betting slips, a couple of bits of paper with birds' numbers on em, a photo of my Capri when I first had her, and a fiver. And she weren't having the fiver. Wages weren't due til next day and you always needs to keep a bit by. 'Fifty. That alright?'

'Oh, aye.' Her smile were almost pretty. If you squeezed your eyes shut tight enough it could be, anyhow. 'Well . . .' she says, coming to her senses and forcing the corners of her lips down. 'If thass all you can manage.'

I got 50p out me pocket and put it atop the counter. Then I blew her a kiss and went walkies. She were kicking up a row again behind us but I chose to ignore it. It were time to stop fucking about and concentrate on the job in hand.

The main bit of the arky were a big square with the change kiosk in the middle of it. Off that were three aisles lined by machines, mainly gamblers but also a few pinball tables and spaceys. I walked down the first, clocking a gander at the younguns glued to them machines as I went by. Fruities had come a long way since my day. Back then it were 10p a go for your top end, 5p and 2p bar. Now most of em took 20p, which were flaming barmy if you asks me. Where's a youngun meant to find enough coinage to see him through the day on them terms? Same place as me and the lads did in our day like as not – robbing. 'Got a light, mate?'

I turned. It were a filthy little scrag-end of a youngun in a black bomber and greasy hair, sort of feller you want to cuff round the ear just to watch him sail off on the breeze. 'Who you callin' mate?' I says.

He shrugged and backed off. 'Alright, mate. Only askin', weren't I.'

I grabbed his sleeve. 'Where's the bird come in here just now?'

'Bird? Ain't no birds in here. Get off us.'

'Don't feed us shite, you little cunt. Not five minute ago she came in here.'

'Alright, alright. Let go me hair. Fuckin' hurts that do. Ah . . . fuck . . .' He rubbed his scalp for a bit then leaned in and starts whispering. 'Only bird in here's Mona, back there by the pinball. You won't get much out of her, mind, heh heh.'

'What the fuck do that mean, you little—'

'Ow . . . Let us go . . . I mean you can't stick yer knob up her. She ain't for sale.'

'Oh, sure about that, is you?'

'Aye, I fuckin' am.'

'Knows who I am, does you?'

'Course I does. Royston B—'

'Royston fucking Blake. I can stick me knob where I wants to. Right?'

'Aye, alright. Let go me ear please.'

'So woss she doin' here if she ain't puttin' out?'

'She's . . . Er . . . Dunno, really.'

'"Dunno"? Fuck off. Tell us.'

'Ask her yerself.'

'Fuckin' cheeky . . .' I picked him up and dangled him by the ankles. Twenties and tens rained down on the carpet. Half a dozen other younguns jumped in and cleared up the mess, clocking nary a glance at their helpless comrade. I held him by one hand and lit a fag with the free one, watching em all. Scragends the lot of em, just like this un here. Nothing like in my day when you had to be born with bricks and mortar in your blood to even walk past the arky. Either folks had been spawning a lot of runts of late or the arky were attracting a lower class of punter. And going by some of the young shite-houses I had to contend with on the door at Hoppers I reckon it were the latter.

I let go his ankle, landing him plum on his swede. He lay on his face rubbing his conk for a bit, then up and scarpered soon as I looked away. He were shouting summat at us from the doorway as I made me way to the last aisle but I weren't paying no heed. Only peg it he would if I went after him anyhow. And I'd already showed him who were boss in Mangel. Besides, I'd just that minute spotted her, leaning against a wall over there, sharing some sweets with her pals.

I flicked me ash and strolled on up.

'Alright, love,' I says.

She clocked us up and down, making out like it were an effort to do as much, then turned back to her scrag-ends, who was stashing the sweets she'd just gave em. She weren't fooling us, mind. I'd seen the way birds eyed us down at Hoppers. Couldn't keep their fucking eyes off of us, they couldn't. I dunno what it were about us. I were a big lad, course, and that always gives you head start with the skirt. Plus there was some reckoned us a ringer for Clint Eastwood, if you can picture him a bit more fleshed out, like. So all in all there were no fucking way she didn't fancy us. Specially what with me being Head Doorman and Manager of Hoppers and her being a healthy young lass and all.

'I says alright, love,' I says.

Her eyes flicked at us and she says: 'Piss off.'

Course, I were as surprised as you by that. No bird ever spoke to us like that except Fat San just now, who ain't a proper bird anyhow. 'Come again?' I says.

'Piss off,' she says same as before only a bit louder and narkier now. The scrag-ends slipped past us, greasy and shifty as they was. She tried to follow, holding her head high and leading with her shoulder. I stuck me arm out.

She walked into it. Just like the other night outside Hoppers. But this time she looked up at us and says: 'Move yer fuckin' arm.'

She weren't so bad to look at now I got a good gander of her. I reckon there'd been summat up with her the other night like the feller had said. Her ginger hair were all shiny and done up today, and the way she used her pale eyes set me groin astir summat chronic. My arm were cross-ways over her chest so I moved it around a bit.

She stepped back. 'What d'you want?' she says, getting a smoke out.

I held a lighter out before she could get her own. 'A sweet,' I says. 'Got a sweetie for us?'

'You what?'

'Go on, giz one. I knows you got em.'

'Sweets? What the—'

'Aye, seen you give em to them lads just now. Come on.' I held out my hand. 'Sweet tooth, ain't I.'

'I don't care about yer teeth. You'll get nuthin' from us. Move.'

'Who's gonna make us, eh?'

She said nothing to that, sense finally seeping through her strop and hushing her up.

'Thass better,' I says, relaxing a bit. 'Now, I'll let you off the sweets. I knows how younguns ain't meant to give sweets to strangers and I wouldn't want you gettin' in no trouble with yer old feller over it. Wouldn't wanna upset him, would you?'

She were looking at us different now. Not quite a smile, but she were interested.

'Alright, fair play,' I says. 'Change the subject, shall us? Who were that feller dropped you off outside just now, eh?'

I reckoned she'd been planning it all along, waiting her moment. There'd been no sign of it leading up anyhow. I were a doorman, weren't I, trained to look out for such things on a nightly basis. But I weren't on duty now. I were chatting up a young bird in the arky. And I thought I were doing alright until she swung her knee full bore in me knackers.

She were long gone by the time I came to. Not that I'd been splayed out on the deck nor nothing. Can't let em see your pain, you can't. I just let meself fall sideways, standing propped up against a fruitie until the stars in me swede faded a bit and the sap started flowing south again. I made me exit with a dignified gait, ruing the fucking moment I'd stepped in that place not half an hour previous. And with fucking good reason to rue as it went on to turn out. You couldn't measure on a weighbridge how much grief

I could have spared meself if I'd only steered well clear.

And a good bit of it were to land on us next, when I went to Hoppers.

6

SWEETS DEFY SCIENTISTS
Robbie Sleeter, Junior Reporter

*Police scientists have completed their tests on the uniden-
tified items of confectionery found on the two youths
arrested for burgling Gromer Wines. 'To be honest with
you we just don't know what they are,' said Dr G. Gumb
in a hastily arranged press conference, attended also by
Dr B. Wimmer and Police Chief Bob Cadwallader. 'Odd
little things they are. Pink and round and quite hard.
Look a bit like them old sweets you used to get. What was
they called? Can't remember, can we, Bri?'*

'No,' replied Dr Wimmer.

*'Anyhow, in composition they are a bit like your typi-
cal gobstopper, with a couple of minor differences. What
differences?' you say. We can't say that for definite
because, well ... I wouldn't give them to my children,
that's all I can say.'*

*Standing up suddenly, Chief Cadwallader said: 'Listen
here, if anyone wants to come in and try one of these
sweets for us, under proper laboratory conditions and*

safety procedures and that, we'd be most grateful. And you'll be performing a public service. Just pop into the station and you'll be looked after.'

Asked about the recent crime wave the chief said: 'What crime wave? What's a flipping crime wave? Spot of robbery's nothing to fret over, is it? Spell inside will sort them two out. And to anyone reading this who's thinking of getting up to no good, let me tell you this: a spell inside will sort you out and all.'

'Message for you,' says Rache.

I were getting started on me fourth pint by way of bedding meself in for the evening. Folks wasn't up to much yet so I were sat at the bar taking it casual.

'You know what, Rache?' I says, shaking me swede and smiling a smile of resignation. 'She can take her message an' stick him up her—'

'It ain't from Sal. From Nathan, ennit.'

I drank half me pint, celebrating it not being from Sal. You might have noticed that Sal weren't top of my list of folks I wants to talk to. Well, that don't make you clever. If you was clever you'd know why. And you don't, does you. So I'd better tell you.

I just couldn't be arsed with her no more.

And that ain't just me being a cunt. She were letting herself go, weren't she. And if a bird don't care about herself then I ain't gonna neither.

So I were glad to hear the message weren't from her. Meant she were getting my message to her. If she wants to be near Royston Blake she's got to take a good long look in the mirror and tidy herself up a bit. Quality goes with quality, dunnit.

But it weren't all good news.

Idea of having Nathan the barman as me boss had been an alright one at first. Fuck only knew how he'd wangled ownership of the place after the last feller'd carked it, and to be honest I hadn't been in a fit shape to give it much thought at the time. I were just happy to get back on me door, and with someone I knew paying me wages. But he weren't half a whinging cunt when he got going. You seen him yesterday at the Paul Pry going on about this and that. What do you reckon? Could you work for a cunt like him? Course you couldn't. Not even if he'd have you. 'Woss he want now?' I says.

'Don't fuckin' swear at me,' she says, flashing fire at us. Been doing a fair bit of that of late she had. 'I only took the flippin' message.'

'Which were?'

She went to serve a feller, leaving us to sink the rest of me pint and look at meself in the mirrored wall behind the bar. Me dicky were a mite straight so I set him askew, just the way a dicky ought to be.

'About fuckin' time an' all,' says someone on me left.

'Oh, alright, Jack,' I says. 'Woss about time an' all? Settin' me dicky askew?'

He couldn't have heard us cos he wiped his mouth and says: 'Fuckin' fuckers. Fuckin' have em, I will, fuckin' lot of em. Fuckers. Telled him I did an' all. I'll have em. Them yonder an' all. Fuckin' sew em up proper. Cunts. I'll—' He started coughing and I knew he'd be busy with that for five minutes.

Rache came back, looking a bit calmer. 'Don't mind him,' she says, glancing at Jack, who were chewing summat he'd coughed up. 'He's been on one since openin'.'

'Aye, alright,' I says. 'But what about—'

'He says,' she says, referring to Nathan now and his phone call. 'He says, "Don't forget to keep the stage clear. And no trouble." You do know what he's on about, right?'

I pushed me empty towards her. Rache were getting on me tits now. Always had reckoned herself a cut above. And now here she were, trying to make a cunt of us.

'You mean you dunno?' She were smiling now. I'm happy to bring sunshine into folks' lives but one thing I don't enjoy is having the piss took out of us.

'Shut up an' giz another pint in there.'

That wiped the smirk off her chops. Then her eyes turned hard and she shook her head slow. 'I dunno why I bothers with you sometimes, Royston Blake.'

'Eh? But you don't bother with us, else I'd have me pint by now. Now come on – shift.'

She pulled us the drink and set it in front of us, slopping half of it over the bartop. By rights I ought to have her up over such shoddy barmanship but there was other matters at hand by then. Folks was starting to come in, see. I could see em in the mirror. And it were no different from last night.

I lit one up and drank me pint. I were doing a bit of thinking, see, and them two helps on that front, I've found. What the fuck was they playing at, them punters? I'd fucking showed em all last night, hadn't I? I'd smacked em black and blue and brown up the back and still they was coming in tonight getting me hackles up just the same way, doing the thing a feller just ain't meant to do, less he's after a shoeing.

Looking at us, weren't they. But not only that ...

They was looking at us ... *funny.*

And if there's one thing any self-respecting head doorman won't stand for it's funny looks.

I've said it before and I'll say him again: the number-one root of aggro round these parts is eye contact. Sometimes a shared glance can't be avoided. Eyes is eyes, and clocking's what they does best even when you don't want em to. Feller can't very well walk about with em shut unless he's aiming to make short work of himself. But anything more than a glance, at a feller you ain't on glancing terms with ...

You gets a smack, don't you.

And they was all doing it, them wankers. I couldn't fucking believe it. I'd have to do em all again for the second night on the trot. I sighed and shook me swede and sunk the lager, trying to wind meself up for it. Don't get us wrong, mind – hitting folks is always a pleasure. But I were getting a bit knackered. And too much of a good thing's bad for you. Still ...

It were only when I squared up to the first one that I recalled Nathan's orders. The thrust of em anyhow. *No aggro,* or summat. Which meant I couldn't hardly do me job proper. You don't really want to mess with Nathan's orders for several reasons – one of em being that no one ever had messed with him and I weren't about to be the first. 'Wanna look at summat, does you?' I says to the lucky feller who I'd decided against hitting. I held up me right paw anyhow, clenched. 'Well, look at this feller here.

Remember him. Next time you comes in here clockin' us like that you'll be meetin' him proper. Alright?'

'But . . .' He looked shite scared, to be fair. But that didn't stop him looking us up and down like I were a bird with no kit on. 'But you just . . . I mean you . . . Oh fuck, I'm . . . Can he . . .'

I weighed him up a moment then says: 'You fuckin' what?'

'No use, is it,' someone says into me right ear. 'J'd up, ain't he, heh heh. You'll not get a bit o' sense out of him.'

I turned, fists clenching even more. Who were this cunt who had the nerve to tell us what were what in my own place? That scrawny little gobshite from the arky is who he were, the one who I'd dropped on his swede just now.

'Likes glass, does you?' he says. 'Heh heh, hang about a bit an' we'll give you a glass show. Heh heh . . .'

'You fuckin' what?' I says. No one were making no sense and I were getting a bit sick of it. I made a grab for him but he ducked and slithered away. And just when I were thinking of going off after him someone else took me arm.

I threw it off and faced em, ready to drop my head. I didn't like the way the evening were unfolding and the only way to make it better were to make an example of some fucker. But it weren't no fucker, were it.

It were our fucking Sal.

'Well,' she says. 'I'm here.'

'Wha . . . Wh . . .' I were so taken aback I couldn't

spit the words out. 'What the fuck is you doin' here?'
I says at last, moving close. She had an inch of slap
on her face and smelled like a tart's window box
come spring. Least she had her coat buttoned up
proper, mind. If there were one thing I couldn't
abide it's fellers peeking down her cleavage. 'I telled
you don't come here. Puts us off me work, dunnit.'

'Your work, eh? Well, *I'm* workin' tonight an' all.'
She started unbuttoning her coat, which set us on
edge.

But I weren't gonna let it put us off. 'You? Work?'
says I. 'Don't make us laugh. You don't fuckin' work.
I looks after you. An' I'll tell you summat else . . .' I
stopped there cos . . . cos . . .

Music started up somewhere. Sort of music I
hadn't heard in Hoppers in a long time.

Tie a yellow ribbon round the . . .

But that weren't why I shut up. I shut up cos . . .
Ah, fucking hell.

She plonked her coat across me shoulder and
made off towards the raised drinking area. Fellers
was already taking notice – cheering, clearing a passage for her and then getting off the stage when she
reached it and started swinging her hips. They
was roaring when she turned her back and fiddled
with the catch of her yellow bra. None of em was
bothered about me no more. But to be honest I'd
rather have em bothering us than clocking my bird
up there turning round with her hands covering her
bare bosoms, which was getting quite big of late I
must say. The music were swinging and so were her
tits when she threw her paws up. I knew where I'd
last heard the song now – strip nights we used to

have down Hoppers in the old days when the Muntons still ran the show. Hoppers hadn't seen a pair of nips in nigh on four year. But it were seeing em now alright, as our Sal rubbed em up all poky and pert. And when she stuck her thumbs down the ribbon sides of her yellow knickers I knew it were set to see a lot more besides.

'Hoy,' I were shouting. 'Hoy, fuckin' cover yerself up and get down here *now*.' But Sal couldn't hear us with all the cheering. I couldn't even hear meself. I shut me eyes for a bit. When I opened em again it were worse. It were about as bad as it can fucking get, mate. She were bending over backwards and . . . She were . . .

You know, her knickers . . .

Ah, fuck.

I pegged it.

Rache were hoying us as I steamed past but I couldn't stop. If I stopped for her I'd have to look her in the eye, which were summat I didn't reckon I'd ever be doing again, the way things was going. I ran past her and headed for the door. Which were where I found me second problem.

'Royston Blake?' he says.

I looked up at his head. Then I looked from shoulder to shoulder, craning me neck. Aye, he were a big lad alright. But he were standing nice and quiet outside the door like a good boy, waiting to be let in. So I weren't fretting too much yet. 'Who the fuck is you?' I says.

'Royston Blake or what?' he says. You couldn't actually see his eyeballs he were so high up. Which were starting to make us a bit nervous if I'm honest.

But I knew his face to look at, just about. He'd been a little scrag-end last time I'd seen him, which must have been a year or so previous. Aye, I'd turned him away from the door on account of his looking no older than a young ten. We never let younguns in Hoppers. They could go to the Forager's. But he'd grown a bit since then. Big cunt he were now, about four times his former size. Looked a bit like that Frankenstein monster, with his bulgy forehead and tree trunk neck and that.

'So what if I is Royston Blake? Who wants to know?'

'You lamped our bruvver just now,' says Frankenstein, all matter of fact like he were telling us the time.

I scratched my head. 'Did I?'

'Aye, you did.'

'Where . . . ?' I were still scratching.

'Outside the arky.'

'Arky, eh? Well, I can't say I—'

'Knocked two of his teeth out, you did.'

'I honestly ain't—'

'And bust his lip.'

'Now come on, mate—'

I should have seen it coming. Me of all folks. I mean, come on, when it came to headbutting I ruled the fucking roost, didn't I. Aye, I fucking did. And there I were, breaking the first rule of good head-butting:

Don't let the other cunt nut you first.

I were pondering on this as I lay on me back watching the ceiling. Summat were wrong with me nose. I couldn't feel much but it were getting warm around there. Frankenstein's head appeared above us, nary a fret furrowing his big smooth brow. He were looking at me gob. Then me nose.

'Fuck,' he says, dribbling some flob on us. 'Missed.'

I saw his arm move a bit. His fist . . .

I were thrashing me arms, trying to get the bastards off. All over us they was, picking and poking and prodding. Don't sound that bad to you like as not, but it were the thought of what they'd do next that had us struggling. It had started with only looking, see. They'd been looking at us from far off. Then from near off. Then . . .

I opened me eyes.

'Blake?' Rache were bending over us, long hair brushing me face and sticking to it. She peeled it away, grimacing. 'Ugh . . . Blake, you alright? Can you hear us?'

'Course I can fuckin' hear.' But I weren't alright. My gob felt all wrong. I poked me tongue around it. 'Where the fuck's me gnashers gone?'

'Oh, Blake, don't try to get up.' She were holding a damp white cloth turned pink from blood. 'I'll call the ambulance . . .'

'Ambulance? Fuck off. Get off us. Piss off.'

Me pins didn't feel too bad once I were back on em. Bore us up alright anyhow. But when I clocked me reflection in the door window . . .

Fucking hell.

'What . . . ?' I started to say. But I knew what soon as I started asking it. The big feller, that's what. I'd had a fight with him. He'd nutted us and I'd got up and . . .

Ah, fuck. I hadn't got up at all, had I. I'd been lying here in the doorway ever since.

'How long I been lyin' there?'

Rache shrugged. But she knew well enough how long and I told her as much. 'Twenty minutes?' she says, hugging herself. It were cold out and getting late. 'Half an hour?'

'How many folks seen us like this?'

She leaned away from us. 'Blake . . . Don't . . .'

'What?'

'Here.' She wiped off the blood I'd just dripped on her cleavage then handed us the damp cloth. 'You best get down the hospital.'

'Fuck the ozzy.' I took a deep one and went inside. There was nothing else for it. Most of em had seen the mug damage already like as not. And if I kept me head down and moved fast I'd reach the bog without em seeing much more. I got halfway there before I noticed summat odd.

No one were there. It were only about half nine and not one fucking punter were in the place. And then there were that strange sound underfoot. I looked down.

Broken glass.

Fucking tons of it. All over the floor. Across the bar and behind it. On the tables and chairs and sofas and that. All along the back corridor. Scattered right across the stage, where . . .

'Where is she?'

'Who?'

'You knows who.'

'I don't, honest. Who?'

'Sal, for fuck.'

'Sal? But you don't . . .'

'Never mind what I don't. Where is she?'

'Dunno, do I. She were up there doing her . . . Blake, I've thought about it and I might as well tell you now – I ain't workin' no place they got strippers . . . Ow, get *off*. Alright, alright – I'll tell you. Fuckin' hell. She were up there, and I reckon by then you was out of it by the door, and then they started up with them bottles. Flyin' everywhere, they was. Smashin' on the walls and—'

'Who? Who were lobbin' em?'

'Dunno.'

Me fists was clenching. I held one up. 'Fuck off. Tell us or I'll . . .'

'Oh aye? Or you'll what?'

I put me paw down. I wouldn't get nowhere with that tack and Rache were only being Rache. 'Alright, what'd they look like?'

'Kids. Skinny little uns. About fourteen, fifteen.'

'How many? Seen em before?'

'There was loads, Blake. They was everywhere. I dunno . . . Maybe I seen a couple of em somewhere in town.'

'Where? Come on.'

'Calm down, Blake. Woss that road down by the . . .'

'The what? The Forager's? The Why Not? The Green Feller?'

'Frotfield Way.'

'Frot . . . Fuckin' bastards.'

'What?'

'Bitch.'

'I've told you, Blake, don't you talk to us like—'

'Not you. Fat Sandra from the arky. Fuckin' Fat fuckin' . . . fuck . . .'

'Blake? Where you off? What about all this . . .'

I saw sense just as I were pulling into Frotfield Way. Instead of stopping I drove on past the arky, clocking a good gander of it. Even through the locked doors I knew they was all in there, whooping it up and getting rid of the free tokens Fat San would have gave em. But there were no point me going in. Not with me face the way it were. I drove home, tonguing the holes where me front teeth used to be.

I remembered Sal when I were halfway there and made a detour for her flat. Weren't so bad when you thought about it in the cold light of a battered face. So what if fellers had got a look at her? Seen her before, hadn't they, when she'd been stripping for proper? Course they fucking had. And it weren't like they was getting the best of her now. Like I says just now, she'd let herself go a bit of late. That's what comes from sitting on your arse all day. But if fellers reckoned she were still worth a look, who were I to naysay em? And she'd be bringing a few quid in for a change.

But instead of taking the turn into her estate I pulled a U and went home. Couldn't be arsed, could I. She'd be alright anyhow. I'd have heard about it if she'd got hurt.

There were no sign of Fin when I got in. In his room like as not, watching his little telly or wanking over them mags he kept under his pit. I went upstairs and stripped and cleaned meself up a bit. Face weren't so bad once you washed off the dried blood. Hooter had been bust every which way over the years, so there weren't much left of him besides gristle and snot. Top lip were a bit swelled up and the empty gums was bleeding. So I'd lost a couple of ivories. So fucking what? Life's a bit shite now and then. But I were still standing, unlike Finney. I still had me facilities. And me brain were still sound despite everything.

I went down the cellar and got stuck into Doug's tinnies. Gums was still bleeding a fair bit and lager were the best thing to rinse em out with, I reckoned. I must have rinsed em out long and hard cos when I woke on the stone floor next morning they was alright, although the rest of me gob tasted like cack. And there were a banging in my head. And it weren't morning no more really. It were half two in the afty. And that banging weren't in me swede, it were the front door. I dragged my weary arse up there and opened it. Doug the shopkeeper.

And he weren't happy.

7

A MOTHER SPEAKS
Steve Dowie, Crime Editor

*I approach the street from the west. The autumn sun dips
behind me. Darkness looms up ahead. It has not rained
for hours but the pavement remains slick. The door opens
on the third ring.*

*A woman of middling years stands in dressing gown
and slippers, eyes red rimmed and shadowed. The woman
is Mrs X. 'You'd better come in,' she says.*

*You probably know Mrs X. You walk past her in the
market, sit next to her on the bus. She is the mother of
Boy X, one of the two teenagers convicted of robbing
Gromer Wines.*

She is every mother in Mangel.

*I ask her how she is coping, now her son is serving a
six-month jail term. 'I don't know what to do with
meself,' she says, pouring tea from a chipped brown pot.
'He's never been away from home before. I hope he's
changing his pants of a morn. Hey, do you think he is?'*

*I tell her that he probably is, then ask her about her
son's character.*

'Well,' she says, pulling her threadbare dressing gown tight around her generous bosom. 'He were always such a sensible lad. An old man in short trousers, you might say, except he never wore short trousers much. But lately he got ... well ...'

I reach out across the cramped living room and pat Mrs X gently on the knee. There there. In your own time.

'He's been behaving so odd of late, sleeping til noon and staying out til I don't know when. It's the friends he keeps. It's them who's the cause of it, you know. He won't wash himself proper neither. Smells like a dead cat, he do. And he's been looking so sick. Tried getting him down the doctor's but oh no, he's off down that arcade. I brung him up proper, mind.'

I reassure her that nobody is questioning her parenting skills. Quite the contrary. Such a fine figure of a woman as she could hardly fail as a mother.

'Oh, ta,' she says, leaning towards me, letting her dressing gown fall open slightly. 'Do you really think so?'

I ask her about the 'sweets' found in his possession. Had she herself noticed strange items of confectionery about his person?

'Oh,' she says, pressing her hand against mine, which is still on her knee. 'Oh, it's been so long since our Ivor passed away. You don't know what it's like for a widow. I've got needs, you know. Needs.'

I try to steer Mrs X back to the sweets, but the thread is gone. I make my excuses and leave.

Outside the sky is black. It is raining once again. A whiff of burning leaves taints the air with a sense of impending doom.

'... made it worse ... all night long, she has. With that feller no doubt ... trusted you ... lager and fags ... little girl, she is ... bastard.'

I knows this is about as clear as a boarded-up window but that's just how it were coming across to us. I'd just woke up, for fuck sake. And think about the punishment I'd took the night prior. Doug's voice were tuning in and out like a bluebottle going after earwax. But I got the strength of it.

He stopped for a bit then says: 'What happened to yer face?'

'What? Oh ...' I let him come in, being as he were shouting and spectators was lining up in the street. 'Pitfalls of the trade, ennit,' I says, grinning at him.

He frowned. 'You'll have to get dressed. I'll not stand for the way things is right now.'

'And what way is they?'

'I told you. She's not come home. Ain't seen her since yesterday mornin'. Never done this before, she ain't. Summat's happened. I knows it. That feller of hers is holdin' her against her will.'

'Now hold up, how old is she again?'

'Fourteen last December.'

'Fourteen?'

'What I said, ennit?'

'Doug, she's old enough to stay out at night. Fuck sake, she's old enough to go out and fuck half the fellers in Mangel if it so pleases her.'

I were just wondering if this weren't the cleverest thing to say when Doug lamped us one right on the nose. Now, I've already said how there weren't much a feller can trouble me hooter with, it being long since defeated from every angle. But that didn't mean it didn't sting. Stinging fit to blind us, it were. I doubled over and held me face.

'Perhaps that'll learn you a thing or two about treatin' folks proper, Royston Blake. And perhaps you'll kindly scrub yerself up and report at my shop in five minutes sharp. You're bringin' my daughter home, you are.'

I didn't have the will to argue, else I would have boxed his ears flat and sent him arse first onto the hard stuff. I went upstairs instead and brushed what were left of me teeth. By habit I'd pull on me bouncing togs after kipping this late, but they stank of fags and dried blood and I couldn't face em right now. I put on some jeans and a green shirt instead, which made us feel a bit better, though half the buttons was missing on the shirt and the jeans hummed a bit. I bundled up the bouncing gear and went down to the kitchen. There was a couple of things to make us a bit more better down there. Two hundred-odd tins of the one and eight packs of t'other. If only I could find em.

But I couldn't.

I went down the cellar. I'd lugged em all down there last night like as not when I got in. But they wasn't there neither. I went all over the house looking for em, until I found meself standing outside the only place they fairly could be.

I held me breath a full half minute, struggling to keep from kicking the door down. The fucking thieving little cunt – having away with my lager and fags after all I'd done for him, putting him up in me own front room and looking after him and that. I opened the door.

He weren't there. Nor was my gear. I looked under the bed and in the wardrobe and behind the door.

Fuck all.

No empties neither.

Where the fuck were he? Finney weren't meant to go out. He were a fucking cripple, for fuck sake. What reason had he to go out? I scratched my head for a bit, then shrugged and went off to Doug's corner shop.

'You can have em back when I gets me little girl back.'

I were puffing hard on me last fag. 'Come on, Doug, just crash us a couple o' packs for now, eh.'

'You heard. Do yer job and you'll get paid. I trusted you with half now, half on completion, and you let us down.'

'I fuckin' never. Been workin' on it I has. Even spoke to her yes'dy.'

'Oh aye? Go on.'

'Well, had a word, like. With your girl. In the arky.'

'What for? I never asked you to have a word with her. I'll be havin' all the words with her that needs havin', ta very much. Asked you to have a word with *him*, I did. And a bit more besides.'

'I know, I know. Been workin' on it, ain't I. Like I says.'

'And?'

'An' . . . Well, he ain't easy to get hold of, is he.'

'Thass why I flippin' hired you.'

'Alright, fuckin' don't shout, whatever you does. Me fuckin' head—'

'I don't care two figs about your head. I wants my

daughter back before summat happens to her. And I wants that feller beaten and drove out o' town. An' I'll tell you what, Royston Blake – if anyone – *anyone* – has so much as bruised her arm, *you're* answerin' for it.' He slammed the door on us.

I dunno how I came to be back out on the street but back on the street I were. And me fag were gone out.

It started raining.

I didn't go straight downtown. I knew what were up with Mona, see. She were only with her boyfriend. And I couldn't blame her. I'd be with her boyfriend and all if I had Doug at home. I'd find her later. Then I'd get me lager and fags back. But first I went round Sal's.

I were feeling low, see. You'd be feeling low and all if you'd had what I'd had. And the best thing for lowness, I've found, is a shag.

'What?'

'Me, ennit.'

'Who?'

'Fuck off. Let us in.'

There were silence for a bit. And, do you know, the thought crossed me mind that she might not let us in. She'd never not let us in before. Not once during all the highs and lows of our time together. No matter how bad it got she always came through with a buzz and a click.

'Sal? Open the fuckin' door, eh. Pissin' it down out here it is.'

Couldn't help herself, could she. Why leave him down there when you can bring him upstairs and bawl his ears out? But it were more than that. She just couldn't resist us. No woman ever could when you came down to it. Except the barmy uns. But Sal weren't barmy. She were just a bit thick at times. And you can't blame a woman for that.

'Fuck sake, Sal. Gonna open this door or what?'

'I dunno.'

'What? Fuckin' buzz us up, will you.'

'I dunno if I wants to, Blake.' She were getting us a bit worried. Her voice were different. She sounded knackered, like she couldn't be arsed with the effort no more. And that weren't like our Sal.

'Alright, love. Let us up an' we'll sort it out.' I went to get a fag then remembered I didn't have none. I flobbed on the floor instead. But even that were soon lost in the rain. I wished I'd stayed in bed. Or the sofa down the cellar, which is where I'd actually kipped. 'Fuck sake, Sal.'

She buzzed us up.

I sat on the white leather sofa that I'd gave her a couple of birthdays ago. Feller down Hoppers had cleared out a posh house and had it going spare. Too white for my place it were. I'd only mess it up with food and lager and fag burns. But Sal knew how to look after nice furniture, so she had it. I could hear her in the kitchen making a drink. I knew it wouldn't be a cup of tea, mind, which is what I could have done with right then, believe it or no.

She came out holding a glass of vod. Might have been water, I suppose. But you'd gamble your house on it being voddy if you knew our Sal and the way she were back then. In the other hand a fag were burning low. She were barefoot and clad in a pink dressing gown that had seen better days though I knew she hadn't had it so long. That's the thing about dressing gowns: they ain't built for general usage. What Sal needed were a pair of overalls to do her lying around and drinking and smoking in. With a leather patch for her arse, considering all the telly time she put in.

Aye, Sal were a rough sight them days if I'm honest. As a rule I tried not to look at her face if I came round too early. Last night were the first time I'd seen her in slap for yonks. Normally took us ten pints before her head stopped looking like an upturned radish with mucky roots sticking out the top. Weren't even noon yet and I hadn't touched a drop, but summat told us to have a gander at her face. I screwed up me peepers and went for it.

And I'll tell you what, mate – I fucking wished I hadn't. Did I say Sal were getting rough? Sailed past the rough stage overnight she had and turned jaggedy. Face were sliced down one cheek and up the other, with a little slanty bit across her forehead. It were all stitched up and that but needlework never had made a face less ugly and it weren't doing here.

I knew I had to say summat. On the spot, weren't I. 'Reckon you won't be doin' much more strippin',' I says, giving her a friendly smile. 'Less you wears a paper bag.'

To be honest she could have done with a paper bag anyhow, even before last night. But she couldn't hardly expect to get by without one now. I didn't mention none of that, course. I were all set to but she turned arse and went into the bedroom, slamming the door behind her and rattling that Elvis painting on the wall. I'd gave her that for her birthday and all. Different birthday, mind.

I sighed and got up. I went to her door and put me ear to it for a bit. She were sobbing, just loud enough so's I could hear it. Weren't the usual put-on neither. She were sobbing for proper this time. I put my hand on the doorknob and left it there a second. Then I came to me senses and stepped away. I lifted her smokes off the side and went out the front door, shutting it quiet behind us.

Oh aye, reckon I'm a cunt, does you?

Well, that's what I am.

And so's the feller who bust my face last night. And so's all them little fuckers done over Hoppers with the glass last night. Then there's me old man, who started us off on the cuntish trail by being such a good one himself. And every other bastard in town. Cunts the lot of em. Sal included. So don't come at us with your finger wagging and your arse in the air, cos if you looks hard enough in the mirror you'll find a cunt there and all.

Alright?

Now shut it or fuck off.

I got back in me Capri and drove townward, feeling lighter in meself the farther I got away from Sal. Had work to do, I did. A bird to find and a feller to do over. Them's two things I knew I could do when I put me heart to em even if nothing else were going right for us. In fact I knew if I could just get them two jobs done then all the rest would foller. All about confidence, you see. Land a couple of lefts and the rights looks after emselves. Here's what I'd do:

1. Sort out Frankenstein. He'd lamped us at Hoppers last night and doing him would restore my standing in the community.
2. Fuck Fat Sandra and her arcade monkeys.
3. When I says fuck her I don't mean it literal, you twat.
4. Fags and lager.

But I'd just pop down the Paul Pry first. It were pay day and I only had a fiver on us. Might have a couple while I were down there and all. Feller needs his strength getting up before performing great feats, don't he.

'No.'

I looked around the bar, sipping me pint. It were a quiet lunchtime in the quietest establishment in town. And that's just how I liked it. I spent enough time in Hoppers surrounded by the cory munts and filthy slappers that passed for townfolk. Outside work I needed a peaceful environment in which to sup me hard-earned. And with Nathan the barman in charge, the Paul Pry were it.

'You what, Nathan?' I says.

Weren't many folks could relax with Nathan around, see. I were one of em, course, but that's cos I'm easy going. I knows he knows everything and I don't give a toss about it. Other folks ain't so happy about that side of him, mind, Nathan knowing every little thing they gets up to and that. So Nathan's gift were also his curse, which were to preside over the least-frequented hostelry in Mangel.

'I says no. An' I'll not say him again. Clean yer ears out. No's an easy word to hear, and I reckon there ain't much of an excuse fer not hearin' him first time.'

The lager trickled down me neck as Nathan's meaning came through. 'What d'yer fuckin' mean, "no"?'

'I've told you before, Blake – kindly control yer language in my bar, ladies bein' present.'

'I don't see none.'

'Ain't the point.'

'What is, then?'

'Principle, ennit.'

'Where's me fuckin' wages?'

'Ain't payin.' He shrugged and went about his barmanlike affairs as if he'd just told us he were out of peanuts.

'Alright, Nathan,' I says, sucking a fag. Weren't like Nathan to play games. But a game it had to be. Made no sense else. 'I'll play. Why ain't I gettin' paid?'

'You ain't gettin' paid, Blakey, cos I ain't no longer your paymaster.'

I stubbed the smoke and plonked my empty glass before him. 'You what?' I lit another and chucked the empty box.

He sighed. 'I don't like repeatin' meself. You wants yer wages, you'll have to ask yer new boss. I'm sure he'll be just as good a paymaster as I were. And kindly pick that fag packet up.' He took my empty and filled her up.

'Eh? You owns Hoppers, right?'

'Wrong.'

'Wha . . . ?'

'Not no more I don't.'

'Course you does.'

'Nope. Not after last night.'

I remembered he were having us on and calmed down a bit. 'Alright, Nathan. Who fuckin' *do* own her, then?'

'Less of yer swearin'.'

Fuck calming down – I wanted to climb over the bartop and break his face. But this were Nathan the barman. You could do that to other barmen but not him. 'Who?'

He were wiping down the pumps, whistling a tune I weren't acquainted with. 'Nick Nopoly,' he says.

'You fuckin' what?'

He went to serve a punter. I started going through all the Nicks I knew. There were Nick Leech from school. He'd disappeared ten year ago and folks who disappears in Mangel don't as a rule ever turn up again. Like as not ventured one too many a time into Norbert Green, hadn't he. Then there were Nick Soil. But he were an old cadger and spent his days putting on tuppenny blads down the bookies. There were no way he'd buy Hoppers and he'd never win enough to anyhow. I tried thinking of other Nicks, well aware that I were wearing out me swede for no good purpose. I knew who Nick Nopoly were. Only I didn't want to face it. If I ignored it long enough it might go away and Nick Nopoly might start being someone else.

But, you know, I weren't quite sure why I were

fretting. He were only a streak of piss, weren't he. And he drove a fucking shite ugly motor.

'Nick Nopoly,' says Nathan, folding his hairy arms and setting em down atop the counter, 'is an outsider.' He gave us a long slow wink, like he'd said all that needed saying on the matter.

'But . . .' I had a lot of buts. I had so many fucking buts I weren't sure which but were best. But as it turned out I didn't need none of em.

Nathan cleared it all up for us, see. 'I'm a businessman, Blake. Businessmen needs to make money, not fritter it away. And Hoppers don't make no money. All Hoppers makes is trouble. The harder you tries to turn her around the more trouble you gets. Look at last night. Meant to be the night everythin' turned around, it were. Folks'd start buyin' and I'd start earnin' at last. But what happens? You tell us what happens, Blake. You was there. What'd I tell you? "No trouble," I says. So what does I get, eh? Trouble. Know what I says to Nick wossname, after he'd signed? "You ought to give that place a new name," I says. "You ought to call her *Trouble*." Thass what I says to him.'

I opened me gob.

But he were off again: 'And as fer him bein' an outsider, what of it? Like I says – I'm a businessman. One punter's good as the next un. Ain't first time an outsider's owned Hoppers. And besides, who else'd buy her? Who in Mangel is barmy enough to buy that place, besides meself once upon a time? And don't say you would. I'm talkin' about folks of means, not the like of you.'

'But . . .' I knew there were a good but in there

somewhere gagging for air. I tongued me bleeding gums hoping that'd spring him out.

'No buts,' says Nathan. 'You wants yer wages – and I've no doubt you does – get em off yer new boss like I says.'

'But . . .' It weren't the one I were after but it were a but. 'But where is he?'

'You'll find him in the Bee Hive,' he says, picking up a *Mangel Informer*. I fucking hated that particular journal and hadn't read it since they'd printed all that shite about us back then. Far as I were concerned that paper were a tissue of bollocks, or whatever they says, and like all good tissues it were fit only for blowing your nose or wiping your arse on. But I couldn't help clocking the headline: INTO THE LION'S DEN.

'Be there til six like as not he will. After which, Hoppers.'

I looked at him a bit longer. There were no point rowing with Nathan. You couldn't win. And even if you could it wouldn't gain you nothing. I necked me pint and got up.

'Payin' fer them, you are,' he says, nodding at my empty.

I glared at him, wishing he'd at least said them last two words the other way round. I couldn't believe he were being such a cunt. Not only were I a discarded employee and deserving of a bit more respect and gratitude – I were one of his top punters, and merited a particular level of service. 'Take it out me wages, same as always.'

'Can't very well do that now, can I.'

'Come on, Nathan. Only got a fiver on us, ain't I.
Put him on the slate or summat.'

'See that sign?' he says, poking thumb over shoulder. 'NO CREDIT.'

'Fuckin' hell,' I says, reaching into me pocket.

'And pick that fag packet up.'

Course, soon as I were back in me car I recalled the
thing I'd been wanting to say, the *but* that'd kept hid
under the shock of everything:

But what about me?

See, Hoppers were all I had. And don't go getting
the violin out and taking the piss. All I means is, you
know, Hoppers is the only job I ever done. Only legal
one, like. And it's more than . . .

Ah, fuck off. I can't be arsed. You wouldn't bloody
understand if I told you.

So go on, fuck off.

Still here? Alright, then . . .

I were headed cross town out Norbert Green way.
I didn't fucking care if I were straying onto dangerous ground and that folks from thereabouts is liable
to put you on a barbie if the sun's just so in the sky.
Fuck em. I wanted me wages, didn't I. And if I had
to go into the Bee Hive to get em . . .

Only thing were, I thought to meself, lifting up an
arse cheek and pumping out a long rattler, what the
hell were Nick Wossname doing in Norbert Green,
let alone the swarming stinking heart of it? Alright,
so he knew Nobby and Cosh. Knowing them would
get him in there no problem if they was still the

vicious cunts I used to know em to be. But how the fuck had he come to know em?

I'd asked meself such questions as these before. None of it had made sense then and it were no different now. I pulled up outside and opened the door of me 2.8i.

There's a feeling in your guts only a walk on the pavements of Norbert Green can give you. I were nigh on immune to it, having got up to a fair bit on them streets in me time and more or less got away with it. Saying that, within twenty or so yard of the Bee Hive I were as liable to cack meself as the next feller.

But I weren't having none of that today. Wanted me fucking wages, didn't I.

I strode across them paving slabs like a bull across his field. I were Royston fucking Blake. I could go anywhere. And who the fuck were gonna stop us? No one, that's who.

Just then the door opened and out comes Frankenstein.

8

INTO THE LION'S DEN
Steve Dowie, Crime Editor

The sun is shining as I walk up the five marble steps of Mangel Amusement Arcade, but the moment I pass through the wide entrance it might as well be midnight. Not only is this a dark place — it is a threatening place.

I am walking into a jungle. I know the natives are there. I cannot see them but I sense them. They recede into the shadows, furtive, suspicious of this stranger. The smell is like a jungle too: flatulence and indifferent personal hygiene.

I go to the booth in the centre of the floor and request change for the slot machines.

'Who's you?' says the large lady ensconced therein.

I shrug and try to look impatient.

She glares for a while longer, then picks up my money.

'We don't change pounds,' she says, pushing it away and shaking her head. 'Nothing bigger on you?'

I offer a five-pound note, which is greeted similarly. I offer a ten.

'More like it, ain't it.'

I pick up the coins and turn away. I count the money: only seven pounds. But I am not here to cause a scene. I pick a machine at random and feed in a coin. It flashes and plays an inane tune, does little else. I put more money in. Suddenly the sour odour of old sweat intensifies. An arm stretches out and leans on the machine. I sense sharp eyes following the spinning icons. The wheels stop suddenly.

'Here, I'll get you jackie from them nudges,' says a male voice, barely broken but roughened already by years of tobacco.

I turn to face this native. I ask him to clarify his meaning.

'Shift,' he says, shouldering me aside and taking the controls. He works the buttons like the pilot of an aircraft, jerking the wheels until three dollar signs line up. The machine plays a fanfare and pumps out coins. 'Nice one,' says the young man, kneeling down to help himself. 'I'll just get me slice.'

Taking advantage of his good mood I ask him casually where I can buy some 'sweets'.

He pauses and looks at me, eyes of a bitter old man staring out of a boy's face. Then he scuttles away.

I pick up what coins remain and move on. The banks of machines form three flashing, bleeping aisles. I take the central one, heading for a machine near the end where two lads are engrossed in their gambling. I put some money into the next machine along. Almost immediately I receive a blow to the back of the head and collapse. Four hostile young faces peer down at me.

'Giz it,' says one.

I ask him to clarify.

He kicks me in the ribs. Small bony hands probe into my pockets and deprive me of my coins. I feel one reach for my wallet.

'Oi!' It is a gruff female voice – the large lady in the booth. 'Get out of it, you. Go on. Let him get up, that's it. Now you there – **** off.'

I get on my feet and step away from the violent youths. An investigative reporter has no use for dignity. I nod my thanks to the booth lady.

'Didn't you hear us?' she shouts. 'I says **** off.'

I mumble my excuses and leave.

Outside the sun is shining and the air is clean. People are going about their business. Dogs bark. Young children squeal and frolic. But the oppressiveness of the arcade clings to me like soot to a chimney. I hurry along Frotfield Way.

Halfway down the High Street I notice that jungle stench again and resolve to have my overcoat cleaned.

'Oi, mate,' says a voice at my side. It is the youth who won me the jackpot. He looks up and down the street, then drops a screwed-up piece of paper in front of me.

I pick up the paper and smooth it out. 'YOU WANT JOEY – SEE THE J-MAN. DOWN HOPPERS.'

'Hoppers,' I say.

But the boy is gone.

Instead of turning into the Bee Hive I walked straight on past, turning me face the other way. I were being clever, see. No point getting into a ruck out in the open, is there. Not when all I'm after is me wages. Course, I wanted to settle it with Frankenstein there and then, but it weren't the right time just now.

'Hoy,' he shouts.

Like I says, the timing were wrong. I trotted off like I were a jogger or summat. It didn't feel too good but I'd look a twat if I stopped. I heard him coming after. Sounded like he'd crack the slabs with them heavy footfalls. He were gaining on us. 'Hoy, come here, you,' he says.

I pegged it a bit faster and started whistling like I were deaf and hadn't heard him. It were hard to whistle, the rate I were shifting at. I can go a bit quick over forty yard but past that and I've had it. I heard him panting behind us and knew it'd be same for him and all. I stuck me head down and gave it everything I had. Not that I were scared of Frankenstein nor nothing. I just didn't want a scene, like. At the end of the road I turned the corner and went down there a few yard. Me pins had packed up by now and I were running on momentum alone. Me eyes latched on an alley a bit farther up. I were nigh on falling apart when I got there. But there I surely did get.

I collapsed, hitting the ground hard. Lungs was working so hard I thought they'd barge past me ribs and come on out. I had to move. He'd be on us any minute if he were still chasing. I clawed meself upright on a rusty old wire fence and stuck my head round the corner. No Frankenstein.

I bent over and chucked me guts.

It's a funny un, life is. I ain't just saying that to make out like I'm a philosophiser and that. I really do reckon life is a funny one.

Fucking hilarious.

One minute you're on top of your game. You're widely considered the hardest feller in town. You're able to ignore your bird for weeks on end and still she's gagging for you. You've got more fags and tinnies than you knows what to do with. On top of all that you've got fifteen sheets in your pocket.

And then what?

Then you're sat behind a tree in a Norbert Green alley, honk all over your boots, scared to come out. Your face is bust and you've lost your two front ivories – all courtesy of a fucking overgrown young-un. Plus half town clocked you getting decked. Your bird won't talk to you and you don't want to look at her anyhow cos she's turned pig ugly. You ain't got no beer nor fags. There ain't even a crafty smoke stowed in your pocket somewhere and you're fucking gasping for one. You're skint.

And how? How the fuck had such a state of affairs come about?

This cunt Nick Wossname, that's how.

Still, life weren't all as shite as all that. I still had me job, didn't I. And my gold Capri 2.8i with black vinyl roof were parked just around the block. All I had to do were get to her.

I'd been sat mulling it all over for about an hour in total. It were five o'clock now and I were getting hungry. I left it any longer they'd be hearing me gut rumblings in Muckfield. I got up.

I staggered around a bit, hurting. Knees was cramped up to all fuck. I hadn't noticed it before but didn't I ever now. After ten minutes or so it were alright and I walked nice and quiet down the alley, aiming to come out the other side of the Bee Hive and not have to go past it again. No one were about. Never really were in Norbert Green. You stayed in your house unless you had somewhere to go. I went down the lane and turned left.

My car were fifty yard up the way and it warmed me cockles to see her. If there's one thing you can rely on in this world it's your motor. She's always there for you, ain't she. Might not start always but she's there.

But I knew she wouldn't let us down on the starting score. Not today. I'd had her serviced and souped up not but two week prior. Better than new, she were. Had been when I'd parked her anyhow. I were still thirty yard off when I noticed they'd slashed her fucking tyres.

Cunts.

I says just now that I were skint. That weren't the case as it turned out. I had 15p. But that weren't enough to get us a bus home. Even if buses did come to Norbert Green. So I walked.

I fucking hated yomping. It were beneath us. Didn't have much of a choice here, mind. I'd never get a spanner man to come out Norbert Green way. Only mechanics works there is your local uns and I weren't trusting one o' them with my Capri. Plus I had work at six. Normally I'd turn up whenever I felt like it, me being Manager and all. But with this new boss I had to set out on the right foot. Just for now, mind.

And that set us to thinking as I yomped down Shire Road past the graveyard. How the fuck were I meant to do right by Doug the shopkeeper if the feller he'd hired us to sort out were me boss? I couldn't, that's how. Not at the minute anyhow. Not even if I wanted to. Not even if Nick Wossname were the thorn in my side I knew he'd be. I'd have to work summat out, mind. No way were I going without me lager and fags.

I were bloody knackered when I reached Friar Street. With a bit of luck it'd be a quiet night at Hoppers so I could sit at the bar and get me puff back. But that hope went the way of morning mist when I clocked the crowd outside trying to get in. What the fuck were going on? It were only a bit past six.

I started pushing em aside when I reached the queue. I were the doorman, after all. And what were the fucking hold-up? Why the queue? I found out when I got a bit nearer. Then before I knew what I were doing I ducked and turned arse. I kept on walking down Friar Street, gasping for a fag and wondering what the bastard fuck Frankenstein were doing manning the door.

My fucking door.

'Alright, fuckin' calm down,' I says. 'Thass it. Just fuckin' take her easy and relax. Nice one. Now, less have a think about this, shall us?'

But it were hard to think. I needed a smoke. I needed twenty of em, chained two at a time. Plus me hands was shaking. This were what it felt like to be an old cadger, I reckoned. And I were only thirt . . . Never you fucking mind how old I were. I were in me prime is how old I were. The trembling were on account of all the shite I'd had to put up with of late. Only so much a feller can take, ain't there. I needed a drink. Aye, that'd steady me nerves alright. Plus I were fucking starving.

I got shifting.

'Fifteen p?' he says.

I didn't bother replying. He could see how much were lying atop the counter. Did I have to do his adding up for him now? Fucking cheek.

'What ... er ...' He were looking at us a bit shifty. Put him on the spot, hadn't I. Alvin were a businessman and as such weren't one to sell himself short. 'Woss you want us to sell you fer fifteen p?'

I sighed and shook me head. 'Just giz a bag o' chips. Giz fifteen p's worth o' chips, why don't you.'

He sort of smiled and shrugged, then started piling em on paper.

'Ta, mate,' I says, taking the full portion off him. 'Owes you one.'

'Right you is, Blakey.'

I walked out of Alvin's Kebab Shop & Chippy and headed back for Friar Street, shovelling chips in me gob. After a minute or so I could think proper again, which weren't such a good thing as it turned out. What the fuck were I meant to do with Frankenstein on me door? I'd have to fight him, wouldn't I, if I wanted in to see Nick Wossname. I knew I could have him though. Experience tells, mate. He were big alright but I had the moves.

'Alright, Blake,' says a passing feller, on his way to Hoppers like as not.

'Alright, Dave.'

I lobbed the chip paper in a bin and wiped hands

on strides, realising that I weren't dressed for door work anyhow. I were dressed like a punter.

'Hold up there, Dave.'

It weren't bad as disguises went. I'd been known to use better, mind. But without a wig there's only so far you can go. Still, it were worth a punt, me being a punter and all.

There weren't much of a queue now. But you could tell from the corner that Hoppers were rammed. I strolled on up, walking funny and keeping me head down.

Frankenstein weren't paying no mind anyhow when I went past him. In a daze he were, sunk eyes off in the distance. Could be he were pondering on the East Bloater Road and what lay beyond it. But I reckoned not. I reckoned it were just meself who gave thought to such matters, Mangel folk in general being happy with their lot. Ain't saying I weren't happy, mind. I were just a cut above your typical Mangel citizen in the thinking department. But you knows that, course. Can't very well talk to us for long without noticing it. Can you.

Anyhow, I reckoned Frankenstein weren't up to the job. Else I wouldn't have sailed past him so simple, would I. Tricky undertaking is door work. Specially at Hoppers. Only your top swedes is up to such a task and I reckon Frankie here fell well short in that area. It were too much for him and his head had shut down. So I got into Hoppers with nary a second glance.

And I'll tell you what, it *were* fucking rammed in there. Hadn't seen it so packed since that time a

while back when my face were all over the *Informer*
and everyone wanted a gander at us close up. No one
were interested in us now, mind, thanks to me clever
disguise. I clocked Dave up the far end of the bar –
where I'd told him to be – and started wending me
way down there.

Weren't easy as you'd think, I can tell you. Folks
was getting in the way more than normal. Some was
walking in front of us, flailing about like saplings in
a storm. Others just stood there, like twats. And they
wasn't your typical puntership neither. Mostly younguns these was, so young I wouldn't have let em in
meself – Hoppers being a class establishment and
the Forager's Arms across town being the favoured
venue for high-knackered drinkers. I'd soon sort that
out once I'd had a word with Nick Wossname and
booted Frankie off my door. But first things first.

'Alright, Dave,' I says, making him jump. I'd forgot
how he were good as blind without his glasses. I
handed em him along with his donkey jacket and
cap.

Course, I felt a bit sorry for him. There were good
reason for him wearing that flat cap. He'd managed
to keep it hid from Mangel folk in general for a
goodly stretch of time and all. But it were out now.
Bald as a plucked turkey, weren't he. Balder, considering most plucked turkeys you gets round here still
has a few feathers on em.

'Alright, Blake,' he says, squinting at us, shiny pate
glinting in the overheads.

I called Rache over and pointed at Dave, who were
just then putting his cap on, arse-about. 'Hiya, Blake,'
she says, giving us a nervy smile. 'You alright?'

I ignored her. She were a good girl, Rache, but I didn't want her fretting over us just cos another feller were on my door. No one had to worry about old Blakey. Sort meself out, couldn't I. Mind you, it were a nice surprise having a smile off her, considering the way she'd been spitting piss at us the past while. I pointed at Dave and winked at her.

'Hiya, Dave,' she says. 'What'll it be?' Smart girl.

'Oh, aye,' he says, still fumbling with his donkey jacket. 'Er, Blake?'

'Pint, ta,' I says, putting my own coat on. Always felt good to wrap meself in leather it did. Like pulling on a suit of armour.

'Right,' he says. 'He'll have a pint. Er . . . me an' all.' When she went to get em he says: 'Blake, what you done to me glasses?'

'Couldn't see through em, could I,' I says sparking one up. I offered the packet to him but he didn't take one.

'Aye, but where's the lenses?'

'Lenses?'

'Aye. Where's me blinkin' lenses?'

I glared at him for a bit, fag hanging out the side of me gob. Summat behind the bar caught my eye. It were my reflection in the mirror, but I'd have sworn it to be Clint Eastwood for a moment there. It were only the leather coat and slightly fleshier head gave us away. And the hat. Weren't wearing no hat, were I. Plus Clint Eastwood hadn't ever been known to show himself in Mangel to my knowledge, let alone working behind the bar at Hoppers. 'You swearin' at us?' I says to Dave.

'Soz about that, Blake, but where's me lenses?'

'Glass bits, you mean?'

'Aye.'

'Had to take em out. Telled you, didn't I, couldn't see with em. Might as well walk round with me eyes shut.'

'You...Y...' He started coughing so I slapped him on the back a couple of times. His false gnashers flew out his trap and slid along the bartop, coming to rest a few yard along in front of a bird. She dropped her drink, let out a little squeal and ran off.

'I kept em for you, mind,' I says, handing him his teeth back. 'Them glass bits. In yer coat there.'

He started rummaging in his pockets while Rache came back with the drinks. 'Where's me fags?' he says.

'That'll be four pound fifty, love,' says Rache.

'Ta, mate,' I says, and went off out back. I'd come here with a job to do after all. I didn't have time to stand about talking shite with the like of Dave.

The office door couldn't have been shut proper, seeing as how it swung open on the first knock. I were all set to apologise – this being our first proper meeting and that – when I noticed the room were empty.

So I went in.

After all, in a way it were more my office than his. How long had he been at Hoppers? A day? Less than that in fact. And look at me – I'd been there fuck knew how many years and I hadn't never had chance to call that office me own. Nathan made us manager but never let us use the office. 'Wouldn't be right,' the cunt said at the time. 'No, wouldn't be proper. And I'm doin' you a good turn there. Lettin' you have that office right now wouldn't do you no favours at all. Trust us.' So what did he do? Did he use it for himself? Like fuck. Left it empty, didn't he. Got new locks put on and shut the place up.

So aye, it were only fair I got to sit in the boss chair for a few moments on me own. And that's what I did.

Ah, I had some memories of that room. You wouldn't believe the goings-on I'd clocked within them four walls. Right up until the last time I'd been in there and all. Although I noticed they'd mopped it up a bit and fixed the window since that occasion. Still had that cigar box atop the desk from the last boss, mind. I flipped the lid – four inside, big fat uns. I took one and lit it using my half-smoked fag, sucking deep and then regretting it when the heavy smoke wanted out again sharpish. Always done that with cigars, I did, forgetting how strong they was compared to fags. I could get used to em, mind. I swung me boots atop the desk and sat back, dreaming like this were my own office and them stogies was mine by rights. Do the place up smart I would. Nice wood panels and a big drinking cabinet built in. I'd have a picture of Clint up there on that side – the one from the end of *The Good, the Bad and the Ugly* where he's stood in his poncho staring the shite out of the other two and making em shit.

On t'other wall I'd have a nice shot of a bird with her kit off. But tasteful, like. Baps but no bacon.

Aye, be happy in there I would, in that office. The rest of them out there could do what they fucking wanted. I'd sit here and count me coinage and let them deal with the punters for once. Maybe I'd let Frankie stay on the door. He didn't deserve it for jumping us like that but I couldn't deny he had door potential. Perhaps I'd even let Rache manage the bar. Long as she served us pronto when I phoned through for me pint.

'Go ahead, make yourself at home.'

It were Nick Wossname.

Fuck knew how long he'd been stood there in the doorway but it put the shite right up us and I dropped the cigar. Fuck it. Leave it burning there on the carpet. His fault for giving us a fright, wernit.

He looked a bit different from the other time I'd seen him up close. Older this time, which you can put down to it being light in here just now and dark the other day when I'd clocked him out front. Seemed less of an outsider and all, which were just him getting used to the place like as not.

Stood at the door with him were Nobby and Cosh, the two I'd clocked him with outside the Bee Hive just now. Behind them were Frankenstein. He towered above em by one head and half a neck and the top bit of his hair were hid by the door frame, which I'd always reckoned quite a high one. He were licking his lips.

'Can I knack him, boss?' he says, not taking his eyes off us. 'Eh, boss? Can I?'

'Look,' I says, half getting up off the chair. 'I were just . . . er . . .'

'Sittin' in that chair for old time's sake,' says Nick. 'I know. I don't blame you.'

'He wants knackin' boss. Bein' cheeky he is.'

'I dunno about that. What do you say, Blake? Cheeky, were you?'

I chewed on a bit of baccy I'd found between me

teeth and squinted at him. Clint did a fair bit of squinting and baccy-chewing and all. You cannot deny there was obvious likenesses between us two. I sat down again. 'How'd you know my name?'

'*Is* your name Blake?'

'Perhaps.'

'"Perhaps"? You mean you dunno?'

Only difference were that Clint always had a gun, which I wouldn't have minded right then. 'Ain't sure if I ought to tell you,' I says instead of shooting em.

Frankie were going purple. 'See, boss? Cheeky bugger wants knackin'.'

'Aye,' says Nobby, licking his ginger tash with his purple tongue. 'Always been cheeky that un has.'

'Always been a wanker an' all,' Cosh says. The two of em started chortling like they'd said summat funny. Oh aye, said I'd tell you about them two, didn't I. Go on then . . .

Nobby and Cosh had always gone round together. Cos of em both being so pig ugly like as not – Nobby with his bright ginger hair and freckles like baked beans stuck to his face, Cosh with his harelip. As younguns they used to stick bangers up cats' arses, you know. Everyone thought that were a great laugh. When they was a bit older they was caught fucking heifers down the Cowie. Now that ain't such a bad thing, you might say. Feller can't very well learn about birds and shagging if he can't fuck heifers first. But these two killed the poor heifer first, before cutting fuck holes in her guts and shagging them. Folks didn't like that so much but it were only a heifer, wernit.

Few years after that a young lass disappeared in

Muckfield on her way home from school. Old feller said he seen Nobby and Cosh take her but he had heart attack and died before summat came of it. Coppers turned up fuck all as usual and let em go. But that don't mean nothing. Everyone knew it were Nobby and Cosh. And the only way they got off from getting strung up a lamp-post were by never straying out of Norbert Green. Not even a lynch mob'll go out there. And Norbert Green folk don't give a fuck about a Muckfield youngun.

'Alright, Nobby and Cosh,' I says.

'Alright, Blake.'

'Alright, Blake.'

'Who says you two nonces could come out?'

They shut up at that. But I knew I'd be paying for it soon enough, if they got their way.

'You hear that, boss?' says Frankie. 'Can't say that, can he? I can knack him, boss, if you just says . . .'

I'd have ignored em and walked on out if they wasn't blocking the doorway. I'd do it anyhow but I didn't want to cause a scene, what with all them folks out there. I were here to talk business, not fuck about.

Nick Wossname were looking at us, chewing his lip. 'Nah,' he says after a bit. 'Leave us alone a while, will you?'

'Eh? But boss . . .'

He ushered em out with nary another word. Looked about twelve he did from behind with them stupid baggy togs of his. Someone ought to take him aside and tell him how to dress proper. Specially him being boss of Hoppers and all. Feller in his position ought to have a clean shirt and a sovereign on his finger.

'Royston Blake,' he says, turning to face us after shutting the door. He sat down in the hard wood chair opposite and got a pack of smokes from out his pocket. I didn't like him sat there. That had always been my chair. Why didn't he tell us to get out of his chair? I would have told him where to go if he did, course. But if he asked nice I might have obliged. Fuck knows I wanted to. I didn't like it this way round. It were like he were taking the piss, him sat there and me in the boss chair. 'Smoke?' he says, holding out the pack.

I took one.

'You don't want those cigars,' he says, making a face. 'They been there ... what, a year?'

'Two year.'

'That long, eh? And how long you been here?'

'Never mind that,' I says. Cos I were here on business, weren't I. 'I come for me wages.'

'Ah, yeah.' He reached behind him and pulled a fat wallet from out his back pocket. 'How much do I owe?'

Fucking hell, I were thinking, this is a piece of piss. And there I were thinking I'd be in for a hard time. I did some quick sums in me head then doubled it a couple of times. Then I took a bit off cos there's only so much piss you can take before the puddle runs dry. Then I made up a number cos I never had been no good at sums. 'Eighty,' I says. I clamped me jaw tight shut. Hold firm. Stand your ground.

He counted out eight brownies and laid em atop the desk. I picked em up. Been a long time since I'd held this much in me paw. Nathan normally kept back most of me wages to cover all the subs. And it were never this much anyhow. I looked at this Nick feller, wondering if Nathan had told him about the subs when he bought the place. Nah, he couldn't have, if he'd had to ask us how much he owed. This feller truly were a piece of piss. 'So I can keep me job then or what?' I blurts.

He started stroking his chin, which normally means the feller's about to talk bollocks. Body language, ennit. 'Sort of.'

'"Sort of"? Woss "sort of" mean?'

'I mean there's work for you. But not on the door.'

'Oh aye?' I were getting interested now. I loved working door at Hoppers but there were one job (only one, mind) I'd pack it in for. 'You wants us to manage the place?'

'Not exactly.'

'I ain't workin' behind no bar, you know. And if it's glass washer-uppers you wants you can go down the job shop.'

'None of them things. Put it this way – what d'you think a bloke like me needs, doing what I do?'

It were my turn to stroke me chin. Doing what he done? Far as I were concerned he were another flash outsider coming to Mangel, reckoning he can clean up. I'd seen em before, mate. They never lasts. 'How the fuck should I know?' I says.

'But you do know what I do, right?'

I shrugged. 'You owns Hoppers.'

'Yeah. And?'

I shrugged again. I didn't like shrugging and it were him making us do it. 'I don't fuckin' know. What you want us to tell you? Fuckin' hell ... Have I got a fuckin' job or what?'

He smiled and shook his head a bit. But not like he were naysaying us. It were a slow shake, like he were recalling an old joke. He were an odd feller alright. But he seemed to like us, didn't he. Can't say I blamed him neither. Quality in a man stands out a mile off, and if you're hiring in Mangel you can't do better than come knocking on my door. Mind you, depends what the work is. 'Mind you,' I says, 'depends what the work is, dunnit.'

'Alright,' he says. 'I'll tell you.' He got up and strolled over to the window. Funny how folks always does that when they got summat important to say. But what could be so important?

What job, I asks you, is more important than your doorman?

That's a question folks has asked emselves up and down the ages without much joy. Truth be telled, there ain't nothing more important than the job of welcoming them what's welcome and sending the others on their way. I mean, imagine a world where unwelcome folks comes and goes as they pleases, lowering the tone for the rest of you. Not pretty, is it. And that's why your doorman is sacred.

But there were one other job I wouldn't have minded doing. Besides managing. And Nick Wossname got it in one, as it happened.

'Blake,' he says, 'I want you to be my minder.'

9

WHAT IS WRONG WITH MANGEL YOUTH?
Malcolm Pigg, Chief Editor

Yesterday saw seven domestic burglaries, eleven car thefts, six muggings, two armed robberies, and eight reports of shoplifting in this town of ours. That's thirty-seven crimes in one day. How many of those do you want to bet were done by grown-up professionals? Two perhaps? Five, tops? Let's say five for bother's sake. That leaves us with thirty-four crimes.

And who did those thirty-four?

Children is who. You know it and I know it. Tell you what, I won't even bother looking at the details of who they caught for them (where they caught anyone at all). I'll stake my reputation here and now that at least nine out of ten of those twenty-five were youngsters.

Now, I'm well aware that kids in Mangel have never got up to much good and oftentimes a lot of bad. In fact I got my assistant Jeanie to have a look at the records and see what she came up with for this day twenty year previous. She came back with this nice chart here comparing like for like today against twenty year back.

Crime	Today	20 year back
Burglary	7	1
Car Theft	11	4
Mugging	6	2
Armed Robbery	2	0
Shoplifting	8	2

Look at that. Go on, just look at it, will you. (Ta, Jeanie.)

Now, we've got the same police force, same folks on the streets give or take a few, same schools, and same water supply. So what is it that makes the youngsters of today so wayward?

Respect for their elders and betters, that's what.

They don't know what respect is any more. And do you know why?

Fear.

It's you lot I'm talking about now. Parents and teachers and folks on the street. You're afraid of them. You know it and they know and they don't respect you for it. So here's what to do:

Tell your kids off. Spank them. And if that doesn't work, send them round my house. I'll teach them a thing or two about respect.

It is an undisputed and widely held fact, according to most folks, that *Minder* is one of the greatest programmes ever to have graced our telly screens. The pairing of Dennis Waterman at the height of his telly powers and that old feller with the hat were a potent brew, and one what had the world and his mate watching every Sunday night come flood or fire. But it weren't Waterman they came to see. Weren't the old hat feller neither. No.

It were the white Capri with a black vinyl roof at the start.

See, your Capri is class. And a Capri on a telly programme is the mark of a class show. With *Minder* you had that theme tune and all which not even a man dying in the gutter could help but tap his boot to. So all in all it were a top bit of telly. Which were why I gave Nick Wossname the nod.

'Aye, go on then,' I says. 'You won't find a better minder round here than Royston Blake.'

'Is that so?'

'Course it is. Who else is there? There's hard lads here and there but they ain't got class like what a minder needs. But I got it, mate. You don't spend ten years in a dicky bow and not pick up class.'

'You won't be needing a dicky bow with me.'

'Ain't bothered. I were growing out of it anyhow.'

'Oh, right. Well, the job is just being around, really, in case anything kicks off. Obviously you'll need to step in now and then, but your presence is more important than your punch. Know what I mean?'

He were a clever lad were Nick Wossname and I were looking forward to working with him. 'A raised eyebrow is as good as a thump in the kidneys,' I says. 'Sometimes.'

'Right. You won't get regular time off as such. You'll be off duty whenever I don't need you. I'll pay you double what you make now.'

I started to smile but pinned it down. Double what I were on now? Were he taking the piss or what?

'Don't worry,' he says. 'I can afford it. I'm doin' alright, Blake. And I'll be doin' a lot better before I'm through with this town.'

I frowned. 'Woss you mean by that?' Cos it were an odd thing to say, wernit.

'Forget it,' he says, shrugging. 'But listen, you ought to think it over first. Sleep on it and let me know tomorrow. I don't want you changing your mind on me.'

Were he fucking joshing or what? I'd been waiting my whole life to be a minder. I just hadn't realised it til now, had I. But it all made sense when you looked at it. I were your perfect minder. Just look at the facts here:

- Hardest feller in Mangel bar none.
- Respect of his public built up over ten year of doorman work.
- Possessing a level of style and sophistication rare in this town, picked up off my old feller, who were a snappy dresser in his day, so they says.
- Drives a Ford Capri, with eighty sheets in me pocket for getting her on the road again.

So no, I didn't need to sleep on nothing.

I were all set to tell him as much when I came to me senses. He were right. You ought never to commit yourself to a tackle unless you're sure you can reach the ball. And it's a blind man who knows how to find his mother in a crowd. So sleep on it I would.

He reached his paw across the desk. I flobbed on mine and shook his, cos I were feeling proper rosy now and there ain't no finer way than that to honour a feller. My life were looking up again, and it were all down to my new mate Nick Wossname.

★

I couldn't be arsed with Hoppers when I came out of his office. I were a minder now, weren't I. A minder ain't chained to one place like I had been as a doorman. A minder gets out and about, getting up to this and that.

Frankenstein were at the door. I stopped and had a gander at him close up, nodding appreciatively at his stiff collar and spotless sleeves. Manning doors is a dirty job but there's no excuse for sloppiness, I always says. Only thing I could fault him on were his dicky, which were straight as the horizon. I reached out to set it askew.

But he weren't having it, were he. He called us a cunt, told us to fuck off, and shoved us away. In that order.

Didn't bother us, mind. I were testing him, see. And he'd failed. He'd got the ingredients right but the recipe were wrong: he should have shoved us away, told us to fuck off, and *then* called us a cunt as I sat in the dust wondering what had come to pass. But I said nothing about it for now. Plenty of time to set him straight. And as for him lacking respect for his olders and betters – I let him off that one and all. He didn't know yet that I were the boss's minder and therefore well above him on the Hoppers career ladder.

I gave him a wink then got back on me feet and fucked off out of it.

I bumped into Filthy Stan outside the Volley and asked him if he'd pick up my Capri first thing the morrer, fix her up and drop her round mine. He were all up for it but when I mentioned Norbert Green he shook his head so hard the grease were flying off it like water off a wet sheepdog. Not even for fifty would he do it. And to be fair I couldn't blame him. Sixty quid and he had a think about it, then shook his filthy head and went to fuck off again. Then I got seven brown ones out.

He gave us the nod at that, cramming the notes in his back pocket. By rights I ought to have gave him a slap for trying to rip us off but I couldn't see no other way of getting my motor back. And what with us being a high earner and all now seventy wouldn't kill us.

And at least I had a tenner left.

I stopped at the offie in Cutler Road and spent that on fags, nuts and a half-bottle of whisky, then headed homeward. I were in a good mood now so I didn't mind the yomping so much, but I'd be a lot happier doing it on a full tank.

The nuts was gone by the time I could smell Burt's Caff and I wished to fuck I'd held firm and only gave Stan the sixty. Steak and chips I fancied if Burt had any in. Otherwise steak and summat else. Pie perhaps. I had a think about it and decided Burt might give us credit just this once, seeing as how I were a minder and all now. Life is all about give and take after all and he'd be sure to need my minding skills sooner or later. Before going in I popped up the alley next to the caff for a quick piss. After I put meself away I twisted the cap off the hard stuff and put him to me lips, closing me eyes and swimming in that golden sea for a while. I got quarter way down before coming up for air. And it's then that I noticed her.

She were sat on her arse not but ten foot from where I were stood. 'Hello?' I says. She didn't hear us so I took a step closer. It were dark up there so I sparked me lighter and crouched down.

Doug's youngun, wernit. Mona.

I shook her foot and said her name. One of her lids opened a bit and she copped half an eyeful of us. A little smirk touched her chops. She said summat quiet.

'You what, love?' I says.

The lid shut and her face went slack. I leaned in and got a cop of her breath. No sauce fumes whatsoever. It were like when I'd seen her outside Hoppers that time – out of it but no sign of boozing. I wondered if there weren't summat wrong with her. Maybe she went mong now and again or summat. There'd been a feller like that at school. Elmer his name were. Used to go mental of a sudden and then lie on the deck, legs twitching and tongue out. Ever so funny it were. Couple of year back he crashed his motor into a wall and carked it. Such a shame that were. She were a beautiful silver Ford Zephyr with nary a spot of rust on her.

Anyhow, there was two reasons why I doubted our Mona here were like that. First off her tongue weren't hanging out. Second off I'd been noticing a fair bit of odd behaviour amongst youngfolk of late and they couldn't all have what Elmer had, could they.

I took another swig and sparked one up, wondering why I were fretting my head over it. Her health weren't my fucking problem. Specially not now I had a new job as Mangel's premier minder. Doug could take his mouldy ale and squirt it up his cock with a pair of bellows for all I gave a toss.

Who the fucking bollocks were he, telling Royston Blake what to do?

I took another swig and a few puffs, then tossed the smoke and picked Mona up. There weren't much to her, to be fair. It were like lugging a rolled-up mat on me shoulder. I went up the far end of the alley and booted the old door. There were a bolt t'other side but it never had worked in the old days and it were no different now. Beyond it were a grimy old yard round back of the joke shop. From there you could step over the low fence and tippy-toe along the big old wall overlooking the Wall Road. So that's what I done.

Couple of motors was passing in either direction but that didn't bother us. Hadn't done nothing wrong, had I. Quite the opposite, mate. My good deed for the year this were. And if Doug didn't give us a big ta – and the four hundred tins and smokes he owed us – I'd get them bellows out meself.

I set her down and jumped off the wall into the car park behind Hoppers. The fucking whisky bottle fell out and smashed on the tarmac. I kept calm about it, mind, and didn't shout – I were after some transport so I couldn't have folks clocking on to us, could I.

Weren't easy getting Mona down off that wall. She were light as you like but there were summat awkward about her arms and legs and I ended up dropping her.

'Oh, soz,' I says. But I needn't have bothered. She were awake but not enough to give a toss. Just lay there on her back, she did, with that daft smirk on her face. Summat were up with her for surely. No one gets dropped like that without crying about it.

Specially not birds. But I didn't have time to fret over that one. I perched her across me shoulder again and strode into the car park.

I set her down and started trying door handles. Normally you'd have at least twenty motors here by this time, but I weren't surprised to find only ten or so. Hoppers were full of younguns tonight and younguns don't drive. Not their own motors anyhow.

Weren't long before I found a door unlocked. A Mini, it were, which weren't ideal. I don't really fit in Minis, never had done nor ever would do. Easy to start em, mind. But just as I were climbing in summat over the far side of the yard caught me eye.

Nick Wossname's flash motor, wernit.

Like I says already, she truly were pig arse ugly. I still stands by that one. But she weren't half shiny. Put the other motors to shame, she fair did. Even that burgundy Austin Princess over there by the bins. Not that I were interested, course. There were just summat about her. I checked no one were near by then went on over.

Ever seen the paintwork on them ugly new motors, has you? Fucking smart it is. Closer you looks at it the more little sparkly uns you sees in it, like they plucked the stars out the sky and lobbed em in a paint pot then stirred it all up and slapped him on. Not that I were impressed, mind. I'd still have me Ford Capri any day. Course I fucking would. And she had metallic paint and all. But not like this un here. Bloody marvellous it were, and I spent a goodly few minutes breathing on her and buffing her up and just plain staring at her. Then a motor started up across the way, over by where I'd left . . .

I stood up, opening me gob to shout summat. Then I shut it and went down again. All me sap drained south. That's what it fucking felt like anyhow. I hadn't seen nothing. I hadn't fucking needed to. Hearing it were bad enough.

And still she never made no sound.

Not a fucking peep.

The engine stalled and whoever it were got out. Who the fuck could be twat enough to drive over a bird lying slap fucking bang in front of his motor? He'd have had to walk right past her to get to his door. Course, it didn't take much to work out who'd done it. And when he started blubbering like a babby I knew it for surely.

'Fuck,' I says, slumping down against the flash motor. The occasion demanded summat a bit grander but that were all I could think of to say. 'Fuck,' I says again but in a slightly grander way. I had a point, mind. I were fucking fucked, I were. And I weren't hanging about to collect me dues for it.

I crept to the back wall and bunked over, dropping down into the scrub and sliding on my arse down to the Wall Road. Dave could sort his own problems. Weren't my fault, were it.

Don't start.

By the time I'd turned into my road there was four things I knew for surely.

First off I were fucking thirsty.

Second off I were dog arse knackered.

Third off I'd blown me chance of being a minder. I mean fucking think about it: if Mona were still alive she'd for surely let on that I'd carried her off and plonked her in the car park, leading to her getting run over. And if she'd carked it I were in even more shite. There'd been a couple of motors going up and down the Wall Road and someone must have clocked us lugging her. Alright, Dave had done the deed so he'd cop the full whack, and rightly so, but I couldn't see Nick Wossname having us as a minder after this.

And the fourth thing I knew for surely – cos if you're paying us heed and not just sitting there picking your nose and wondering what you'll have for tea you'll recall me saying there was four things I knew for surely – is that I were fucking thirsty.

That's right. I said that one already. Give yourself a gold star and shut your fucking hole. I says it twice for a reason, see:

Thirsty enough for two fellers, weren't I.

Anyhow, you can be thirsty as you likes, but if you ain't got a penny to your name nor a drop in the house you ain't gonna get far. These was desperate times alright. And you knows what desperate times calls for.

'Alright, Doug,' I says when he popped up behind his counter at last.

'Alright, Royston,' he says, eyes narrowing. Not enough so's I couldn't see how bloodshot they was, mind. 'Well?'

'Come for me fags and lager, ain't I.'

His lids widened a bit. But not in any jovial way. He shouldered past us and looked both ways out the door, then came back in front of us and says, stubbly chin thrust out at us: 'You what?'

'Fags and lager, ennit.' I started whistling but it didn't sound right so I stopped. 'You know, me dues. I done what you hired us for, ennit.'

After a bit he says: 'How's that then?' He weren't smiling.

'Your feller – Nick Wossname. Done him over, ain't I. "Smack him around a bit," you says t'other day. "Then you can have this little pile here. In payment, like." Well, cough up then. Fair's fair. Done my bit, ain't I.'

I were getting a bit fed up with Doug, if I'm honest. And his stary eyes and silent approach to conversation weren't helping matters. Alright, so I were feeding him a plate of shite with nary a flicker of shame. But shame don't help you if shite's what you're feeding. And these was desperate times.

'Where's my girl?' he barks at last.

'Ah, right . . .' Cos I'd forgot about that bit. 'In town somewhere.'

'You what?'

'I says in—'

'I told you go on an' bring her back here. Where is she?'

'I had her. I swear I did. Got her away from Nick Wossname, didn't I. All set to come home with us, she were, but the fuckin' cow slipped us and hared off. She'll be alright, mind. Turn up here in an hour or so like as not. Right then . . .' I says, rubbing me paws and peering over his shoulder. 'Out there, is they?'

He did some more staring at us. And I'll tell you summat – I didn't much care for Doug's stares. Staring's a fine art in Mangel. Some can do it, some can't. But that ain't the end of it. There's staring, see, and there's staring fit to turn a feller's blood to black pudding. And that's what Doug the shopkeeper were doing there for a minute or two.

'Alright,' I says, feeling me pudding turning black. 'Alright, Doug. Keep yer fuckin' hairpiece on.' I turned arse.

'An' I'll tell you summat,' he says as I opened the door. 'You'll get nuthin' from us until that little girl is back here where she belongs.'

I started crossing the road, feeling a bit sick. 'Tell you what,' he says behind us from his open doorway. His voice had softened somewhat so I stopped. 'Bring her back before sunset the morrer an' I'll double the bounty. How's that sound?'

'Eight hundred tins? And fags?' I says.

'You've had some already.'

'A round eight hundred of each, you says?'

'Go on, then,' he says, pulling the door shut as he spoke. 'Just bring her back safe.'

Doubling the bounty were a marvellous thing, but the cob in me pants were drooping already by the time I slotted key in door. I were stepping into a home bereft of life's comforts. Weren't even no whisky in there far as I knew. I'd been meaning to tax another bottle off Hoppers but hadn't had chance what with this and that. So it were with a heavy heart, a knackered pair of pins, a sore set of gums and a bruised arse that I shut the door behind us.

I sat said arse gently down at the kitchen table and buried face in paws. I ain't one to yield easy to self-pity, I can tell you. But there's only so fucking much a feller can take, ain't there. I mean, ain't there. Put up and shut your face, I heard a feller say once or twice. And I reckon he had it about right. But I'll bet me trousers he hadn't got as low as meself without having a glass and a smoke to keep his nose above water. Or some coinage to get it with. Or a mate to share his woes with.

And that gave us an idea.

I cleared me throat and knocked on Finney's door. He'd surprised us earlier by not being in, but he'd be home now for surely. Cripple can't stay out for long on his tod. Who's gonna wipe his arse for him?

But there were no answer.

I knocked again. He'd be fast akip in his pit like as not. And there was nothing stopping us walking on in. But if you're aiming to tap a feller for a few quid you'd best be polite. 'Come on, you cunt,' I says politely, knocking a bit more. Still no sound. I went in.

He weren't there. Nor his cripple chair neither.

I stood in the middle of the floor scratching my head. It worried us a bit, him being out so long. He were a cripple, weren't he? What's a cripple doing out and about at night?

Still, no good fretting over Finney.

Next morning I woke up on the floor. I sat on the bed and took a few deep uns for a while, getting used to not being akip no more. ''S alright,' I were saying to meself. 'Just another one o' them flyin' cunt dreams.' I repeated that a few times then got up and made me way across the landing.

Like all dreams the flavour had wore off by the time I'd had a slash. I brushed me teeth, splashed me face and threw on some gear. None of them things made us feel the way they ought to. I couldn't recall the last time I'd got washed up and dressed that early, so the novelty ought to have had us whistling and frolicking. But it weren't. Felt like shite, didn't I. Not your normal shite, mind. It were on account of it not being your normal shite what made it so shite, in fact. Know what I mean?

No?

Fucking hell, you're hard work, ain't you. Alright, I'll paint him black and white, just for you:

I'd had fuck all to drink last night, ennit.

One pint in Hoppers and a sip of whisky is all. My head were clear, thoughts buzzing round it like little buzzing fellers. But I didn't like it that way. Felt like I had a beehive for a brain. No, I liked me thinker nice and fuzzy of a morn. I liked to start off rough and ease meself into the day gradual. I were a fucking doorman, for fuck sake. A doorman, up at half nine with a clear head? I were letting meself go is what I were doing. I went down the stair.

I opened the fridge and reached for that bag of sprouts over there. Big old bag he were and you never knew what were lurking behind, me having plonked it and forgot it weeks ago. The paper gave way and summat looking like sprout soup and stinking like landfill spilled out and onto me boots. The bit of shelf it had been on were black with mildew. I found that a bit odd cos you ain't meant to get mildew in your fridge, are you. Mind you, I'd been wondering for months if that fridge weren't bust. The seal around the door were coming off anyhow.

But I forgot all about all that when I found a tin of lager there, right in the corner.

I reached for him.

He didn't want to come at first. The mould and fungus and what have you had growed up around and fused him to the fridge, like. I tugged hard and at last popped him from his furry cradle. It were only half a can as it turned out and I swore a bit as a few drops sloshed out the open top. Finney'd put it there like as not after I'd dropped off at the table one night. Course, it'd be flat by now. But flat lager's better that no lager in my experience. I got a knife from the sink and cleaned up the outside of the can, then put it to me lips.

Ah, it were lager alright. Not even the onslaught of nature could take that away from it. And it hit the required spot quite nicely if you made a few allowances. But I weren't sure about them crunchy bits. Specially not when one of em started wriggling under me tongue. And when a big old eary wig crawled out the can and waggled his feelers at us I heard a female voice piping up somewhere inside us, saying: *Royston Blake, you got a drinking problem.*

I got the sieve out the cupboard and used it to get all the bugs out of my lager. That were the first use I'd ever had for that sieve. Been me mam's at one time, I supposed, if you went back far enough. Fuck knew what she'd used it for, but straining eary wigs and woodlices out of pop weren't it, like as not.

Ah, if she could see us now.

I leaned back on the sink and supped the lager out of a mug. I'd never seen her, mind. Not even a photo. But I still felt a twinge of shame at the thought of her up there, looking down on her only begotten young-un drinking such manky beer.

I tipped the lager down the sink and went to the door. Mam were right, bless her. I did have a drinking problem. No son of hers ought to be reduced to drinking that old cat spray. No, I ought to be drinking proper lager, out of cans that ain't been opened yet. And far as I could see there were only one way I could get hold of some:

Find Mona and collect me dues off of Doug.

10

SWEET TEST INCONCLUSIVE
Robbie Sleeter, Junior Reporter

Police scientists Dr G. Gumb and Dr B. Wimmer were forced to abandon the controversial testing of unidentified sweets on human subjects when all four volunteers fled the laboratory.

'I just can't understand it,' said Dr Gumb. 'They were all here the one minute, sucking and chewing on the sweets. I turn around to drink my tea and read the paper and next thing you know they're gone. I just can't understand it. You can't either, can you, Bri?'

'No,' replied Dr Wimmer.

'To be honest I thought it might have been down to the tea. Me making a cuppa for meself must have put their noses out of joint, I reckon. But I couldn't have given them tea. Laboratory conditions don't allow for the drinking of tea, do they, Bri?'

'No,' replied Dr Wimmer.

'But I would have made them some after, honest I would. Looks like I won't get the chance now, though.

Anyhow, we'd just like to say this to those volunteers if they're watching. Please come in and tell us what happened after you left here. Did your hair fall out? Did you start talking funny? Perhaps you experienced strong sexual urges? Please come in and tell us so we can write it down. Anyone who does so will get some tea.'

'Right,' I says, opening the front door. 'No more fuckin' about.'

I were right, you know. That's what I'd been doing of late, ennit. Fucking about. Royston Blake, letting an overgrowed youngun swipe his job from under him? Getting his tyres slashed in Norbert Green, thereby stranding his Capri there? And allowing the cruel wossnames of fate – with the help of Dave – to fuck up the things I had done proper, like getting a new job as Mangel's top minder and helping out Mona? Fucking about is what I calls that. From now on I were doing things proper.

I waited twenty minutes for a bus before recalling how I didn't have no money anyhow. I thought about going back to blad some off Fin, who'd rolled in after I'd crashed like as not. But it'd been hard enough getting past Doug's without him clocking us and I didn't fancy risking it again. I cursed my bastard luck and started walking.

Tell you what, mind, there's summat to be said for being skint and having your motor stuck in Norbert Green. I were getting used to walking, weren't I. In a way. As I've said before and like as not will say again – fellers ain't built for yomping. Yomping's for tramps, housewives and boot coppers, as everyone knows. But that morning I were almost enjoying it.

Air were clean and not so stinking as it were by habit. Nice and crispy and all, nigh on stinging me nostrils with crispiness when I sucked too much too fast. But that might have been on account of the flattening Frankenstein had gave it t'other night. Me pins was bursting with beans and all. Felt like I could walk halfway round the world without stopping, I did. And I would have and all, if leaving Mangel were summat a feller could reasonably do. But it weren't, ain't, and never will be.

And besides, I were fucking knackered by the time I reached Mangel Infirmary.

Doing me own headwork I were, see. My custom were to visit Nathan the barman when summat needed knowing. He'd always furnish us with the required nugget if I made a fair exchange of it. But since him being my boss I'd stopped requiring them sorts of nuggets. Nathan casting his portly shadow over my affairs had the effect of keeping us out of shite, and when your nose is clean you've got no call for Nathan's help. And besides, last time I'd called on him for that I'd ended up with me face splashed over the *Mangel Informer* with the word KILLER under it. But that's a story I already told and ain't telling again.

So like I says, I were working things out for meself this time. About time I started doing that, I were thinking as I staggered through the glass doors. Though me pins was knackered and wobbling my head were alright, up for tackling any of life's shite. Me thinker were feeling sharp, and though I hadn't liked it that way upon getting up, the walk downtown had blew air through me ears and settled it all down a bit.

'Alright, love,' I says to the bird there. She were a lass in her twenties with nice shiny dark hair tied up behind her head. Tits wasn't up to much but her face made up for it a bit, though no amount of prettiness can truly balance out that kind of shortage.

I waited for her to say hiya and flash us a little smile perhaps, but instead she says: 'You're banned.'

I looked behind us to make sure she had the right feller. There were only meself near by so I says: 'Come again, love?'

'Royston Blake, aren't you? Says here you're banned.'

'Says where?' I says, leaning over the bartop.

'You ain't meant to . . . Get off.' She were off and running out back before I could get a proper hold of her arm. I shook my head and got the bit of paper she had down there. Next to a photo of yours truly – the one from the papers a couple year back – it said: *ROYSTON ROGER BLAKE. DO NOT APPROACH OR ENGAGE IN CONVERSATION. LIKELY TO BE VIOLENT. CALL SECURITY IMMEDIATELY.*

Well, fuck me, I were thinking as the bird came back out front, security guard in tow. 'Well, fuck me,' I says as the guard moved to the fore, egged on by the bird. 'Alright, Don.'

'Alright, Blakey. How's you?'

'Not so bad. Where's Burt?'

'Dunno. We ain't married, you know.'

'I knows that but I always sees you two . . . Ah, never mind.'

'Shame about Hoppers, eh.'

'Aye. How'd you hear?'

'Hear what?'

'Lost me job.'

'Lost yer job, have you?'

'Aye.'

'Sorry to hear that, Blakey.'

'Aye, fuckin' bastards.'

'Fuckin' right.'

'So how'd you hear?'

'You just told us.'

'Did I?'

'Anyhow, shame about Hoppers, ennit.'

'Aye.' I reached in me jacket pocket for a smoke then recalled how I were hungry, skint and fagless. 'What is?'

Don gave us a fag and had one himself. I were grateful for that cos it fucking reeked in there as usual. Reeked of shite and death and open wounds left to go manky. Don offered one to the bird but she didn't seem to notice, so wrapped up were she in our conversation. 'Hoppers I'm on about,' says Don. 'Shame what iss come to, ennit.'

'What, you mean that feller on the door?'

'Feller . . . ? No, the punters in there now. Younguns, ain't they. Full o' fuckin' younguns, ennit.'

'Aye, well. Could be you gettin' old, that.'

'Ain't just me says it. Everyone else do an' all.'

'Who's everyone?'

'Everyone who drinks in Hoppers. Proper punters, not them screamers you has in there now. Time were you could rely on Hoppers to keep younguns out. Forager's Arms is where they goes, not a proper drinkin' place like yer Hoppers. But look at it now – all younguns and that stuff . . . Woss they call it? Joey, aye.'

'Joey? Who the fu—'

'Aye. Your fault an' all, I says. You on the door, ennit. Younguns can't get in without your say-so, can they. Well, ta very much, Blakey. Ta for fuckin' up Mangel's only decent piss house. Always knew we'd lose Hoppers one day with you on the door, what with your mental pro—'

'Excuse me,' says the bird. She looked upset about summat.

'What?' says Don.

'You gonna chuck him out or what?'

'Who?'

'Him. Royston Blake.' She didn't look happy.

'Why?'

'Cos he's banned. Here on this list he is,' she says, grabbing it out of my hand. '*ROYSTON ROGER BLAKE . . . LIKELY TO BE VIOLENT . . . HISTORY OF MENTAL ILLNESS . . . CALL SECURITY IMMEDIATELY*. Well? You're security, ain't you. Chuck him out.'

Don looked at her for a bit, smoking his fag and blowing it in her face. Then he says: 'Nah—harmless, ain't he. Poor old cunt,' and went off out back again.

She turned to us and set her chin firm. 'Kindly leave. Else I'll call the coppers.'

'Look, love . . .'

She picked up a blower, dialled, and started murmuring. After that she says to us: 'I'd go now if I were you. Coppers on their way.'

'Look, you dunno what I'm here for yet.'

'Ain't interested. Banned, you are.'

'But what if I've broke me leg or summat?'

'*Banned,* I said.'

'What if I got a lurgy, and the whole town gets it if you don't cure us?'

'Ain't interested.'

'Alright,' I says, 'alright. I'll come clean. I ain't got no lurgy. I'm in top health and fit as a farm cat, as you can see. All I wants to know is . . .'

But she'd turned away to deal with a punter who'd slied up on me left. I turned to give the punter what for, but it were a young feller with a pan stuck atop his swede, mam standing behind him with a face like concrete. I let the bird sort em out while I finished the smoke and looked around at the folks waiting. It were busy in there for a morning, most injuries tending to occur after sundown by tradition. One or two gashes here and there along with a bust this and bent that, but with most of em you couldn't tell what the problem were. Just sitting there they was, faces white, some with head in hands. Even recognised a couple of them arcade monkeys, I did, though they was wearing different togs this time. Baggy jeans and hooded jogging tops they was decked in now, a bit like—

'I dunno why you don't just go,' the bird says.

'Alright,' I says, cos I'd just about had enough of her and her lip. 'I will. I'll piss off an' not bother you again with me violent ways. Long as you answers us one thing.'

'I ain't meant to talk to you. Coppers'll be here soon.'

'Juss tell us if a particular young lass is in here.'

'No.'

'Come on, me niece, ennit. Worried sick her mam is.'

'I can't,' she says, shaking her head hard.

'Go on, love, look her up in that book you got down there. Mona her name is.'

'Mona who?'

'Dunno. How many Monas you got in?'

'That ain't the point,' she says, opening a big red book like the one they did your register in at school. 'Needs a last name, don't I.'

'She'd of come in last night. Run over. Bust bones and that.'

'Well . . .' She were running her finger down the names now. I leaned over far as I could but the writing were small and you could hardly read it close up, let alone from where I were. 'Hang on,' she says, slamming the book shut. 'I ain't meant to talk to you.'

'Aye, I knows that, but—'

'Woss we got here then?' comes a voice behind us. You could smell copper a mile off. Even the way the ozzy were stinking already.

'Come on,' I says, ignoring him and talking to the bird. 'She in or not?'

'This the feller givin' you trouble?' says the copper.

'Aye,' she says, folding her arms. 'Banned he is an' he won't go away. Told him, I did. Told security an' all and what'd he do? Eh? Know what he done?'

'Hoy you,' says I. 'Just tell us about Mona, fuck sake.'

'Come on, Blake,' says the copper, taking my arm.

'Fuck off, Jonah,' I says, shrugging him off and walking up a corridor. 'Mona,' I shouts, loud as me lungs let us. 'Eh girl, where's you?' I got fuck all answer except me own echoes. 'Hoy, Mona.'

'Right, you.' Jonah the copper were behind us again. He pulled a sly one and twisted my arm up me back. Not bad considering the useless fucking broomstick he'd been at school. Must have learned him good when he joined the coppers.

'Not bad at all,' I says to him, wrenching my arm free and smacking him full bore in the gob with it.

Odd feeling came to us as I walked through the car park behind the Paul Pry. Weren't the time of day that were odd. It were gone lunch by now and I were in the habit of going down there any time after then. Weren't sure what it were to be honest. Not until I'd walked right past it and stepped inside the back door.

Motors.

Alright, it were a car park and by nature such places tends to harbour motors. But you just didn't ever get more than the one or two behind the Paul Pry. Not even on a Saturday night, which this weren't. But today, on this particular weekday afternoon, there was nine of the fuckers. I turned about and looked at em, scratching my head. Nothing unusual about the motors emselves. Just motors they was – Marinas, Cortinas, couple of Maxis and a Zodiac there in the corner. Even recognised one or two of em from the Hoppers car park. But what the fuck was they doing here?

I strolled on in, wondering if the car park on Strake Hill were shut for roadwork. Aye, like as not. But I were wrong there as I found out when I entered the bar area. Cars was parked out back cos the drivers of em was inside.

You might think that obvious yourself, you being a bit of a smart alec, but you didn't know the Paul Pry like I done. It were a quiet pub. You never saw more than eight or so in there of a Saturday night, let alone weekday afternoon. 'Alright, Nathan,' I says, taking a stool by the bar. He didn't hear us at first, unaccustomed as he were to the level of backchat. 'Hoy,' I says, 'Nathan.'

He finished up polishing a tankard, placed it back careful on the tankard shelf, hung the rag on the rag hook, took the damp cloth off of the damp cloth peg, and sidled over to us. He stopped a couple of yard short and started mopping the bartop. 'That you hoyin' us, were it?' he says.

'Aye, I says "Alright, Nathan".'

'Ain't what I heared,' he says. '"Hoy, Nathan," what I heared.'

'Come on, Nathan.' I weren't feeling too sharp of a sudden. Not like I'd been earlier during me townward yomp. Maybe I'd used up all me sap for the day. Maybe I'd got a whiff of lager and noted the shortage of jangle in me pocket. 'Giz a pint, eh?'

'Gonna pay for it?'

I ought to have known. There's me standing there with no coinage, reckoning no one knew about it besides meself. But Nathan always caught you unawares like that. It were easy to forget about his special abilities.

'What special abilities might they be?' he says.

I felt me face drain white as I looked back at him. Fucking hell. Everyone knew about him knowing everything that came to pass in the Mangel area, but it were news to us that he were tele . . . you know, tele . . .

'Phone,' he says, plonking a full one in front of us. 'Tele-phone.'

I were a bit confused now so I had a sip and says: 'Hang on . . .'

'You gonna take him or what?'

I put the empty down. 'Take who?'

'Telephone. Call fer you, ain't there. Go on an' take him.'

He pointed over to the phone out back. 'Oh, right,' I says, getting off me stool. I were halfway across the floor before I started wondering what Nathan were on about. The phone were sitting quiet in its cradle. So Nathan were trying to make a cunt of us, were he? I were just turning around to have him up about that when the phone started ringing. I looked at Nathan. He nodded at the blower and went to pull a pint for Greasy Joe the burger man, who'd just come in.

'Hello,' I says into the handset. 'Er . . . Paul Pry here.'

'Paul Pry, is it?' says a feller's voice. 'Got Royston Blake there, have you, Paul?'

'No, *I* ain't the Paul Pry. I'm *in* the fuckin' Paul Pry, like.'

'Well, I knows that, don' I. Else you wouldn't be pickin' up when I rings the Paul Pry number.'

'Aye, well . . . So woss you want?'

'Already told you, ain't I. Royston Blake there, is he?'

'Who's askin'?'

'Dave.'

'Alright, Dave.'

'Alright . . . er . . . Who's you?'

'Oh, for fuck . . . You knows who I is.'

'Paul Pry, you says just now.'

'Royston bastard Blake, ennit,' I says, loud enough so's a few punters turned and looked at us. I glared back until they started chinking and yakking amongst emselves once again.

'Oh. Alright, Blake.'

'Alright, Dave. So you gonna tell us woss you want or what?'

He said nothing for a bit. A wood pigeon somewhere near him filled the gap. 'You alone?' he says.

'I'm in the fuckin' Paul Pry.'

'Alright, alright, don't shout.'

'Where's you?'

'Well . . . anyone near you?'

'Fuckin' spit it, will you.'

'Alright, I'm . . . You sure no one's harkin'?'

'I'm hangin' up. Later . . .'

'*No*, I'll tell you, I'll tell you. I'm on the Barkettle Road, phone box up—'

'What end?' I says, though I could have guessed the answer.

'North.'

'North?'

'Aye.'

'Thass Hurk Wood.'

The pips started going and him cursing. Then I heard some coins spill on the floor and him cursing some more, a bit further away now. I thought about putting the blower down right there and then. Dave were in shite and I'd only get meself dragged down with him. Why the fuck were he in Hurk Wood, for fuck? No one went to Hurk Wood unless they was looking to plant a carcass or get planted emselves. 'I'm back,' he says. The pips was gone now, along with my last chance of enjoying a quiet life. 'Aye,' he says, 's'pose it is Hurk Wood.'

'Woss you there for?'

'Hidin', ain't I.' An engine trundled past followed by some more twittering and maybe a sheep or two going baa. 'Blake,' says Dave. But he didn't sound like Dave of a sudden. Sounded more like one o' them there sheep, as it happened. 'I'm in a bit o' trouble, you could say.'

Course, I knew what the trouble were. I'd known it the second I'd picked up the blower and heard him the other end. 'You topped her,' I says. 'You fuckin' squashed her under your wheels like a bag o' chips.'

I could hear him thinking out his answer. I hated that. I dunno why he didn't just spill the fucker since I'd guessed him anyhow. But that weren't what he done.

'Topped her?' he says. 'I ain't topped no one.'

'Come on,' I says. 'Don't give us that—'

'But I ain't.'

'Oh aye, where is she, then?'

'Here.'

'You what? Where?'

'Right here, with me.'

'In Hurk Wood?'

'Aye, in Hurk Wood. Well, back there in some trees, to be particular.'

'But . . . Woss she doin' there? How is she? She's alright, right?'

'Well ... not really. Her leg, she ...'

'Ah, fuckin' hell. But she's talkin', right?'

'Er ... No.'

'Fuck.'

'Got her gagged, ain't I. Had to, screamin' an' bawlin' as she were.'

This were all I needed. How the bastard fuck could I bring Mona to her old feller with her leg busted? My long-term plans was lying at me feet, ripped up and pissed on. It were my fault, course. Long-term planning never got no one no place.

'Blake? Blake, you still there? Blake?'

'Aye,' I says. 'Well, looks like you got it all sorted. I'll leave you to it, then ...'

'Blake. Blake, hold up.'

'Look, Dave, I'm sorry for you an' all but—'

'Sorry, is you?' he says, his tone going a bit different now. Gone were the sheep voice of just now, replaced by ... I dunno, summat more lairy. Like an angry goat or summat. 'I should blinkin' hope so. It were you bust me blinkin' spectacles, wernit. Weren't for that none o' this'd of happened. No, you're helpin' us, you are.'

'Dave, but—'

'But nuthin'. You ain't here in one hour I'll tell the coppers it were you bust them spectacles, set that lass under me wheels, then hid behind a nearby motor and laughed as I went over her.'

'Dave, that ain't—'

'One hour, Blake. I'll be behind a clump of larches thirty yard back from the phone box.'

'Dave ...' But he were gone.

I put the blower down careful. I wanted to slam

the fucker but I knew that'd get folks wondering. I kept my head down and walked back through the bar heading for the back door. This were all I fucking needed, wernit. I didn't even have no motor to get to Hurk Wood in. She'd be down Filthy Stan's by now, or maybe he'd fixed her up and dropped her off at ours already. But I didn't have time to yomp home and look. Least I knew where Mona were now, mind. And perhaps she weren't so fucked up as Dave had made out. Aye, once you got reflecting on it none of it seemed quite so bad. Even though Dave had pushed us around a bit there, the cunt. The path of life is paved with many a busted flagstone, and sometimes all you needs is a shove from behind to jump over em, or summat.

'Hold on right there,' says Nathan, just as I were disappearing down the back passage. But I weren't quite disappeared yet. And I'd heard him.

And he knew it.

'What?' I says, stopping still but not turning.

'You ain't paid fer this un here yet.'

11

HOPPERS: AXIS OF EVIL?
Steve Dowie, Crime Editor

Hoppers squats menacingly in Friar Street like a beggar more interested in kicking at the legs of passers-by than soliciting loose change. It is a place rich in history, and none of it good.

It is here that I have come in search of Joey.

JOEY: a code name, a euphemism employed by the dispossessed youth of Mangel for the sweet solace they all seek.

JOEY: a teasing legend scrawled on the walls of alleys and the doors of public conveniences across the town.

JOEY: the unidentified confectionery found on two young petty thieves last week.

Joey, my friends, is an illegal drug.

'Not in this town,' you say. 'Folks in this town don't need none of that. Drugs is for big city folk.'

Well, think again.

Drugs are here and now. Drugs are right there on our streets, waiting for your children to come and get them.

Drugs are the driving force behind the crime wave that has lately been bringing this town to its knees. Drugs, unless we do something about it, will change this town for ever.

YOU WANT JOEY – SEE THE J-MAN. DOWN HOPPERS

Founded three decades ago by legendary local bandit Tommy Munton (using for capital the spoils of extortion and armed robbery), Hoppers quickly became a magnet for the rough underbelly of Mangel's populace. The venue thrived for many years, putting on entertainment events that drew crowds from all over the Mangel area. But then Munton senior died, and control was passed to his hapless progeny.

Within a few years the three brothers turned a thriving – if disreputable – business into a vomit-spattered vice den teetering on the verge of collapse. They attempted to cut their losses by resorting to arson, that time-honoured contingency plan. Sadly (if inevitably) for them their make-or-break move failed spectacularly, resulting not only in firm shakes of the head from their insurers, but also the death of their head doorman's wife, Elizabeth Blake. Somehow avoiding custodial punishment for their crime(s), the Muntons then sold this scorched Jerusalem to one James Fenton, a mysterious businessman from the big city with a fat wallet and a death wish.

Amazingly, Fenton managed to turn Hoppers back into the thriving if disreputable concern of old, bestowing upon it a fancy if unoriginal new moniker: 'Hoppers Wine Bar & Bistro'. Despite keeping his new enterprise on the straight and narrow, within two short years Fenton fell victim to his own criminal past. The FOR SALE sign went up yet again.

The next two years saw Hoppers sliding into a black pit of failure featuring all the desperation of the Munton tenure but none of the colour. Through a combination of wilful omission and suspicious rain damage, official records defy all attempts to identify the owner during this period. Whoever it is, one would have to question his judgement in employing as day-to-day manager one Royston Blake, erstwhile doorman of Hoppers, widower of the aforementioned arson victim, and chief suspect in the subsequent murder inquiry (acquitted on grounds of mental unfitness to stand trial).

And now Hoppers enters a new dynasty, as she once again feels the weight of a big city exile at her stern. As I approach the darkened door I wonder where new skipper Nick Nopoly could possibly steer a ship which has already charted all manner of rocky water. Could he be heading – unwittingly or otherwise – for a sea more treacherous still?

YOU WANT JOEY – SEE THE J-MAN. DOWN HOPPERS

'Not tonight, mate,' I am told as a huge arm blocks my passage.

And why? Is it because I am a reporter? Is it because I might just bring down this whole sticky, greasy house of cards if I can only get in?

'Greasy?' grunts the gargantuan doorman. 'You want Burt's Caff, down the road there. Now **** off.'

So ends my search for Joey. For now. And so continues the unhallowed history of Mangel's rankest corner.

For now.

'Fuck sake, Nathan,' I says, wanting to fuck off out the door but not being able to.

'I've told you before, Blake: I'll not have obscenities uttered in my bar, ladies bein' present an' all.'

I looked around, shaking my head and clocking no ladies. There was no reasoning with Nathan sometimes.

'And there's no special favours fer you here.' Somehow I'd been drawn to the bar again. And his voice were a bit lower, for which I were grateful considering what he were saying and all the other punters being near by. 'You'll pay fer your pint like everyone else.'

'Come on, Nathan.'

'Come on conkers. Ain't my concern if your new boss won't pay you. Wanna come back here an' wash the glasses instead, do you?'

I rolled me eyes. 'I'm a doorman, Nathan. Doormen don't wash up.'

'Who's a doorman?'

'I ... Alright, I'm out o' work right now but ...'

Nathan were looking at us, waiting for us to finish. But I couldn't. What were there to say? I weren't a doorman no more. I weren't a minder no more neither what with recent Dave-related events and that. I could handle not being a minder, though. I hadn't ever been one o' them before so I weren't missing nothing. But I'd been a doorman all me grafting life.

And who were I kidding anyhow, reckoning I'd get meself back on the door at Hoppers? Frankenstein were there now, weren't he. He were bigger than us, younger than us, and ... I sucked me gut in far as it'd go, then looked down. It were no use. I still couldn't see me belt.

'Alright, Jack,' says Nathan to someone behind us. 'Pint, is it?' He went to pull one while Jack waited by the bar.

'Alright, Jack,' I says.

Jack nodded at us, which told us that he were sober. Jack hardly ever said a word when he were dry. Which were good really cos when he did open his mouth he stunk the place out, him with his breath. You couldn't blame him, mind, not for his breath nor his drinking nor his untalkativeness and that. Had a hard life, hadn't he. You had to go easy on the poor fucker. One day in Mangel Jail is too much for most men, so they says. And Jack had spent six year in the fucking place.

I breathed easy when he fucked off to a quiet corner with his pint and paper. Jack were harmless enough. If you didn't spill his pint. And you held your puff while he spoke to you. But to be honest I didn't much like being around him. It's cos I'd knowed him before, see, before he'd gone inside. And seeing what Mangel Jail had done to him always got to us a bit. Mind you, weren't so low he couldn't buy himself a pint, were he.

I sat on me stool, twiddling me thumbs, thinking about that fact. I noticed a dead pint a little ways along the bar. About a third left inside there were. Never could understand them who don't finish off their pints knowing full well there's folks in shite countries has to go without. Good lager it were, if a bit flat by now. I edged along the bar until the pint were bang in front of us, then sat tight til I felt confident that no one were clocking. They weren't, course. Why would anyone want to look at a doorless doorman?

I picked up the pint and drank it slow. While I done that I tried to make out what they was all carping on about behind us. I couldn't. Talking too low they was, one after t'other like they was having a meeting or summat. What was they all here for anyhow? Hoppers were their pub, for most of em. Not the Paul Pry. I had a reason to drink here meself: Hoppers were a place of graft for me and I needed a change of air in me off hours. But them? What right had they to come here, whispering like a bunch of fucking . . . bunch of . . . you know, whisperers or summat. And what was they on about anyhow?

Bet they was talking about us.

There I were – Mr Dozy Fucking Twat Ex-Doorman – thinking no one were paying us heed. And all the while them cunts behind us was pointing and having a laugh at us.

Hark at old Blakey over there, out of work and penniless, unable to pay his way, supping leftovers.

Bastards.

'Eh, Blakey,' one of em calls out. 'What d'you say to that?'

'What?' I says, spinning to face em. 'Woss I fuckin' say to what?'

No one answered us for a bit and I weren't sure who'd asked anyhow. I sat there nice and calm, waiting for me answer. But all I got were nervous looks. And not too many of them neither. Most of em looked at the floor or swilled the beer around in their glasses.

'Now now, Blake,' says Nathan behind us. 'We're all on your side here.'

I looked back at him, wondering what he were on

about now. The punters started chattering again. I noticed my heart were beating hard, but starting to slow a bit.

'What you sees here,' says Nathan all low and confiding, 'what you sees in this here bar, Blakey, is what is known as an exodus.' He nodded over my shoulder. 'These lads here is the dispossessed of the Mangel drinking community.' Someone put an empty atop the bar and Nathan went to serve him.

While he were gone I thought hard about what he'd said just there. When he came back I says: 'You fuckin' what?'

'Exiles, Blake. Good honest punters exiled from their natural habitat, which happens to be your former place of employ.'

I wished I had a fag. And another pint. 'Hoppers, you means?'

'Aye, Blake, I means Hoppers. Folks has stopped drinkin' there of a sudden. Been restin' yer eyes of late, has you? Open em, Blake, and you'll see that Mangel is changin' under our very hooters.'

'Well,' I says. Nathan had put another one in front of us so I drained half of it off. Mind you, I still hadn't coughed up for the first so I dunno what he were playing at. Ain't my place to question Nathan's motives, though, is it. 'Well,' I says, licking foam off me top lip. 'Well ...'

'Gat summat to say, Blake? Besides a preamble, that is?'

'Aye ... I mean no, you're right. I mean this Nick Wossname ...'

'Nopoly.'

'Wha? Anyhow, this Nick Wossname ... Iss him,

ennit, all this bollocks. Since he comes along iss all gone to shite, like.'

Nathan were smoothing down his tash. 'I ain't disagreein' with that, Blake.'

'I mean, fancy gettin' someone else on the fuckin' door. Woss he fuckin' playin' at? *I'm* the fuckin' Head Doorman of Hoppers. You knows it an' I knows it and so do every fucker else. These fellers here is disprocessed, you says? You knows why that is, right? Cos I ain't on the door there no more. Cos of fuckin' Frankie there instead, standin' there like a . . .'

'Blake . . .'

'. . . a fuckin' . . . You know, a . . .'

'Blake, just—'

'An' you knows what? You fuckin' knows what, does you? Cos I'll fuckin' tell you, I will. See this? See my face here where he bust it? Here an' all. An' there's this bit here . . .'

'Blake, listen . . .'

'Catched us by surprise he did. Bein' nice to him an' that I were, givin' him the doubt of his benefits an' that, an' he fuckin'— Wearin' dusters an' all he were, else he'd never of— Plus he were clutchin' some lead or summat . . .'

'Shut it and listen.'

I hadn't ever heard Nathan the barman shout so loud. Voice-raising weren't part of his repertoire, you might say. Had no need of it, did Nathan. Which were why I did like he says and shut me gob. And so did every other fucker in the Paul Pry on that particular weekday afternoon, going by the silence that ensued.

'Carry on,' he snapped at the punters, waving his arm. 'Go on.'

They went on and carried on.

'Now,' he says, leaning his hairy arms atop the bar and putting his swede not far from mine. 'This here's a quiet establishment by reputation, as well you knows. Always has been that way and always will be, that bein' the way I likes things. Folks in large number means trouble – and trouble, as well you also knows, I don't much like. But right now – at this moment in the long history of this here pub – the Paul Pry ain't quiet.'

He took a sip of his drink and wiped the froth off his tash. It were only lemonade, mind. Nathan never touched lager to my knowledge.

'Now I don't like that, Blakey. I don't like that at all. I wants peace and quiet restored. And the only way I sees that happenin' is when them over there gets their Hoppers back.'

'But, Nathan . . .' I says.

'What is it?' he says, all impatient like.

'Can I have another pint, mate?'

'Never you mind that,' he barks, eyes ablaze. 'You'll get your beer soon enough. But you does what I says first. Right?'

'But . . .'

'But what?'

'I . . .' But it were no use. Nathan were a higher being, weren't he. And as such I were powerless in his presence. 'Dunno, really.' I shrugged.

He picked up a cloth and started mopping the bartop like I weren't there. I were starting to regret asking him for that pint there now. I mean, I fucking needed one and that. To be fair I needed one like I'd never needed summat before. But it looked like I'd stuck me chin out too far and made him go quiet on us. His flow were broke beyond repair. And now that he were holding it back, I wanted it. I wanted to know what he had in mind.

But I were fretting needlessly. He turned to us all casual and says: 'I wants you back in Hoppers. On the door.'

I nodded. 'Too fuckin' right. I belongs—'

'No, not like that,' he says. 'I wants you on that door so's I can get that feller out. He's a bad un, Blake. This town will come to no good with him here. Look at my pub already,' he says, almost spitting at the punters behind us. 'Look at em. Blinkin' layabouts to the man. They can do what they wants in Hoppers but they ain't doin' it in *my* pub.'

'But Nathan,' I says. 'Why not just turn em out if you don't want em?'

'How can I? I'm a fair man, Blake. I knows when a debt's owed and right now them lot's due summat from us, bein' as it were me sold Hoppers in the first place.'

'Aye, thass true,' I says. Cos I'd been meaning to mention that.

'Thass true? Thass flippin' true? Who's you to blinkin' say woss true or ain't. Woss you know about arcane knowledge and covert machinations, eh? Eh?'

'Well, er . . .' I says, wanting to scratch me ear but fighting it. 'Mashed what?'

He shook his head and drained his soft drink. 'Just listen here,' he says. 'Here's how you'll get yer job back . . .'

Course, I were fucked now, weren't I. Nathan had kept us there yakking the best part of fuck knows how long, and I were meant to be up Hurk Wood way in that much shy of an hour. As I've said many a time, walking ain't one of the many things I does best. Don't worry, I won't go on about it again, even though it is one o' them things that just can't be gone on about enough times in my book. And this is my fucking book, ennit, so . . .

Ah, fuck you.

Anyhow, what I were trying to get at there is how I came to be trying handles along the Cutler Road that day, and how the only one that weren't locked were the one belonging to the Hillman Imp. Alright? So no fucking taking the piss. Necessity is the mother of all evil as they says, or summat. And four wheels is four fucking wheels. They says that and all.

Mind you, by the time I had her pointed north on the Barkettle Road I were starting to come round to that little Imp, believe it or no. What you loses in nigh on every area, you gains in headroom for the taller driver such as meself. Plus that little engine in the back there were revving like a Catherine wheel with nary a tremble, and I just knew she'd keep it up long as I asked her to. I'd even go far as to say she were moving slowly up my rankings. Against all the odds she'd hauled her ugly arse off the bottom spot and gone one above your Avenger, and were just now holding back for a go at your Viva. But then I clocked our reflection in the windows of Cullimore Storage & Distribution, and the dream of glory were over for her. Seeing yourself in a Hillman Imp is like when you're in bed trying to get to kip and you feel a big spider scuttle over your face.

I pulled up there and then. I weren't driving that nail not one minute longer. And no four-eyed cunt were making us do it. No matter how many daughters of Doug the shopkeeper he'd run over and kidnapped.

But then it started raining.

And it's a foolish man who ignores his omens.

I swallowed hard and got going again. Least no one would see us. And even if they recognised us they'd talk emselves out of it. Every fucker in Mangel knew where I stood on Hillman Imps so no one would believe I'd drive one. And besides, by the time I caught sight of the phone box in Hurk Wood I were getting used to her again.

The rain were easing off as I pulled up. I checked me watch: ten minutes late. But not even Dave'd be so barmy as to call the coppers out. I might get collared for aiding and abetting but what about him? He'd fucking ran her over, hadn't he, so phoning the coppers'd be like eating shite to make your brother chuck up.

'Time d'you call this?' he says, stepping out the phone box.

'Thought you says you'd be over by yonder larches?' says I.

'Were, weren't I, til you failed to turn up at the agreed minute.'

'Joshin', ain't you?'

'No I ain't. You was late.'

'Only a couple o' fuckin' minutes. Woss you gone an' done?' I could feel me fingernails cutting into me palms. Dave were wearing his glasses again, held together by some old chongy by the looks of him. But hitting a speccy feller never had been a problem for us. Why should four-eyed cunts get away with it? A four-eyed cunt's asking for it, he's asking for it. Fuck him and his glasses. 'Come on, spill.'

He thought about it and says: 'Who says I done summat?'

'On the blower, wasn't you?'

'Never says that, did I. I— B-Blake, come on, mate ... Put us down.'

'Fuckin' tell us *now*.'

'I ... Take it easy, Blakey. I never done nuthin', honest. Just havin' me little laugh is all ... Let us go, Blake. You'll rip me coat.'

I knew I wouldn't cos them donkey jackets is like chainmail, unless you puts a Stanley to em. But I let go anyhow. You could see in them big speccy eyes of his how he were givin' us it straight now. 'Windin' us up, then, was you?'

'Aye,' he says, setting his glasses right. 'Soz, Blake.'

'And what the fuck for should I help you now, eh? Reckon I drives Imps for fun, does you? Reckon I comes out to Hurk Wood cos I likes lookin' at trees?'

'I says I'm sorry. I just wanted to ...'

'Go on.'

'Well ...' He made a choking sound, like he had a chicken bone stuck down his neck. I were all set to wallop him on the back when he done it again, a bit different this time. I looked in his big goldfish eyes and saw that he were crying. He sniffed hard, took his glasses off, then rubbed his eyes and pulled himself straight. I were glad of that. If there's one thing worse that a Hillman Imp it's a feller bawling. You asks me, fellers who bawls ought to be made to drive Hillman Imps. They deserves each other.

Dave put his glasses back on and says: 'Everyone takes advantage of old Dave, don't they. Every blinkin' one of em. And they all expects us to take it. Well, I've had it, Blake. I've blinkin' had it. I ain't takin' no more of it, I ain't. An' I'll show em. I blinkin' will, you know. Next feller pushes us I'll . . .'

He reached inside his donkey jacket and pulled summat out. At first I thought it were one o' them posh fag lighters you keeps on the table. Then the barrel glinted and I knew it were a pistol.

He waved it around, tears streaming down his ruddy cheeks. 'I'll blinkin' . . .' he sobs. 'I'll blinkin' show em . . .'

'Dave,' I says.

He stopped crying and gun-waving and clocked us like he'd forgot I were there. Then he put the gun away and wiped his eyes and says: 'Soz, mate.' But you could tell he were still upset.

I were stumped for what to do. I wanted to ask him where the fuck he'd got that firearm. And what did he have it for anyhow? But I couldn't even believe he had it. Dave waving a gun around? It were like having a sheep growl at you – it don't make no sense and you ain't sure how to take it. So I says: 'Fuck sake, Dave,' and walked off towards the larches.

There'd be summat coming along the road sooner or later anyhow and I didn't want to be clocked. Dave had already been spotted like as not, twat that he were, but just cos he were in shite didn't mean I had to jump in with him, as I've said before. He were walking alongside us anyhow by the time I'd crossed half the twenty-odd yard to the larches. Which were a good thing as it turned out. Cos I'd had an idea, hadn't I.

I stopped and says: 'Dave.' Well, I more whispered it than said it.

And Dave answered same way. 'What?' He were back to normal now.

'You ain't mentioned us to her?'

He looked thick for a bit then says: 'No, ain't said nuthin' to her besides "it'll be alright", and "there there", an' that.'

'Nice one. Right, well, we got a problem.'

I explained it to him nice and simple. He were a bit confused, but seemed alright about it. I made sure he knew what to do and what I had planned, then sent him ahead while I stayed back a few minutes.

Weren't like it were a shite plan nor nothing. As plans went it were alright. But it were the details what done for us, out there in Hurk Wood that day.

If you want to er-change the . . .

I tried hard to work em out, them details, but that fucking *Minder* tune were back in me swede and I couldn't think for toffee nor sprouts. I'd spotted a way of getting back in with Nick Wossname, see, which meant my minding career were back off the ground. And not only that neither. The way he tossed coinage about I were set for a nice little bonus, weren't I.

Right people, right time . . .

I tried shaking me swede and sticking thumbs in me eyes, but it didn't work. Dennis Waterman wouldn't fucking shut up with his warbling. After a bit I gave up on the details and got on with it. Which were a pity, considering the amount of grief I'd have avoided by turning arse and going home. But like I says just now, it weren't like the plan were shite. It were the . . .

I've got a good . . .

Ah, for fuck sake. There he goes again, round and round me swede like a lost tapeworm without a road map. Fucking shut it, Dennis, will you. I'm trying to tell em about how you and your fucking tune fucked it all up for us out there in the woods. No disrespect, mind. *Minder* were a fucking smart telly programme wernit. Even if you never saw much of that white Capri after the opening bits.

She didn't look too happy. On her back she were but her eyes was wide and bulging like eggs set to plop out a chicken's hole. Arms was tied afore her with leccy cable, and her gob were gagged with what looked to be an old sock strapped in with more cable. So no, she didn't look happy at all.

Dave were sat on the trunk of a fallen tree, leg bouncing up and down. Looked like he were waiting for summat to happen – which is what I told him not to look like. Cos summat were about to happen, and Mona were meant to think he knew fuck all about it.

I'd been spying through the thinning branches of one of them larches. I took a step back, aiming to walk round t'other side. Summat big cracked underfoot. Dry branch under the fallen leaves like as not.

But knowing Hurk Wood the way I knew it I wondered if it were a leg bone. Anyhow, the crack were loud enough to set Mona off. She started wailing, though she couldn't get much of a noise through that sock. I had a quick gander and Dave hadn't budged.

I crept round the other side to make a run at em, then had a thought. Perhaps it'd look more real if I were holding summat. She had to believe I were saving her from him else it wouldn't help us with Nick Wossname. I got me monkey wrench out and ran into the clearing. Felt good in my hand it did.

Just like it always done.

'Dave?' I says a few moments later, after the darkness had cleared from in front of me eyeballs. I prodded him with me boot. Then I recalled how he were meant to be a villain and me come to save Mona, so I says, more gruffer: 'Hoy, get up, you cunt.' I kicked him hard this time.

But it made no odds. He weren't budging. I looked at Mona, who were still staring goggle-eyed but making no noise now. Then I looked at the monkey wrench in my hand. It'd all been a bit of a blur to be honest. I sometimes gets like that in the heat of battle, even when it's a bit parky and the other feller ain't fighting. I suppose you could say I'd applied the wrench a bit harder than I'd meant to. You could say I never needed to use it at all. Any cunt could look at Dave and meself and see there weren't no match between us. But like I says just now, I'd got the plan sorted but not the details.

I grabbed one of Dave's arms and pulled him over. Mona made a little squeal under her gag as the sun hit t'other side of Dave's face. I tutted and shook my head. This one here needed more than a plaster and a couple of pints. I knelt down and put me ear next to his face to check his breathing. After a bit I stood up and looked at him again.

Dead, weren't he.

I looked at me wrench, wondering how that had happened. But I'd been in this place before and there's only so much wondering you can do before moss starts growing on your boots.

'Oh well,' I says, shrugging. 'Soz about that, mate.' Cos he were alright, were Dave. Bit of a twat, and blind as a lump of tar. But he were harmless by and large and hadn't ever gave us grief on the door at Hoppers, which set him apart from most fellers in Mangel. But you reaps what you sows, so my old feller used to say, which meant Dave must have been a bit of a cunt on the quiet, like. And there's no good crying over spilt blood, as my old man also used to say, after he'd gave us a bust lip.

I looked at Mona and sent her one of my professional grins, the sort like I've perfected over my many years spent dooring at Hoppers. If there's one thing I knows it's how to put a bird at ease. And if there's one bird who needed it, this one here were her.

But she just went on staring at us.

'Well,' I says, going over to her. 'Lucky for you I were passin', eh? Else who knows what this here feller'd of done. Eh?'

Aye, she were fucking hard work alright. Saved her life, I had, and all I got back were that nasty look. Alright, she were gagged and that, but a bird can use her eyes when she wants to, and to be honest I reckoned I were due summat for me troubles. I were starting to wonder if this here Mona weren't one o' them lesbians. I mean, she just weren't interested. I know she were going out with Nick Wossname and all but he did have long hair, didn't he.

Anyhow, it were her I'd come for so I had to take her as I found her, gratitude or no. I knelt down to untie her. My leg were up against her side and I felt her go stiff as a gatepost. When I reached behind her head to get her gag off there were no give at all in her neck. ''S alright, love,' I says, winking. 'Have no fear. Blakey's here.' I pulled the gag off.

She screamed.

'Alright,' I says, putting my hand over her gob. 'No need for that, right? When I takes my hand away just now I wants no more. Right?' I took my hand away.

She screamed again.

Like a cage full of hungry babies.

I put the gag back on. I couldn't be doing with that, not with Dave lying there dead. What if someone were passing by? 'No need for that,' I says to her. 'It ain't friendly. Saved you, I done. Look at him yonder with his face all fucked. Done that for you, I done. But woss I get in return? Bawlin'.'

I walked up and down the clearing a few times, trying to calm down. No good getting het up, were there. I ought to have known summat like this would happen. After a bit I got me breathing under control and turned to her with a new-found resolve. 'You wait here,' I says.

Then I went to sort Dave out.

I found his motor about thirty yard deeper into the wood in a dark hawthorn-hid spot. On a brighter day you might have clocked the sun glinting off the chrome from the road. But on this gloomy late afternoon here I could stand across the bush from her and not know she were there. It were only us knowing she must be near by that gave her away. That and the tyre tracks.

She weren't half a nice motor, mind. I'd always had a soft spot for them Rovers and his were the only decent one in Mangel them days. To be fair she could have done with a sand down and respray, and even in the poor light I could see how much work the interior required. But your Rover P6 is a plush motor whatever nick she's in, and sends shivers up and down the hardest man's spine when he sees her cruise by. Which were why Dave had come to be driving her like as not. Everyone likes a bit of attention, and for Dave this were the only way. I tried her doors.

Fucking locked, weren't they.

I went back to Dave, starting to chew me lip just a mite. With them keys I could make it look like an accident. Idea had come to us while I'd been looking for his motor, and I reckoned it were one of the best uns I'd ever had. But without the keys I were fucked. I breathed easier when I found em in his donkey jacket. I got him by the ankles and started tugging for a yard or two, then thought about all that mud and grass getting on his back and set him across me shoulder instead. He were a bit of a lump but I'd shifted heavier loads than him in me time. When I got him to his motor I set him shotgun and got in the driver side.

I started her up with nary a glance at him. I'd

never been that keen on corpses at the best of times, and this weren't that by a long stretch, me being out of work and stuck in Hurk Wood and all. The gentle rumble of your Rover's 3.5-litre engine went some way to soothing my frazzled nerve endings, mind, and I just sat like that for a bit, letting the vibrations massage us. After a length of time I noticed it were getting dark, so I took the stopper off and taxied her across the grass to the Barkettle Road.

I pointed her north and let the Rover's V6 ticker do the rest, which happened to be not far shy of nine seconds up to your sixty. I knew what top end she were capable of and all. We'd swiped one off Culver's Scrap Yard as younguns and I swear she clocked a ton thirty down the East Bloater Road before blowing a gasket. Had to walk home in the pissing rain we did but it were worth it to have come so close to heaven. Anyhow, last thing I wanted right now were a copper taking a professional interest, so I kept her under eighty all the way to Rudge Valley.

Most Mangel folk ain't ever even seen Rudge Valley. No reason to go up that way, is there. Not unless you're sightseeing. But I'd always made it my business to know about the border areas. Not like I were planning on escaping, mind. Mangel folk is all leaves on the same tree, so they says, and if a leaf drops off he withers and dies. We can't get by without the tree and it can't live without us, they says and all. Alright? Got that, have you? Well, I had it and all. I'd had it since day fucking one and if there's one thing I knew, besides where to find my arse, it's that Mangel folk stays Mangel folk come what might. So no, I hadn't come out to Rudge Valley looking to slip away. I hadn't stood at the top of the slope and dreamed of what adventures lay beyond. I hadn't spent hours on end pacing by the side of the road, wondering what might happen if I legged it out of the Mangel area and headed for the big city.

Just liked a bit of sightseeing is all.

I pulled up on the rim of the valley and got out. It were a nice little elbow bend in the Barkettle Road where the armpit were a bank of firs and off the shoulder were a sheer drop down the valley. I went to the edge and looked. A long stretch of grass so steep not even a goat would use it led you down a quarter-mile or so to the River Clunge, which were tree-lined along that stretch and not visible to the naked eye. Dangerous bit of road it were. But like I says, no fucker ever came out this way so it never made no odds. I went back to the Rover.

I hauled Dave out of the shotgun spot and set him in front of the wheel. Couldn't get his paws to stick to it but that were alright. I put her in fifth and turned the key, letting her stall.

'Well,' I says, squatting beside the open door. 'I'm sorry iss come to this. I mean, I'd like to of got to know you a bit more . . . And perhaps we would of done that, circumstances bein' different. We could of had fun alright, oh aye . . .'

I closed me eyes and pictured the two of us having fun together.

'Fun? More than fun it would of been. You knows it an' I knows it an' all. We could of been . . . special.'

I had to stop there cos it were all getting a bit much. I wiped me eyes and pulled meself together.

'Right,' I says. 'None o' that, eh? Feller's gotta do

what he's gotta.' I stroked the steering wheel a few times to show her I meant every word I'd said, then I let the handbrake off and shut the door.

'Oh, and see you, Dave,' I says, remembering he were there and all.

Then I went round back and shouldered man and motor into Rudge Valley.

Course, I were stuck yomping again now, weren't I. Two mile it were back to that phone box and by the time I'd got there it were dark. The Hillman Imp were hardly a pretty sight but just the one I'd been wanting at that particular time. I'd not been able to lock the doors, see, so there were no banking on her still being there. I should have put her behind them trees like Dave had done with his, I suppose, but to be honest I couldn't recall hearing one motor come past all the while I'd been here, so I were alright.

You could hardly see that clump of larches. The wood proper were behind em, and the last drops of light washing over the sky behind that, so all I seen were a big black blob looming in front of us. Still, when you started walking over there the trees slowly came clear, and before you knew it you're stood next to what you could have swore were that very same clump of larches.

Only Mona weren't there, were she.

I had a good poke about to be sure she weren't hiding nearabouts. She'd fucked off alright. Even found the cabling she'd been trussed up in and the damp old sock Dave had gagged her with. Silly tart. Told her I'd come to save her, didn't I? Why couldn't she just sit tight and wait for us? Then I could have took her back to Nick Wossname and got started as a minder. Fucking birds for you, that is. Never does what you wants em to.

I shrugged and went back to the Imp. Fuck her. If she'd gone into the woods she were fucked anyhow. And if she'd took the road townward I'd never get her neither. Jump into the trees, she would, first sound of a motor coming behind her. She'd limp back to Nick Wossname like as not, which wouldn't be so bad when you stopped and thought about it for a bit. Saved her, hadn't I. She'd sat there and watched us knock her kidnapper dead. Alright, she'd found it all a bit scary and scarpered. Couldn't blame her for that, though. She were only a bird and it can't be pleasant watching death come to a feller. But she still knew I'd saved her. And she could tell that to her feller Nick Wossname, who'd be even more keener to get us minding for him.

I were thinking that as I walked across the clearing, watching a motor start up and pull a U-ey over there on the road. By the time I'd worked out it were my Hillman Imp she were forty yard off Mangelward.

Fucking birds for you, that is.

No gratitude.

12

READERS RESPOND

Dear Mangel Informer,

What was your man Steve Dowie on about the other day in his article about Hoppers and sweets and crime and God knows what else? We don't have them 'drugs' in Mangel. Ask anyone. We like a drop or two and a bit of tobacco here and there but drugs are for thickheads, being as when you takes them you go funny for a bit and then die. Everyone knows that. That's why we don't have them in Mangel.

Mrs Vera Trandle
Mangel

Dear mate,

I just want to take umbrage here about what you said in your paper about Hoppers. A 'sticky, greasy house of cards', you called it. Well, I did some repair work on the building a few year back after that fire and I can tell you straight that it's built of brick and mortar like any other building. I tried making a shed out of cardboard once and

*they just don't work, sticky or no. Soon as the rain comes
you're swimming. I just wanted to set that straight.*
  Bob Gretchum
  Gretchum & Sons Building and Clearance
  Mangel

Alright,
  *I went to school with your Steve Dowie and he never
had no mates. He was always the one up front sticking his
hand up and licking teacher's* **** *and that. My mate
John knocked into him once and the little* ****** *only
went and told on him to the headmaster. Always looking
at books and that he was, reckoning himself more clever-
er than the rest of us. Books is for folks who ain't got no
mates and can't stick up for emselves.*
  Michael Tinch
  Mangel

Dear Editor
  *Do you realise your feller Steve Dowie can't even spell
properly? 'Moniker', he wrote. Have you not got diction-
aries there?*
  Monica Fleigh
  Mangel

'Where's you fuckin' been, you fucker?'
  Jack had been drinking. He must have been drinking cos he never said nothing at all when he hadn't
been, like I already told you. I weren't sure if I were
happy about that, about him being pissed. He were
too quiet by half when he weren't pissed but at least
he couldn't pollute folks' ears that way. I mean, just
you have a listen to him:

'Hoy, you, you cunt. I'm fuckin' talkin' to you. Where's you fuckin' bin?'

Come on, that ain't no way to talk, is it? But like I says previous – you had to go easy on the poor old cunt. You can't blame a feller for using choice words after spending all that time in Mangel Jail. No, Jack hadn't always been so foul of tongue. Always been a lairy bastard but he used to have class with it. He'd deck a feller then turn and check his hair in the mirror. Not that he needed to. Used to sport one o' them barnets you can't ruffle with a crowbar, he did. Fuck knew what he put in it to get it that way but the birds never seemed to mind. Always one hung off his arm there were, when he weren't scrapping. And not your usual mingers neither. I'm talking the top birds – big tits, nice round arses, long yellow hair, alright faces . . . the fucking works, mate. You wants a bird like that, you got to show a bit o' class. And Jack had it. Bit like meself in that respect.

'Alright, Jack,' I says. 'Calm it, right?'

But there were no comparing us now. Jail had been rough on him alright. You couldn't hardly see his face for scar tissue. And his eyeballs was so shot you couldn't tell which way he were looking. Rumour were he hadn't closed his eyes once in all his time inside, which is how he'd kept himself ticking. I wanted to ask him what the fuck happened to him in there, but looking at him here down that alley next to Burt's Caff I weren't sure he were in the mood. And I weren't sure I wanted to know neither.

'Fuckin' half past fuckin' nine, Nathan said,' he says, lighting a match on his shaved head and sparking up. 'Not ten o' fuckin' bastard clock.'

I weren't sure I wanted to hear it anyhow, even if he'd wanted to tell it. Some things it don't do to yak about, and the inner workings of Mangel Jail is one of em. Besides, you could tell he hadn't ever really got out of there anyhow. We was stood down the alley having a chat but his eyes was flicking all over the shop.

'Alright, alright,' I says. 'Heared you the first time, didn't I.'

'Stood here like a fuckin' cunt I were.' He kept looking behind him, like someone were trying to get at him through the brick wall. 'Smoked nearly all me fuckin' smokes an' all. Know how many I smoked? Fuckin' seven. Seven fuckin' smokes. Thass seven smokes you owes us, you fuckin'—'

'I says alright, didn't I?' I says, wafting his breath away from me face.

I were gonna say more but you had to be careful with Jack. Like I says, he weren't in the best of shape. Specially the way he'd been pickling himself non-stop since getting out. But he had homemade tats up and down his arms that'd have you crossing the street. And you don't spend all that time surviving in Mangel Jail without picking up a move or two, does you. No, you don't.

'Look,' I says, getting a bit narked with him now. 'What we had planned, right? Forget the lot of it. It's off.'

Jack grumbled summat else and lit another up without offering us one. What a cunt, eh. Could have bunged us one, couldn't he. Yomped all the bastard way from Hurk Wood North I had, and a little smoke would have gone a long way to getting us feeling rosy again. Then again he smoked Lamberts, which I fucking hated. Smoking a Lambert is like smoking an old dogshite rolled up in chip paper.

'Did you hear us?' I says. Cos to be honest he didn't look like he had. He were muttering under his minging breath, blowing smoke and squeezing them big old fists tight.

Looking at him here, stood in the shadows like we was, I found it hard to believe I'd been on the point of entrusting my future unto Jack. He were a fucking spanner, weren't he. 'Wait til you sees Blake comin',' Nathan had said to him back there in the Pry. 'Then breathe hard in the incumbent doorman's face, thereby decapacitatin' him for just long enough so's Blake here can step up and floor him.' That were the plan to get us back on the door. Alright, so it looked a bit shite when you peered too close. But it had sounded alright at the time. All Nathan's words sounded right at the time when he said em.

But it were all off now. I didn't even wanna get back on the door no more. Destined for a higher station, weren't I, and the way to it were clear now. Mona would have a chat with Nick, and he'd come to us with arms and wallet open.

'Hey?' I says. 'You hear us or what?'

You had to see it from Jack's angle, course. He'd been asked to do a little job. That ain't an everyday summat to a feller like him, so now he wanted to do it. And here I were knocking him back into the gutter, telling him he weren't wanted after all.

'Look,' I says, taking pity on the poor old tosser. 'Go down an' tell Nathan. Tell him Blake says it's off. He'll pay you anyhow. Alright, mate?'

He said summat I couldn't hear. Didn't sound too happy, mind. But he wouldn't be, would he. Can't be much fun being Jack. He turned and went roadward.

I stood where I were for a bit, sucking in the baccy smoke he'd left hanging in the air behind him. Then I remembered that his breath would be mixed up with it and all, and started coughing. A minute or so later I hauled meself straight, wiped me eyes, and hopped off down the Hoppers.

'*I could be so good for you . . .*' I sings to meself, boots slapping pavement like steak on a butcher's board. '*Love you like you wants us to . . .*' I didn't give a toss who heard us, neither. In a good mood I were. Best mood I'd been in for fucking donkeys. And who gave a toss if I weren't Head Doorman of Hoppers no more? Doorman's a shite job when you thinks about it. Stood there all night looking like a cunt, fielding pot shots from lairy cunts and fighting off pissed-up old slags who can't cop off with no one else. And what about them fucking daft togs a doorman got to wear? Dinner jacket? You're stood on the fucking door, not sat down for steak and chips. No more of that for me, mate. Minders wears minding gear, which is usually blue jeans, leather bomber and black boots. Minders gets out and about, poking all the top birds and taking shite from no fucker.

Royston Blake, Minder.

Aye, I didn't mind the sound of that.

'*I'll do anythin' for yooooooooo, I'll be so good for . . .* Fuck.'

I were about twenty yard off from the Hoppers door but I could see summat were up. I halted, hark-

ing a tiny voice inside us that told us I were once
again in a deep, deep pool full up of brown, brown
shite. What the fuck were Jack doing yonder, scurry-
ing off up the road? Looked like he were trying to get
summat back inside his coat on the trot, like he
didn't have time to stop and do it proper. I opened
me gob to hoy him.

But the tiny voice inside made us shut it again.

I looked at the Hoppers door. No Frankenstein
there. All I could see were half a fag smouldering
away there on the pavement, and a dark puddle by
the entrance where some twat had spilt his snakebite
and black. I looked at the puddle while I mulled
things over, watching it spread slowly from the doorway. All I wanted to do were go inside and start
minding for Nick Wossname. But summat big and
dark and horrible were blocking my path and I
weren't sure what it were. I were thinking about what
it might be when a bird screamed.

Then another bird.

Then folks was running past us up to Hoppers,
cos where there's birds screaming there's summat
worth copping an eyeball of. And I were going with
em, floating more than walking. I knew I ought to be
floating the other way but I had to see.

'Frankenstein,' I says, looking down at him there
on the hard stuff. His back were up against the door,
legs splayed out. His white shirt were glistening red
from chest down.

'Frankenstein?' says someone a fair bit younger
than meself. 'What the ... ? Ah, *Frankenstein*, heh heh.
He do look like him, though, don't he. Odd-lookin'

fucker, wouldn't say it to his face, though, mind. Don't matter now though, do it. Heh heh—'

'Fuckin' shut it, you,' I says, nice and calm.

Another feller of about fifteen looks at us and says: 'Woss you fuckin' care? You're Royston Blake, ain't you? Swiped your job, didn't he, this un? So woss you care?'

I looked at him, this fucking youngun who reckoned he knew what were what. I wanted to answer him, I surely did. I wanted to tear off his swede and bark the news down his neck. But I couldn't. Not with all them other cunts crowded round and about, looking from Frankie to meself and back to Frankie. And what were the point anyhow? He wouldn't understand. None of em would. All younguns they was. And what do younguns know?

'He done it,' says a bird behind us. And I just knew she meant me. 'Royston Blake there. Done it before an' all he has. And got away with it. Mam told us.'

'Aye,' says someone else. 'In the paper it were.'

'Hey, Blake, how'd you do this un here? Fishin' knife, were it? Can't do that kind of job with a lock knife. Blade'd snap off in him.'

'Woss you gonna do now, Blake? Can't hear no coppers comin' yet.'

'Where'd you . . .'

I pegged it. I shifted pins fast as you like, down Friar Street and back up the side of Burt's Caff. I hopped over the wall at the end – knocking part of it over – and dropped down into the Wall Road, landing a bit funny but not being inclined to fret over that just now.

I could hear sirens. Seemed to be coming from all

sides they did. But it weren't the coppers that were bothering us ...

I suppose you're sat there reckoning it's a bit rich, me getting all hoity over one dead feller, what with my past and all. And I'll readily admit to you here and now:

I've killed.

I've killed more than some and less than others. But in this day and age who can put paw to chest and say they ain't? Sometimes a feller's got you cornered and sticking him in the ribs is the only move you've got, or pinging a wrench off his swede. Or running him down with a robbed motor. As that feller says the one time (I forgets who): 'The journey through life is blocked by many a tree. You can walk around some but others is too big. So you got to chop em down.' I reckon that about says it all. Don't you?

Anyhow, the point here I'm getting at is that when folks is just folks it don't do to make a fuss over one or two of em getting dead. But when folks is a doorman ...

Well, that's different ennit.

There is a land far, far away where the folks there reckons cows is sacred, so I hears. That means you can't kill one nor fuck it nor do nothing with it besides looking after it. I dunno where that far-flung land is (Barkettle, I think) and it don't matter anyhow – you got to respect their beliefs and let em get on with it. But come on – a fucking cow? Where'd you get steaks and burgers from if you can't hack a fucking cow down?

But a doorman . . . You ever had a doorman burger? No you ain't. And I'll tell you for why:

Doormen is sacred. Ain't they.

Alright, so this Frankenstein here hadn't been a doorman all that long. Plus he'd swiped my job from under us and that. But he were still a doorman. He were still wearing the black and white of the entertainment security industry. Only it were black and white and red on him. Or just black and red by now, like as not.

That much on its own were enough to place a chill in any doorman's heart. But it weren't the worst of it. I'll tell you what the worst of it were in a minute or two. Well, actually I won't – you'll hear us telling it to the party I were headed to see, if they're in. But I've got to get there first, ain't I. And that's all part of the yarn I'm spinning for you here. I can't just jump from A to B and skip the to and fro, can I. Stories don't work like that, mate, and you can't expect life to neither. I mean, what kind of a world would it be if you could click your heels and get where you wanted to be? There'd be no motors in that world for starters, which means no Ford Capri. And what kind of a world would that be?

But my Capri were still in Norbert bastard Green. So I'll skip the yomping and take you straight to the doorbell, shall I.

'What?'

'Alright, love.'

'Who zat?'

'Me, ennit.'

'Who's you?'

'Fuck sake . . . Blake, ennit.'

'Oh, Blake, is it?'

'Aye, it fuckin' well is. Now let us up.'

She went quiet for a moment or two. But I knew she weren't thinking. Sparking up, weren't she. I could hear her. She sucked deep and says: 'Fuck off,' then fucked off.

I buzzed her again. I weren't yomping all the way out here in the pissing rain with coppers hanging off my arse like shite off a sheep just to hear fuck off. Actually she could tell us to fuck off all she liked. Didn't mean bollocks to us. Told us to fuck off all the time, she did. I hadn't ever listened to it before and I weren't planning on starting.

'I says fuck off,' she says.

'Alright, Sal, you've said yer piece. Now buzz us up and put the kettle on. Alright?'

'Put the kettle on? I'll put the fuckin' kettle on your head. I says fuck off and I means fuck off. Now piss off.'

I looked behind us. Some lads was knocking about on the scrub up yonder, but they was trying to chat up a couple of birds there so they wouldn't have noticed us. Other than them no one were about. Not that I gave a toss anyhow. You knows Royston Blake better than to reckon him a nervous person. I just didn't want to get seen is all. I'm a well-known face round here and, what with the coppers after us and all, I had to keep me profile low.

There were a little window beside the door. I got a half-brick up off the floor and put it through it. But it were one of them windows with wire in em, so I had to bash it a few times to get a hole big enough for me arm. I reached through and opened the door, scratching me wrist on the wire as I pulled it out and cursing the cunt whose idea it were to put the fucking wire in them windows in the first place. I shut the door behind us and went up the stair, bleeding and frowning. But by the time I were rapping on Sal's door I'd thought of a way to get summat out of it. That's what your swede's for, see. Take your opportunities and make the most of em. Watch and learn, mate.

'Come on, open the door, will yer?'

She didn't. But she would.

'Sal, I'm losing blood here. I dunno if I can... I... Aargh...' I leaned on the wall and waited. Course, I could be kicking her door down and gaining rightful entry that way. But I didn't want Sal with a strop on. I were shook up, fuck sake. I'd just come from seeing a doorman with his guts flopping out. Sometimes a woman's touch is the only thing to bring you out of it. The door opened.

Just a crack, mind.

'Sal...' I says, holding out my arm. 'I'm hurt, Sal.'

'Woss happened?' she says. But you could tell she were thawing. There's two sorts of birds and Sal were the better sort, despite appearances.

'I, er... Fuckin' let us in, eh? Please?'

For a minute there I thought she weren't going to. I thought she'd finally turn us away for proper, maybe laugh in me face or flob on us and then slam the door. And do you know what? Gave us a moment of panic it did. I hope you appreciates my honesty here cos I wouldn't tell no other fucker this. I thought of a life without Sal and I panicked. Fucking barmy or what? Cos it weren't like we was wedded nor nothing. Just shagged each other now and then we did. But we was mates and all. And right now I needed her.

She opened the door and went off to the kitchen. I followed her, making noises like I were in pain. To be fair on meself I were suffering. The wiry glass had spiked a juicy vein by the looks of him, and if Sal here couldn't sort it I'd have to go down the ozzy, which I didn't fancy at all. But when Sal took me paw in hers and started mopping all the blood off it I knew she'd see us right. Had the touch, did Sal.

She dried us off with one of her best tea towels – not saying a word about the blood getting all over it – and bandaged the feller up with a bit of gauze under it. Felt alright after that I did, as if by patching up me wrist she'd fixed all them other little buggers that kept my life from flowing straight and true. I kissed her on the cheek and says ta and patted her on the arse, then went to the fridge, leaving her to pick up the mess.

There was nothing there besides some butter, half a block of lard, four old spuds and half a bottle of sparkling. I fucking hates wine. It's strictly for birds and arse bandits and don't do no good at all for a real man like meself. I shut the fridge door and looked around the kitchen, wondering where she hid the voddy. 'Got a fag, Sal?' I says.

I could feel her eyes on us so I added: 'Needs summat for me head, don' I. Feelin' a bit faint, like.'

She took us by the arm and led us back into the living room. 'Rest is what you needs.' She pushed us back on the sofa and started unlacing me boots.

'Got any voddy though, Sal?' I says. Cos I really

did need some now. I mean enough's enough – I couldn't even remember the last sup I'd had. 'An' how about that fag?'

She breathed deep through her nose and shot us a tight-arsed smile. 'I'm turnin' over a new leaf, Blake. You won't find no vodka here. Fags neither. All that's behind us now. An' I means it.'

She looked scared, like she'd built a big old house out of cards and I'd walked up looking to knock it all down. And to be honest a bit of us wanted to do just that. I mean, alright, she were trying to give up the pop. Fair play to her. Sauce never had done her no favours and looked to have got the better of her of late, what with that belly of hers. But fucking come on – fags? What's wrong with fags? And what about me? I hadn't had a smoke in fuck knew how long and the least a bird can do is give a feller what he needs. But I never knocked down her house of cards.

You should know I ain't like that.

I pulled her to us instead, trying to block out the stitches on her face and the way her flesh felt like cold dough. 'Know what?' I says in her ear. 'I'm proud of you. Right fuckin' proud, aye.'

She clamped her paws behind me back and squeezed us so hard I thought the bandages might pop off and me wrist start squirting red. After a while she let up a bit and started sobbing.

'Eh,' I says, holding her face to me chest. Last thing I wanted to do were look at her. She looked rough enough already without all the redness and blotchiness from crying. ''S fuckin' matter with you?'

She weren't really up to answering so we just stayed like that, me rocking her nice and gentle and her calming down slow. To be honest with you I weren't too bothered about what were the matter with her. Birds can turn odd now and then and them's the times a feller's best steering clear. He can ask and listen all he likes, but he'll never understand. Fellers ain't built for understanding birds and the same goes t'other way, although birds might tell you different. Your typical feller knows he don't know and don't give a toss when all's said. So when Sal started to say summat I hushed her up and pushed her face to me chest a bit harder. 'Plenty time for words,' I says. 'All the time in the world there is.'

She seemed alright about that so we stayed hugging each other for a bit. Somehow she'd managed to get her knickers off and before I knew it my hands was working her arse cheeks. It were just as well she were on top cos I didn't have the energy to do much jumping about, what with yomping here and there and all the other shite I'd been putting up with of late. But I weren't so far gone I couldn't rise to the occasion.

Course I fucking weren't.

'I loves you,' she says afterwards when we'd been lying still a fair old while. I'd been doing a bit of thinking about this and that and I'd worked out a bit of a plan. I knew what to do next anyhow. I'd always found that thinking comes easier right after you've shot your muck, see, when your tadger's lying limp and contented up a bird's fanny. But the sound of Sal's voice shook us out of it. Which weren't a bad thing to be fair on her. You can't lie there thinking for ever, can you. Sooner or later you've got to pull out and do summat.

'Aye, nice one,' I says, giving her another squeeze. When you got used to it her plump body weren't so bad, long as you kept the lights low. Still weren't so keen on her belly, mind, which were a bit lumpy and not so soft as it ought to be. 'Couldn't do us a favour, Sal?'

'What?'

'Go up the shop an' get us a few tinnies, eh?'

She went all still, like she'd heard someone come in the kitchen window. But there were no one else here. Just her and meself.

'Only I ain't really up to it, like,' I says. 'You know, me injury an' that . . .' I rolled her over so I were on top, dick soft but still in place. While I were still up her I knew I could get her agreeing to anything. 'An' you knows I loves you.'

At them words she clamped her legs around us so hard I went a bit stiff again. 'Oh, Blake,' she says, kissing us all over the face. 'I'll go to the shops for you. And when I comes back I got summat to tell you. Summat important, Blake.'

'Nice one,' I says, laughing and wrenching meself free. I were busting for a slash and me lower back were giving us grief beyond belief. I went and had a long piss, humming 'Don't Cry Daddy' by the King himself. Mind you, if I were crying it's cos it stunk of puke in that bathroom and I wanted out sharpish.

When I came back she were all set for the shop, though I knew she had fuck all on under that coat. Sal were lazy that way. She kissed us again and went to the door. 'Oh, and some fags,' I says as she stood in the doorway blowing a kiss. She frowned a bit but I knew she were alright about it.

Soon as the front door were shut I sat down and picked up the blower.

'Hello. Paul Pry. Fine selection of ales and—'

'Nathan?'

'Aye. Who zat?'

'Me, ennit. Blake.'

'Ah, Royston Blake.'

'Aye, Blake. So?'

'So what?'

'So you heared or what?'

'Heared what?'

'Come on, I thought you knows everythin'?'

'I never said that, Blakey.'

'You knows iss true, though.'

'Seems not, don' it. So woss I meant to have heared?'

'Well, that plan o' yours . . .'

'Oh aye. Worked, did it?'

'No.'

'No?'

'No.'

He were quiet for a bit. You could hear all them voices in the background. The disprocessed of Mangel, he'd called em. Well, they'd be disprocessed a bit longer, the way things was turning out. 'Ah well,' says Nathan. 'Can't win em all, can us? Anyhow, I'm busy . . .'

'But Nathan—'

'But nuthin'. I can't help you, Blake. There's some things a feller can get help on and others he's on his own for. You can't see how the world works but she's always turnin' nonetheless, takin' us on to the next day come what may. Other times she stops, Blake.

Know that, did you? The world stops and she ain't goin' nowhere. She's waitin' fer summat to happen, Blake. She ain't happy with the way things is goin' up there on her skin, which is where this here town of ours is located. She's waitin' on a feller while he gets a job done for her. Them's the times, Blake. Them's the ones you got to pull yer finger out for. You hearin' us?'

'But—'

'That's too many buts, Blake. Physician says I gotta cut down on me buts. Bad fer the kidneys. Bye, Blake.'

'Bu . . .'

But the cunt had hung up, hadn't he. And fuck knows what he'd been going on about anyhow. So I were left with no plan, being as the plan had been to ask Nathan what to do.

I turned on the telly and tried watching that for a bit. There were fuck all on that I hadn't seen already. I picked up the blower again and rang me own number. I weren't turning barmy, mind. I wanted to see if Fin were back. Not that I were after his help. Any man asks Fin for help is beyond helping. No, I wanted him to have a gander out front and see if my motor weren't there. Filthy Stan had had long enough. Specially considering the premium rate I'd bunged him. But no one answered.

The bastard were still out, weren't he. I couldn't understand it. What reason did he have for going out? You goes out after nightfall you're drinking, shagging or doing a job. Fin were a cripple, so he had no one to drink with, no bird to shag, and no one were thick enough to give him summat to do.

I put down the blower and scratched me swede. I dunno why I even bothered phoning folks. If there's one thing I always knew in me heart it's this:

You want summat doing, do him yourself.

Don't never expect help from no fucker. Oh aye, most times they'll be falling over emselves to hold your cock for you while you has a slash. But when there's a whiff of shite in the air they'll drop you, and you're pissing down your strides and all over the floor.

And there's no such thing as a mate neither. Folks is all cunts, every last fucking bastard of em. Aye, that's what I've learned in life.

I went out.

Even caught meself whistling on me way down the stair. Just as I reached the front door Sal comes through it clutching a couple of placcy bags. I'd forgot about that. Could have murdered a few right then, but I had it all sorted in me swede now and I couldn't let Sal put us off me stride. 'Where's you off?' she says.

'Out,' I says, going past her. She shouted summat behind us but like I says, I had it all sorted in me swede.

I were knackered when I reached the top of the hill. It were right late and all. I were used to coming home late after a hard night down the Hoppers, but not on foot. Still, I were hoping Filthy Stan had come through and parked the Capri outside my house. If he hadn't I'd fucking have him. A deal's a deal and seventy sheets says that's what it is. I stopped on our corner and peered up the road.

A motor were parked outside our house alright. But she weren't mine. Unless Stan had sprayed her white.

I started walking towards her, guts tightening. What the fuck had he done to my motor? 'Pick her up and fix the tyres,' I'd said to him. Not 'Pick her up and fix the tyres and spray her white'. I fucking hated white Capris. Mine were gold. Mine were the only gold Capri in Mangel and I liked it that way.

Mind you, Minder had a white Capri, didn't he.

'Ah, it's you, is it,' says Doug the shopkeeper from the open doorway of his shop. 'Go on then, woss you got to say for yerself, eh?'

13

LOOKING FOR JOEY: PART ONE
Steve Dowie, Crime Editor

At last, after four hours of waiting, my patience is rewarded. He comes out of the arcade and makes his way towards the High Street – hands in pockets, hood up, narrow shoulders hunched. I thank the gods of investigative journalism that he is alone. But then, I always knew he would be alone.

He stops to stick a cigarette in his mouth as I reach him.

'Here,' I say, holding out a lighter.

He takes the light, then glares at me with the same narrow-eyed furtiveness I have seen in him before. '**** d'you want?' he asks.

I just want a chat, I tell him. But I read in his eyes that I'm losing my chance. I reach into my overcoat and flash the brown leather of my wallet.

'Alright,' he says. 'But not here.'

It is ten minutes later. I am sitting on a wooden bench. A high wall is behind me. In front of me are the brown waters of the River Clunge. The only passers-by are old men and their dogs. My eyes light on a pair of white swans on the water, twin beacons of purity in a town whose innocents are few in number and rapidly dwindling. A waft of stale sweat assaults my nostrils. The bench creaks as it takes another occupant.

The boy is sitting next to me. 'What?' he asks.

Can we talk about Joey?

'Joey who?'

Ah, games.

I pass him a folded-up banknote.

'Oh, that Joey. What d'you wanna know about him?'

Where did he come from?

'**** knows.' His eyes seem to look in every direction at once, ready to flee at the first sign of anyone but old men approaching. 'Just turned up, didn't he.'

When?

'Dunno. Few weeks ago. Few months.'

How often do you use it?

The boy shrugs. His face, snow white in the glare of the autumn sun, shows no evidence of the hot summer just gone. Faint lines encircle his squinting eyes. 'When I can get it.'

Do you know what it is?

He shifts uncomfortably. A leg starts jumping nervously. No answer comes.

I offer another banknote.

'Sweets, ain't it,' he says. 'Fancy sweets what does your head in.'

But you don't really believe Joey is a sweet, surely? You realise you're taking an illegal drug, and you have no idea what it does to you?

'Dunno nothin' about no drugs, do I. Joey does what it does, dunnit. It's a sweet and it does your head in.'

What do you mean by 'does your head in'?

He is looking around more than ever now. Both feet are jumping. 'Gotta go.'

Just tell me.

His eyes narrow as he looks at me. Suddenly I am an enemy.

'You likes it here, does you?' he seethes. 'Mangel's a nice place for you? Well, lucky old you. For me and everyone I knows it's a ******* *****-hole. Not just cos it's borin'. I could put up with just havin' **** all to do. But it's worse than that. It's bad. I've seen the telly and Mangel ain't nothin' like places you sees there. There's Mangel here on the one side, right, and on the other there's the telly place. But you can't get to the telly place. And then a feller comes along with a bag o' sweets and they ain't normal sweets. They'm sweets that'll take you to the telly place, ain't they. What you gonna do?'

I open my mouth to answer, but nothing comes out. I have no argument. And by the time I realise that, I am sitting alone again.

'What about?' I says. To be honest I didn't have nothing to say to Doug. But I had to say summat.

'About what, you says? About what? About my bloody daughter who ain't been home. About that little bastard who's led her astray. That's what about.'

'Oh aye, well . . .' I looked at Doug. He weren't so scary really. Must be getting on for sixty if he were any age at all. One of them who always looked same no matter what age he were. It's them you wants to watch out for, so they says. But I'd had enough of Doug the shopkeeper and his demands. And like I says, he weren't so scary really. I took a deep un.

'Knows what you can do, Doug?' I says. It were dark in the street. There were one lamp flickering over the way there but that were too far off to be much help. And no light were spilling from the shop behind him. So all in all Doug weren't much more than a lanky black shape in front of us. But I guessed where his eye were and gave him a look in it, saying: 'You can take yer lager and fags and—'

'I'd stop right there if I were you.' And I did. Just to be on the safe side, like. Cos he were Doug the shopkeeper and there'd always been stories about him.

'I'd consider your position before openin' me big fat trap, if I were you. I'd think of others for a change. Like me and my Mona. Like that mate o' yours, Finley.'

'Finney,' I says. Cos I knew how Fin always hated being called that. 'Not Finley.'

'Finney he might be,' he says. 'But he ain't your mate.'

I didn't like this. I wanted to go home and watch the telly. I didn't care if I didn't have no drink in the house. I'd put the kettle on. 'What?'

'He can't be your mate. He were your mate you'd look out for him.'

'Who says I don't?'

'Does you?'

'Aye, course I—'

'Know his whereabouts, then, does you?'

'Aye, he's . . .' I looked up the road at my house.

There was no lights on. He'd be in bed fast akip. I knew he weren't, mind. That were plain as the gibbous moon hanging up there over our heads, or the whiff of old cheese coming from Doug's shop.

Doug took a step forward, folding his arms. There were no sound in the street besides his breathing and my breathing and the thumpety thump of my heart. I wanted to step back but I were froze to the spot like a dog turd in February. Doug put his face not half a foot from mine. He were tall as meself and about half as heavy. But heft didn't count for shite on that night, stood there outside his shop.

'I got him,' he says. 'Until you gets rid of that Nick feller and I gets my Mona back, I got Finley. An' I'll tell you summat else – I'm only keepin' him one more day. After that you can forget about him. Midnight the morrer, Royston Blake. Midnight the morrer.'

'You fuckin' what?' I says after a bit. But he were long gone. There were no sign of Doug and the door were shut.

I stood alone on the pavement, trying to think.

He had our Fin? That what he were saying? That where Fin had been the past day or so, locked away in the back of the shop, wheels took off his chair like as not? I went to hammer on his door. I'd get Fin out of there and teach Doug a thing or two besides. That's what I'd do alright. But me fist stayed where it were, stuck out before us like a toffee apple.

Listen, I weren't being straight with you before, when I told you about Doug and Sammy Johnson and them sausages back then as younguns. All the lads went in for their tea and that, but not meself.

Didn't have no mam to call us in, did I. It were a good day when my old feller brung us home half a bag of cold chips. Went round the block instead, I did. Down the alley and over the high brick wall behind Doug's back yard. It were nice and quiet back there and I felt smart, like I were on a mission or summat. I crept up the side of the house and peeked through a window.

It were the kitchen. Light were on in there and I could see how clean he kept it. I thought that a bit odd at the time. Doug weren't married back then so why the fuck were his kitchen clean? The one in our house weren't clean. I moved to the next window.

Living room by the looks of it, but the light were off. I could see a telly and a couch and not much besides. I stood back and had a gander at the upstairs windows.

All dark except the one.

I had a quiet poke around the yard and found a ladder behind Doug's shed. Weren't a very long one but it'd get us high enough. I took him over and leaned him under the lit window. It were an odd room I found when I got up there. Weren't a bedroom cos there weren't no bed in it. Weren't much else in it neither, besides a few boxes and a wood chair, Sammy sitting on it with no kit on.

Funny old sight he were, skinny as a sapling and pale as pigeon shite. I had a quiet chortle at that. But I soon stopped and started wondering why he had no kit on. I mean, fair play to Doug for locking the thieving bastard up for a bit, but why strip him? I rapped on the pane.

Sammy looked at us. His eyes was wide and red

rimmed, like fried eggs with tommy sauce round the edge. I could see he wanted to say summat to us but he wouldn't come out with it. He kept looking at the door and then back at meself. 'Open the window,' I says, nice and quiet. 'Got a ladder here, ain't I.'

But he wouldn't move. Just sat there looking from door to me to door again.

I tried the window meself but it wouldn't budge. 'Open the fuckin' win—'

I stopped there and ducked. I didn't move for a bit, thinking about what I'd just clocked. Couldn't be true, could it? I stuck my head up again, nice and slow.

Aye, it were Doug alright. Had a mask on but I could tell it were him. Odd mask it were and all, made up of red rubber by the looks of him and stretched across his whole head except for the two peeping holes and a big round one for his gob. Red rubber covered the rest of his body and all, except for a big hole where his tadger came out.

I didn't hang about after that. I climbed down and put the ladder back and pegged it home.

Course, all made sense next morning when I seen the SAUSAGES sign in the shop window. Doug had stripped Sammy cos he were getting him ready for the sausage machine. And his rubber kit were his sausage-making outfit, wernit, to keep the blood off of him. The hole for his tadger were so he could have a slash.

But no (getting back to many a year later), I didn't knock on Doug's door as I stood there thinking about Fin locked up inside. I'd leave it a bit first and then come back for him. I mean, I had promised

Doug, hadn't I. I had said I'd get his youngun back and sort Nick Wossname.

You what? Calling us scared, is you? Me? No I fucking is not. Told you already – I ain't scared of nothing. Not even Doug the shopkeeper, who drags folks out back and makes em into bangers.

I went back across the road trying to get it all out of my head. I tried to concentrate on that white Capri parked outside my house, which weren't mine as it turned out cos the reg were different. And it weren't no 2.8i anyhow – it were a fucking 1.3.

If there's one thing I cannot stand it's a fucking 1.3 Capri. Alright, shape's the same and a Capri's a Capri . . . But a Capri ain't a Capri, is it. A Capri is a 2.8i. A 1.3 is a fucking embarrassment. Whose idea were it to fit the world's greatest automobile with a lawnmower engine? How can you get satisfaction from that?

Mind you, a motor's a motor when you thinks about it. Ain't the car's fault she's got a lump of cack under her bonnet. No, it's the folks who drives em that I despairs of. I mean, what kind of cunt would drive a 1.3 Capri?

'Alright, Blakey.'

'Alright, Blakey.'

I watched em come out my front door. I were watching em but I couldn't take it in. By habit I'm good at copping on to situations sharpish, but I'll admit here that I were struck dumb as a slaughtered calf.

What the fuck was Nobby and Cosh doing coming out my front door?

'Eh . . .' I says. I know I ought to be saying more

but my head were just then starting to catch on. Nobby and Cosh was coming out my front door – course they fucking would be. Hadn't their mate Frankie just got bladed? Hadn't folks been saying it were us who done it?

'Alright, lads?' I says, judging it best to take a friendly tone. Them two was anything but my mates, but you had to be careful with em.

They just stood there looking back at us. The door were still open behind em. You could see right through the hall to the kitchen. Stuff were lying all over the floor and the blower were hanging off its cradle. The bastards had turned the place over, hadn't they. Mind you, I couldn't swear blind I hadn't left it that way meself.

And then I clocked the big brown Mr Whippy slap bang centre of the hall carpet. I keeps an informal household but not that informal. 'Right,' I says, starting round the 1.3 towards the two of em. I weren't standing for that. I didn't care if they was tapped in the head and handy with sharpened steel – no fucker was allowed to do a shite on my floor. 'Come here, you fuckin'—'

Nobby had a blade. I dunno if he'd had it out ready for us or what, but it were out now. A blade changes matters. Not for permanent, like, but it makes you stop and weigh up your options. I stopped and weighed em up.

There weren't many of em.

See, Cosh had his cosh out and all, which were no great surprise to us. One man with a blade is a problem. You can get over a problem. Specially if you got a monkey wrench on your person. But one man with a blade and another with a cosh is a dilemma. And I don't like dilemmas.

I reached for me pocket. But I didn't go in it. 'Come on, lads, less just—'

'Get in,' says Nobby, pointing his knife at the excuse for a Capri.

'I ain't gettin' in there,' I says.

He nodded at the 1.3.

'I ain't gettin' in,' I says, looking at Cosh now.

'Boss wants you,' says Cosh, pushing his filthy black hair out of his eyes then wiping his hand on his jeans. 'Best get in the car.'

'Why'd you shit in my hall?' I says. No one were making a move just yet so I were alright to chat.

They smirked at each other. I thought about reaching for me wrench again but I didn't do it.

'All square now, ain't us,' says Nobby. 'Called us names you did.'

'I called you names?'

'Get in the fuckin' car,' shouts Nobby.

'Hang on a sec, Nob,' says Cosh, tonguing his harelip. 'You called us nonces, Blake. That ain't a nice thing.'

'Call us names again an' I'll cut yer arse off.' Nobby were looking well lairy. Red hair were glowing like a gas fire and his freckles was up. If he put on a green shirt he'd get work as a traffic light. 'Get in the fuckin'—'

'You fuckin' shit in my hall,' I says. I were a bit upset now, and rightly so. 'You shouldn't shit in fellers' halls.'

They looked at each other again, not smirking now. I reached for me pocket and didn't hang about this time. I pulled the wrench out and went for Nobby, who were closest to us. I knew it were touch and go but I could smell that shite now and it just weren't on. I brung the wrench sideways at Nobby's face. He ducked and lost his footing. Cosh were still a couple of yard off so I pulled me leg back ready to give Nobby some shoe. Sometimes you got to show folks what they can and can't get away with, and this were one o' them times. Nobby curled into a ball as my boot closed in on his face. But it never got there, did it.

I went down instead.

Some things is hard for a feller to take. Specially a man o' reputation like meself. I don't mind coming clean that certain folks has got the better of us at times. And it's the Muntons I'm referring to there. But they ran Mangel at one time and there ain't no shame losing ground to such as them. Nobby and Cosh never ran Mangel. Nobby and Cosh was scum. Always had been, always would be. You shouldn't go down to scum. You just fucking shouldn't. So that were one of the hard things I had to take.

The other were nigh on too painful to mention. But mention it I will:

I were sat in the back of that 1.3 Capri.

Mind you, I were glad it were such a late hour. No one were on the streets so no one clocked us slumped in the back with scum up front and scum at me side. Scum was under the bonnet and all, and that's why it took us so long to reach Hoppers.

Cosh parked out back and got out. Nobby didn't budge. He hadn't budged the whole way in, just sat there with his beadies on us and his blade pointing at me right thigh. He hadn't spoke and nor had Cosh. So it had been a pleasant little trip all in all. Specially with the blood dripping down the side of me swede. Cosh opened the shotgun door and shoved the seat aside.

'Shift,' he says.

I didn't shift straight off. You shouldn't, with scum the like of them. It were bad enough being carted hither and thither by em, and I weren't about to make it worser by being their dog. I gave him a nasty look, letting him know I'd have him later for lobbing that cosh at us back there. He might be handy with hardware but I'd seen off harder'n him with me bare fingers. And if you don't believe us go ask anyone. Nobby pressed the knife in me leg.

The denim held for a sec, then gave. You could have woke a graveyard with the holler it wrenched out of us. But no one came, dead or otherwise. I stopped bellowing and got out.

"'S matter?' says Cosh, clocking us from head to leg. I were losing sap from both places and not happy about it. 'Can't stand sight o' blood or summat?'

'We can't stand sight o' you.' It were Nobby, out of the motor now and flashing us the blade again. 'So go on – *move*.' He kicked us in the leg where he'd just stuck us. Didn't hurt so bad as you'd think, mind. It were all getting a bit numb there. I started walking.

We got round front and Nobby unlocked the door. Looking at the key he were using I reckoned the locks had been changed. I went in first. I weren't waiting on being told this time. I didn't want no more aggro from them two until I were ready to dole

some back, which I would do by and by and don't
you worry. If I'd been brung here to answer for
Frankie getting sliced I didn't have much chance of
getting out again, unless it were in the boot of a
motor. So aye, I had aggro in mind. Only question
were when to get started on it.

It were dark inside so I turned some lights on
sharpish. I don't mind a scrap but not if I can't see
who I'm scrapping with.

'Ah, alright, lads,' comes a voice from across the
way.

Nick Wossname were sat all on his tod at one of
them tables along the back wall, feet up on the table,
arms behind swede, smiling and looking like he'd
just woke up. Perched on his face were a pair of sun-
glasses, which were a bit odd considering he'd been
sat in the dark. There were a glass of summat or
other on the table but it didn't look to have been
touched. Next to that were a glass bowl with some
little white round things in it. Next to that were a
pistol, long and pointy like on a cowboy film.

My heart went thumpety at that. Why'd these outsiders always have to bring in guns? Why can't they
go about their business the proper way like the rest
of us, with knives and clubs and that? I'd had deal-
ings with guns before and let me tell you – they don't
leave much room for bargaining. I knew I could handle Nobby and Cosh, but how were I meant to get
past a bullet?

'What the fuck did you do?' says Nick. He weren't
smiling now. He started to stand up.

I were trying to think. It were hard to think with
that gun there and them two nonces behind us.

'Well?' he says. He hadn't picked up the pistol but he hadn't moved away from it neither. 'Come on, spill.'

I opened me trap to say summat.

But Cosh got there first.

'Had a go at Nob, didn't he.'

'Aye,' says Nob. 'Came at us with a big spanner or summat.'

'Monkey wrench.'

'Aye, monkey wrench. Lethal them is.'

Me eyes and ears was going from feller to feller. My head were going from confused to confuseder.

'We told him you wanted to see him but he wanted to fight, didn't he,' Cosh says.

'An' I ain't gonna stand still an' let him hit us with a lethal spanner, is I.'

'So I coshed him.'

Nick took his shades off and clocked us. 'Blake? What have you got to say about it?'

I shrugged and looked at the floor.

'Alright,' he says. 'Alright. You two – beat it.'

They looked at each other. 'But, boss . . .' says Nobby.

'Go on, piss off.'

'But . . .'

'*Go.*'

They shuffled out and shut the door behind em. That left meself and Nick Wossname, him with his pistol and us without a fucking clue what were going on here. I knew I were doing alright, mind, else he wouldn't have told them two to piss off out of it.

'Drink?' he says.

He went behind the bar, leaving his gun all long

and pointy on the table. That settled it for us. No way would he leave his hardware unattended if he wanted to do us for topping Frankenstein.

Unless it were a trick, course. What if that one on the table weren't loaded, and the one with bullets were in his pocket or behind the bar or summat? See, I'm clever. I thinks of these things. That's how I'm here now telling you all this, and not full of worms under Hurk Wood. But you knows I'm clever already. You couldn't hardly sit there listening to us for more than minute or so without knowing it, could you.

Being one step ahead of the game I were able to relax a bit, so I sat on a stool. 'Lager,' I says.

He pulled a pint and put it in front of us. There were more head than lager so you could tell he hadn't ever been behind a bar before. 'Smoke?' he says as I watched the froth go down.

'Aye, alright.' I took one from his pack and lit it, then lit his for him. All very civilised, ennit. Two pillars of the Mangel community having a quiet lock-in after a hard day's summat or other. Except he had a gun in his pocket and I were looking to grab him and knack his swede on the bartop soon as he come close enough.

'That looks nasty,' he says, clocking the side of my head. He got some paper towels and put em under the tap for a bit, then gave us em.

I held em to the cosh wound. I wished I hadn't when cold water started dripping down me collar and making us shiver. But the damage were done now so I left it there.

'What about your leg?' he says, peering over the bartop.

'Aye, well . . .' I moved me leg out where we could both have a gander at it. I'd taken a few knocks and it were nice that someone had noticed for a change.

'You'd better take your trousers off and let me take a look,' he says.

I pulled me leg in sharpish. 'Fuck off,' I says. 'Woss you on about?'

'Hey, chill,' he says, stepping back and putting his hands up. 'Keep them on if that's what you want. No skin off my nose.'

I narrowed me eyes and looked at him, wondering if he were an arse bandit or no. He'd been shagging young Mona but he had long hair so there were no telling. Either way, I weren't so relaxed now. 'Right, I got me half-pint. And I got me fag. You got summat to say to us, say it,' I says. Cos there's only so much fucking about you can do, ain't there.

'Alright,' he says, leaning on the pop fridge, well out of my reach. 'I dunno if you've heard,' he says, 'but something happened here tonight.'

'Oh aye,' I says, laying it on.

'Yeah. Someone got killed.'

'Killed, eh?'

'Yeah. Murdered.'

I took my hand away from me swede. Not much blood coming out now so I put the soggy mess down. I picked up me glass and drained it. 'Murdered?' I says. 'Well, fuck me.'

'You haven't heard?'

'Should I of?'

'I dunno. Should you have?'

'Fuck sake . . .'

'Alright. Look, I might as well tell you that people

are saying it's you. There was a whole posse of them gathered out front after it happened, saying how you stabbed him because he took your job.'

'Fuckin' lyin' bastards,' I blares, slamming me empty down on the bartop and smashing it. 'Always gangin' up on us they is.'

'Who is?'

'Them cunts,' I says, nodding back at the door.

'Which cunts?'

'You know, cunts in general. Folk. Every fucker in Mangel.'

'Come on, man, you know what rumours are like. They'll be saying something different by now anyway.'

'Who will?'

'These cunts you're fed up with.'

'They fuckin' will not, you know. I've had it before, mate. Next thing you knows your face is in the paper with KILLER next to it.'

'I heard about that.'

'About what? Woss you heared?'

'That stuff a couple of years back. The Muntons, wasn't it?'

I looked at him, not sure what to make of it all. It's one thing Mangel folk knowing your business, but the thought of an outsider asking questions about us got me wick up summat chronic. Mind you, there were summat different about this un here. He weren't your typical outsider, you might say. But I couldn't tell you just how.

'Look, I might as well tell you – I know you didn't kill Dean. I don't know about that old stuff and it's not my business anyway, but I know you didn't do this one. You wouldn't kill a bloke in cold blood for a little thing like that. And I've told the police as much.'

I were scratching my head. 'Who the fuck's Dean?'

'De— Fucking hell, Blake, keep up. Dean was my doorman. It's Dean who got ki—'

'Woss you gone an' telled the coppers?'

'Blake, *chill*. I told the coppers you didn't do it.'

'Why?'

'What d'you mean "why"? It's good, isn't it?'

'Aye, but how'd you know I never killed him? I mean, you don't know us from Larry, right?'

He didn't answer. I watched him chewing his lip and closing his eyes. Luckily for him I were no longer looking to smash his face on the bartop. He'd got the coppers off us, and that were the main thing. But there weren't half summat odd about him.

After a bit I got bored of wondering about him and pulled meself another pint, using a dead glass from up the way. It were nice to sit down and refuel meself for a change, and I could feel the sap seeping back into me limbs. I sank that one and got another. I had a powerful thirst on and I hadn't even skimmed the surface of it. I sank me current one and got another.

'Truth is, Blake, I need your help,' he says. I'd forgot all about him for a minute there and to be honest I'd quite enjoyed the break.

'Oh aye.' I rounded off the dregs and pulled meself another.

'You know I do. I already asked you. In a way.'

'You what? When?'

'Yesterday. Remember? Asked you to do some minding for me. You said you'd sleep on it.'

'Did I?'

'Yeah, you did. You alright, Blake?'

'Alright? Aye . . . Just a bit . . .' I knew the word I meant but I couldn't find it. Dis . . . summat. You knows the one – where you don't know north and south from your belly button, and you're dizzy like you just spent half-hour in a tumble dryer. Dis . . .

'Disornamentated,' I says.

Nick looked at us funny and then nodded. Some folks is clever and some ain't. If he didn't understand long words, that were his fucking problem. I weren't bringing meself down for him nor no other bastard.

'Maybe you should slow up on the beer there, man.'

It were my turn to look at him funny now. 'Woss you on about?' I says, pulling meself another. Cos I'd only had a couple.

He knew he were on shaky ground so he changed the subject. 'Thing is, Blake, I need you to start now. I need you to do a little job right now.'

I looked at me watch.

'I know it's late and you're tired and beat up. Believe me, Blake – I never meant for you to get hurt tonight. All I did was ask Cosh and Nobby to go and get you. I thought all you lot knew each other.'

'I does know em. I knows they'm cunts.'

'Well, I didn't know.'

'No, you fuckin' don't know, does you.'

'You got a problem with me, Blake?'

He were fair to say that. I didn't particularly like the bastard but I had to watch me tongue about it.

He wanted us as his minder still, so I couldn't fuck him about too much yet. I had to get meself established before I started doing that. I shrugged and says: 'No.'

'I hope not, Blake. I'm your friend. You know we were talking about trust just now? There's two people I trust in the whole world. One of them's myself. If you can't trust yourself you won't last long. Especially doing what I do.'

I nodded. My own experience of running Hoppers had been same – if you can't trust yourself to lay off the lager you'll have none left for the punters. And then where'd you be?

'The other person I trust,' he says, 'is you.'

I were midway through pulling meself another when he says that. There's none who can pull a better pint than meself. Not even Rache. But suddenly the fucker were brimming over with froth and only an inch or so of drinkable at the bottom.

I mean, I knew the legend of Royston Blake had spread far and wide. And I ain't just talking about Mangel here. When you're a legend like I am Mangel ain't big enough for you, even if you can't get out of it. So bits of you pops out the seams and folks as far flung as Barkettle and Tuber gets to hear about what a top doorman you is, and how you came out on top the one time though the whole town were gagging for your blood. So it stands to reason folks from the like of East Bloater knows how handy you is. But big city fellers like Nick Wossname here?

Fucking hell, eh.

'Blake? Are you OK?'

I tipped the froth out and pulled a proper un. It

ain't every day a feller finds out he's world famous. I celebrated by downing it in one.

'Blake – please, please stop drinking now. I told you, I got a job for you.'

'Oh aye, woss that, then?' Them last two words there was part of a big old belch who wanted out sharpish and went on another five or so seconds. 'You wants a job done, there ain't no fucker more suited to the ... You know, if you're ...' I were feeling a bit light headed of a sudden. Bad pint like as not.

Anyhow, I sat tight and listened while he told us what he wanted doing and why he wanted it done. Seemed fair play all in all, so I says: 'Right you is, boss,' and belched again. Nick went for a piss out back so I had another couple for health's sake. I took one over to the table he'd been sat at. Like I says, I don't approve of guns, but you got to admit – they're nice, ain't they. All shiny and hard and heavy as fuck. I picked her up and pointed her round the place, lining up the optics behind the bar and pretending they was coppers. When I'd had enough of that I put her down and had a look at the little bowl of sweets beside em. I picked one up, held him to the light. Summat familiar about em there were. But young-uns spends their days scoffing sweets so I'd like as not had these many a year ago.

I heard the bog flushing out back so I popped the sweet in me gob and fucked off, swiping a bottle of whisky on me way out.

14

Steve Dowie, Crime Editor

'Well?' I say to my landlady as she tries to squeeze past me in the hall. 'How do I look?'

She grimaces and makes for the nearest escape route, as usual. But I do not need her approval. I only have to glance into the mirror to see that I look like a teenager.

No, this is not a premature mid-life crisis. Nor is it fancy dress. I am going undercover. If 'Steve Dowie, crime editor' cannot gain admittance to Hoppers, maybe 'Steve Dowie, anonymous teenager' can?

It is 6.30 p.m. – that twilit time after the workers have gone home, before the drinkers have come out in force. But already Friar Street is humming with the energy coming from Hoppers. I fall in behind some youths – three boys, two girls – and take my chance. The youngsters are walking unsteadily, as if their feet barely touch the pavement. The effect of Joey perhaps? Whatever, I must do as they do.

The brutish doorman nods and lets them into the dark

enclave beyond. My pulse quickens as I follow them over the threshold, praying my stagger convinces. 'Oi, you,' the doorman grunts. A huge hand covers my chest, holding me back.

I look at him with eyes both quizzical and addled, I hope.

'Summat wrong with your legs or summat?' he says. I notice for the first time how young he really is. This is a boy in a giant's body. But he still stands between me and my investigation.

I look at my legs and shrug.

He seems concerned about my smell. He sniffs the air around me. I flush slightly, remembering that I forgot to wash this morning. Can a case of mild body odour be grounds to deny entry? I realise this is my moment. Either I will reach the place beyond and find out what is destroying the youth of Mangel, or . . .

Or I will fail.

Suddenly the granite hand falls off my chest as the doorman appraises the next customer. My passage is clear. I slouch onwards.

Inside I don't know which way to turn. Children — aged ten to eighteen — are everywhere. I am so manifestly not one of them, and I feel sure they will sense me. But none does. They are too busy: dancing, wandering, talking to each other, talking to themselves, or just sitting still as if watching some imaginary television.

I cannot just stand here and watch. I must do something. I go to the bar.

There I ask the handsome barmaid where the cigarette machine is.

'Empty, ain't it,' she says. 'Been empty for weeks.' She offers me one of her own.

I light up and immediately start coughing.

'Summat wrong?' she says. 'Hang on, you don't smoke, does you.'

I shrug. There's no point in hiding it.

'Why'd you have a lighter, then?'

A reporter should always carry a lighter. But I cannot tell her that. I notice the Mangel Informer *she has been reading and wonder if she has already rumbled me.*

'Here, I knows you,' she says, settling the matter. 'You're that—'

I put my hand on hers and wink at her. It is a risky move. She will either understand me and shut up, or I will be thrown out. She moves away and starts pulling a pint. I wonder if I shouldn't just leave. Maybe I really am out of my depth here. Maybe I shouldn't have studied so hard at school.

She puts the full pint before me. I am teetotal, but I don't tell her that. She leans towards me. She is a generously proportioned woman and I find myself lusting after her, despite myself. I take a gulp of beer to cool myself down. 'I think you're alright,' she says. 'You're the only one who gives a toss.'

About what?

'About this town and the way the kids is going. Look at em all,' she says, nodding to the seething, deranged mêlée behind me. 'They're all in here. This is their home, ain't it, where it all happens. What took you so long?'

I look into this woman's eyes and realise that, for the first time, someone shares my wavelength.

Who is the J-Man?

She giggles nervously and steps back, fingers to lips, eyes flitting. She seems slightly inebriated. Not on alcohol but on the precariousness of her situation. Satisfied that no one is within earshot, she leans in again. 'He's me boss.'

The J-Man. Nick Nopoly.

'Makes them sweets, don't he. I seen him doing it, out back in his office. Never used to see them sweets in Mangel, we didn't. Only since he's been . . .'

She stops suddenly as a customer arrives for a refill. I know this is the end of our interview, and feel an unexpected twinge of sadness. She takes the man's empty and moves away. He has greasy black hair and a cleft palate. He grins at me, exposing an expanse of glinting pink gum. It makes me feel bad inside, as if he'd tricked me into eating his own excrement. I leave a banknote on the bar to cover my drink, and step away. The man pockets the cash, but I am not about to argue.

I glance at the doorman as I hurry out, wondering if he will notice my suddenly improved gait. But he doesn't even see me. He's staring at the sky, as if contemplating chariots of angels coming down to take him away.

I were dreaming. I knew that much. I knew it cos I were in me bedroom at home and I could hear Mam and the old feller downstairs having a go at each other. But Mam had died when I were only a babby, hadn't she, which is how I copped on to it being a dream. Cos I weren't no babby here. I weren't a big feller neither but I were big enough to rob. I knew that cos I were watching the little portable I'd robbed out of someone's house with Legs and Fin the one time. It were black and white and you couldn't hardly get a proper picture on it. But it were better than being down there.

Clint were on. I think it were *A Fistful of Dollars*

but I weren't sure. He's hid behind a horse or summat, watching the goings on across the way, which sounds like a feller and bird having a row. I know it's Mam and the old feller before it shows em. When it does show em it's funny and not funny. Funny cos the old feller's wearing a cowboy hat and Mam one o' them red strappy things what all the prozzies wears in them films. Not funny cos he's strangling her.

Back to Clint again, and he's going for his gun. Only it ain't there. Some cunt's took it and he ain't happy. But you can't hold Clint back. He reaches down his sock and pulls out a fucking great big bowie knife. His eyes narrow and he starts to get up, nice and slow.

I'm in the kitchen now. It's a dream so I don't have to tell you how I got there and you ain't bothered anyhow, are you. The drawer's open and I'm getting summat out. It's a chopping knife, ennit. I takes it and goes to the stairs. Halfway up the stairs and it ain't a chopping knife no more – it's a bowie, just like Clint's. The old man's up there in his bedroom shouting about Mam, calling her a tart and a slag and that. Mam's making a gurgling noise and it don't sound good. But I'm Clint, ain't I. I got narrow eyes and a brown hat and a big fucking blade. I go up to the bedroom door, aiming to open it nice and slow. But I don't go through with it. This is a fucking Clint Eastwood film, ennit. So I take a run-up and break the fucker down.

He gets off her sharpish. Knows he's for it, don't he. He's got Clint on his arse now and he'd better tuck his shirt in. But it's too late for him, ennit. She's lying there on the bed, dead. It's me mam, with her long blonde hair and red lips. Her gob's hanging agape and her big blue eyes is wide with the horror of it all. And it's the old feller who done it.

He's cowering in the corner there trying to get behind that wardrobe. I go to him. I got a blade in my hand and the blackness is coming over us . . .

I dunno what time it were when I came to. I were stretched out on a bench and I could hear running water. Took us a few minutes to work out I were in Vomage Park up the far end by Shatter Crescent, and the sound were coming from the Piss Fountain a few feet away.

The Piss Fountain were so called on account of the three little statues of younguns in the middle of it, slashing into the water no-handed. They'd been slashing like that long as I recalled and showed no sign of slowing up. Between em was a bird with her kit off, but you couldn't see her nips nor fanny nor nothing. Could have seen em when they first put her there like as not, but that had been long ago and the weather had wore her smooth since.

I sat up and tried to think.

The whisky bottle were lying empty on the floor. The label looked dirty, like I'd rolled it in dogshite or summat. My hands was dirty and all but it weren't no dogshite. Sticky and greasy it were, like paint or summat. Fuck knew how that had got there and to be honest I didn't give a toss. I gave a toss about my head, mind, which felt fucking awful. I needed water sharpish else I didn't know what I'd do. There were a drinking tap somewhere in the park but I couldn't recall whereabouts, it being so long since I'd last been in there. I picked up the bottle and went down to the Piss Fountain to fill him up.

After that I felt a bit better. But I still didn't know what time it were. So I looked at me watch. It were a bit dark and I had to squint. 'Look at you,' said me mam. 'Wonderin' what time it is when you don't even know what you're doin'.'

I looked up and sure enough there she were in the middle of the fountain, surrounded by the three pissers. 'Oh,' I says. 'Alright, Mam.'

'Don't Mam me. I'd of known he'd be sleepin' on park benches, I'd never of had a child. Three hours you been lyin' there. Three hours.' Her face softened a bit, despite her being hewn of stone. 'I used to watch you in yer cot when you was only little. Did you know that, Royston? Do you remember?'

'I remembers, Mam,' I says. 'I remembers it all. An'—'

'Do you, though, Royston? Do you remember when I used to stroke your soft cheek and whisper "I loves you"?'

'Mam, I does. I—'

'You was my little man.'

'I still am, Mam. I'm still—'

'I stroked your hair too, Royston. I used to love that hair. Even got to cut it once, before . . .'

'Before what, Mam?'

'Before I went away.'

'Where'd you go, Mam?'

'Everyone goes away, Royston.'

'I know but—'

'And when they go, you've just got to let them.'

'But, Mam—'

'Bye, Royston.'

'Hang on a min, Mam. Mam?'

I stopped pressing me face to her chest when I noticed it were bleeding. Blood were dripping down between her tits and running out of steam down by her belly, sucked in by the thirsty stone like as not. Cos it weren't Mam no more. It were a statue again, of a bird with her bits worn smooth by the tick-tock of the clock. I waded out of the fountain and started walking.

I walked down the main path through the park. Next to the big old weeping willow about halfway down I spotted the drinking tap. I were parched again and wanted a sip. But someone were there already. He stood up, wiped his gob, and squinted at us.

'Alright, Blake,' he says.

'Alright, Clint.'

We sat down on a bench near by. There's a lot of benches in Vomage Park but I don't reckon I'd ever sat on one of em before now. And here I were trying two out in the one night. Fancy that, eh.

Clint offered us a stogie.

'Cheers,' I says.

I checked me pockets. I knew I had me lighter somewhere, but before I found it Clint struck a match on his boot and held it out.

'Nice one,' I says. He were alright, Clint.

'Been waitin' on you,' he says, brushing some ash off his poncho.

It were a decent cigar. Much better than the one I'd had in Nick Wossname's office. And I smoked this un proper and all. Instead of sucking it right down I let it play around me gob a bit first, then took a bit down nice and slow. It were a whole new experience, and one I truly reckoned were down to me being sat there with Clint, and not the usual breed of wanker I sat down for a smoke with.

'You know summat, Clint?' I says. Then I told him what I just told you. About the usual breed of wanker.

'Well, that's nice, Blake,' he says. 'But you oughtn't to be usin' language like that to describe yer townfellows. This here town is made of folks, right? You treat the folks bad, you treat the place bad.'

'Got summat on yer mind, have you, Clint?'

'Aye, matter of fact I have. Thass why I'm here.'

'I reckoned as much. We don't see you round here too regular like.'

'Blake . . .'

'I mean, we gets you on telly and that. I got all your films on vid at home. Mind you, I taped over *Hang em High* by mis—'

'Shut it and listen,' says Clint.

And I did. Cos Clint shoots truer than no man never did.

'The natural order of things has been broken,' he says, squinting through the smoke. 'And you broke it. The sanctity of this here town has been jeopardised, and it's your fault. This is why I'm here, to try and set you on the straight road. Do you hear us, Blake?'

'Clint, can I ask you summat?'

'What?'

'You got one o' them hip flasks?'

'Eh?'

'Hip flask. You know, one o' them little fellers you keeps yer whisky in. You got one? All the cowboys has em.'

'No, I ain't got a fuckin' hip flask. I'm tryin' to tell you summat important here.'

'I knows that, Clint, I knows that. But us sittin' here havin' a nice cigar an' chat I thought—'

'We're not havin' a nice chat.'

'—I thought right here's a good time to have a little heart-warmer, you know? You sure you ain't got one?'

Clint were looking a bit itchy, and you knows what cowboys is like when they gets itchy, with their trigger fingers and all. So I shut up and let him say his piece. I weren't looking forward to it, mind. To be honest, when I first clocked him there I thought he'd come to give us a few tips on minding, not have a go at us about breaking the natural wind of what have you, and that.

'Royston Blake,' he says in a voice that didn't sound like him. To be honest he hadn't sounded much like himself all along. He'd sounded more like Finney. But I knew it were Clint and not Fin because Fin were a greasy-haired streak of piss and this here feller were . . . well, Clint.

'You have killed,' he says. And I'm shutting up now and letting him talk. 'You have killed in the past and you will kill again. But this time, this last one here, that's one too many. It ain't on. It just is not on. I'm talkin' about the natural order of things here and you breakin' it. You followin' us so far there, Blake? You looks lost.'

'Well,' I says. And I were a bit lost as it happens.

'I'm just wonderin' who it is I'm meant to of killed, like. Cos if it's Frankenstein you means then you got the wrong feller. I never killed no Frankenstein. That were Jack, wernit. An' if you means Dave there in the wood, I never meant that un. It were his idea and I just went a bit far, like, by mistake. An'—'

'I don't wanna hear it, Blake,' he says, blowing smoke into the air. 'You've killed, and now you must set things straight.'

'But how?' I says. 'I mean, if a feller's dead—'

'Shut up. Just fuckin' shut your big face for once and listen. I got summat to say here and I'll say it. Alright?'

'Alright, alright. Fuckin' hell, Clint . . .'

'Right. Here it is . . .' He flobbed some nasty black stuff on the grass and cleared his throat, which was a bit arse-about if you asks me, but there you go. 'There is a cancer in this here town. A cancer spreadin' through the veins of Mangel, trapping innocents and making the strong go weak. And there's only one way to fix a cancer. Do you know what that is, Blake?'

'Cancer?'

'Aye.'

'But there ain't no cure for cancer, is there? Our Aunt Betty caught it and—'

'Cut it out.'

'No, I'm just sayin'—'

'I mean cut it out. The fuckin' cancer.'

'Ah, right.'

'And pray it never comes back.'

'But . . .'

'I gotta go now.'

'Hang on, Clint . . . Clint? Where's you off to? Hoy, Clint.'

But he'd fucked off, hadn't he, and I were left on me tod again. I sat there thinking about things for a bit. A goodly while I should say, cos when I heard a noise and looked up it were a milk float going by out on the road. I got off me arse and went home.

When I got there I climbed in me pit and fell fast akip.

15

HOPPERS DOORMAN SLAUGHTERED
Robbie Sleeter, Junior Reporter

Dean Stone was knifed to death last night as he kept door at Hoppers in Friar Street. The 16-year-old head doorman, of Blickett Lane in the Norbert Green district, bled to death before ambulances could reach him. He had only been in the job for three days.

A large, flabby, moustachioed man was spotted running from the scene. Witnesses described a scruffy individual in a very tatty black leather jacket, with a red nose and some teeth missing.

'Can't say I knew him,' said Mr Bruce Arkle, a witness. 'But he looked like a **** to me.'

'Yes,' said Miss Penny Trandle. 'A ****, that's how I'd describe him and all. But I couldn't put a name to him.'

'Fuckin' what?' I says.

But they'd hung up already. I put the blower down and fell back on the pillow. My head felt like shite shovelled up and scooped into a placcy bag, then slung against a wall a few times and fashioned into the shape of my head. And you know what? I were glad of it. I hadn't felt that way for a goodly few days now, and I'd missed it. I nestled me face into the warm sack of feathers and savoured the sweet ache of it. But it didn't last. Things was popping up behind me eyelids, making us toss and turn like bedsprings was sticking into me arse.

Questions, I'm talking about here. Like who were that trying to call us just now?

And what the fuck had I got up to last night?

I knew I'd got up to summat. Sometimes you knows, though you dunno what it is. All I could recall were leaving Hoppers and yomping off up the road, singing 'The Wonder of You' by Elvis. But the way I were singing it were 'The wonder of me . . .', not you. Cos you're a cunt and I were a minder. To be fair on meself the night had turned cold of a sudden, and the particular air that were about at that time didn't do me swede no favours. Plus I'd had that bad pint back there, which couldn't have helped. So what you're left with is a blank spot between then and now, during the which I'd done summat that didn't sit well in me guts come light of day.

Mind you, not knowing what I'd done weren't the worst of it. It were not knowing what I'd set off from Hoppers to do that had us fretting more. I knew Nick Wossname had asked us to do summat for him, see. But fuck on a stick knew what it were.

I got up and had a shower. It were well hot and came down hard on me eyelids, doing a fine job of chasing away them nasty questions I didn't want to answer. By the time I got out I were scrubbed up and clear of conscience. There's no point letting a rough swede ruin your morning, is there. And if I couldn't recall what I done last night it weren't worth recalling. I started brushing me ivories. The phone went again.

'What?' I says, still doing the ones at the back.

'Woss you doin'?' says a voice like Nathan the barman's.

'Who zat?'

'You knows who zat. Woss that noise?'

'You knows woss that noise. What else a feller do first thing he gets up, besides piss?'

'First thing he gets up? I got folks eatin' lunch here.'

'Woss on special?'

'Pie.'

'Again?'

'Aye. Look here, you, I wants a word. Woss you been up to?'

'Me? Not much. This an' that,' I says like a fool. Nathan knew everything that happened in Mangel, didn't he. But I couldn't very well tell him what I didn't know. And the bits I did know didn't bear the repeating of em.

'"This an' that", you says? This an' blinkin' that? I knows what you been up to an' I don't care fer it. There's a fine balance in this here town of ours and we all plays our part in keepin' things just so. There's a higher purpose to the lot of it, Blake, a pattern that some of us is witness to but not the like of you. And this thing you done yesterday . . . You gone an' tipped the scales, Blakey. You get down here sharpish an' don't let no one see you, least of all coppers.'

'But . . .' I says as the line went dead.

I put the blower down and went back to the bathroom with me toothbrush. I couldn't use it no more. My hand were shaking too much. I rinsed me trap out and sat down on the pan.

The shaving mirror were turned sideways, letting us know just what I looked like as I sat there heaving one out. 'Fuckin' look at you,' I says to the mirror. 'Get it together, you big fuckin' ponce. Yer a minder now. Minders is hard as nails inside an' out, and don't take no shite off no fucker. What'd Clint be doin' now if he were a minder, eh? Reckon he'd be sat on the throne like you is, wishin' all his troubles'd flush down the pan with his cack? Eh? No he bastard would fuckin' not. He'd be out there in his motor, er . . . mindin', an' that.'

Which reminded us . . .

'Filthy Stan the Motor Man,' he says. 'Can I help you?'

I were dressed and shaved and dapper now. 'Where the fuck is my motor?' I says down the blower.

'Whose motor? Who's you?'

I were dapper alright but still rough in the head. And I weren't enjoying that no more neither. Pie and chips and a pint or two ought to set that one straight, mind, which were the main reason I'd decided on taking Nathan up on his invitation. I mean, he couldn't ask us down the Paul Pry and not put summat on for us, could he?

But I had to sort out a means of getting there first. 'Who's me? Who's fuckin' me? I'm the cunt gave you seventy bastard notes is who I is.' I were thinking like

a minder now, see, taking it from no fucker and dish-
ing it out like a dinner lady.

'Ah, Royston Roger Blake. Been readin' about you
here in the paper.'

'What . . . You . . . Where's me Capri, you fuckin'
cunt?'

He were quiet for a bit, then I heard him mumbling summat. Then the line went dead.

I called him back.

'Filth—'

'You hang up on us again, you fuckin' wanker,' I
says nice and calm. 'You hang up again an' I'll—'

He only hung up again, didn't he.

I felt a mite aggrieved at that, and I don't mind
telling you I took it out on the blower. Weren't long
before I calmed down, mind. A professional keeps
his place tidy, so I went downstairs to get the broom
from under the stair. After I'd swept all the bits of
blower up I went looking for summat with a hood to
wear. There were nothing like that in me wardrobe or
under the stair with the other coats, but I found an
old parka in Fin's room. It were well tight round the
shoulders and gut and chest and arms and head and
neck but otherwise it were a good fit. I zipped it right
up and clocked meself in the mirror. You couldn't
hardly see through the snorkel bit at the front but
that's how I wanted it. I didn't want no one recog-
nising us in town, things being as they was, and this
were spot on for that. Right smart I looked. Bit like
an Action Man. You know, the one with the parka.
Only thing letting us down were the trousers. So I
went and put some on.

Then I went out.

'Oh aye,' shouts Doug from across the street as I went past. He were stood in his open doorway in his white coat. 'Take more than an old anorak to hide you from us.'

I looked away and trudged on. I couldn't be doing with him and his bollocks right then. I know he had Fin in there but I couldn't sort every fucker's problems out, could I? A man has priorities. I had so many priorities I could put em in a pan with some water and make soup out of em. There was too many to think of, and the only one I could look in the eye just then were the one about pie and chips and a couple of pints.

'Be sure to drop by the morrer,' shouts Doug. 'I'm puttin' on a new special – sausages.'

But I weren't listening.

Things was a bit odd as I walked into town. I weren't quite sure why. Could have been cos there weren't so much traffic. Could have been the dark shadow hanging over everything and painting it dark grey, despite it being lunchtime or thereabouts. Could have been either of them, but when I got downtown I found a few other things to make it all a bit odder.

Smashed windows, for starters. Shopfronts mostly but also houses here and there. Some was boarded up but others was left with the glass lying about and the wind blowing in. It were like the shopkeeper or feller who lived there had clocked on to the way things was going and couldn't be arsed to fight it.

Then there was your beggars. Mangel ain't ever had beggars. Not cos no one were ever skint. Plenty of folks is skint in this town. But Mangel folk is proud folk. You wouldn't catch me holding me paw out for scraps. I'd rather work for me crust, or hop through a window and swipe some other fucker's crust. But these uns here didn't look up to that much work. Looked half dead, they did. Some of em a bit more than half. I went past four or five of em down the High Street, sitting on their skinny arses in their baggy jeans, some of em with their hoods up, backs propped against brick and stone. Not one of em could have been more than seventeen or so.

'A few coppers, mister?' says one, holding his hand out.

I stopped and looked down at him, then up and down the High Street. 'You what?' I says.

He turned his face up to us. His skin were like flour and lard, except round his eyes where it were like soot. 'Coppers, mister. Just a couple? Cup o' tea, like.'

I had another glance up yonder and the other way. 'Where?' I says. Then me eyes set on summat else across the way and I moved on.

It were Mona.

On crutches.

She were wearing a little skirt and her right leg were like a pipe cleaner next to the other un, which were in plaster up past the joint. Didn't seem to bother her, mind. She were shifting like the clappers and I found it hard keeping up. I would have hoyed her but summat told us to keep it zipped, like me parka. Folks'd recognise my deep and powerful voice, wouldn't they. And I were doing so well at keeping meself hid so far, apart from Doug. So I just followed her.

I reckoned she were headed down the arcade at first. But she sailed straight past Frotfield Way and turned right. I huffed and puffed after her.

All the way to Hoppers.

I stood in the doorway of Margaret Hurge Twentieth Century Hair Design and watched Mona go in through the unmanned doors of Mangel's premier piss house. 'You just stay there, my love,' I says. 'You just sit tight with your manky pin an' I'll come back for you in a bit. Alright? Bit o' business first, ain't I.'

'Gonna stand there talkin' to yerself all day, is you?' comes a voice from behind.

'Alright, Marge,' I says turning about.

'Oh, hiya, Blake.'

She were alright were Marge. Used to do me dearly departed wife's hair in the old days. Can't say it made much difference but Beth seemed to like it. Marge were a bit of alright, though. Had the goods she did and she carried em well. Bit too much to say for herself for my liking, mind.

'You still workin' over there?' she says, nodding at the Hoppers. I'd thought it a question but it couldn't have been, cos she carried on talking: 'Only I ain't happy with it. This street has turned bad of late an' it's all on account of your place over there. Comes up and down here all day long they does, makin' their noise and droppin' their litter. And then there's the robberies. You seen Mr Fillery's up yonder? Emptied it, they did. Not one single ornamental figurine left in the whole shop. It's a disgrace. And you ought to ...'

But I weren't listening no more. I'd like to stand there slying glances at Marge's tits all day, but I couldn't. Had Nathan the barman waiting for us, didn't I.

'Ah, the feller himself,' says Nathan.

And I'm glad he did cos I were all set to turn arse and fuck off out of it. The Paul Pry were rammed with the disprocessed of Mangel again, except most of em was reading the paper this time instead of sitting around talking bollocks. But that weren't the problem. They all knew us and I knew them. That's what the problem were. I were their doorman of old and they was my punters of yore. But you'd not have knowed it, the way they went all quiet and gawped at us soon as I unzipped me parka. I gandered in the mirror behind the bar. I still looked like Royston Blake far as I reckoned. 'I stink o' shite or summat?' I says to no one in particular, checking the underside of me boots.

No one in particular answered. They turned back to their papers and started cooing amongst emselves again. And that were when Nathan came up behind us saying: 'Ah, the feller himself,' like I says just now. 'Took yer time, didn't you?'

'Fuckin' had to yomp here, didn't I. That cunt Filthy Stan's got my Capri.'

'We'll have no swearin' in here, Blake, ladies bein' present and all. And don't blame your woes on Filthy Stan the Motor Man. Ain't his fault yer head gasket's went. Didn't tell him about that, did you. He can't do the work before you agrees to pay fer it, now, can he? How many times he gotta ring you before you'll answer him? And answer him with a civil tongue, I might add.'

'Head gasket?' I says. 'I only wanted the tyres . . .' But it were no good arguing the toss. I hated that about Nathan sometimes. The odds was stacked on his side cos he knew all about you and you knew jack shite about him, besides him having a sparse tash and hairy arms.

'Well, there it is,' he says. 'You'll talk to him about monies or you'll tow her away yerself.'

'Here, Nathan,' I says, trying to peel the parka off.

'Best leave that on,' he says. 'You'll need it where we're headed. Come on, you.' He went through the door beside the microwave, leaving it open behind him. The door, not the microwave.

I scratched my head and looked over me shoulder. You ain't never seen so many eyes turn away so quick. Every bastard one of em looked down at his paper or found summat of interest on a beer mat.

'Just off to splash me boots,' I shouts to Nathan.

He shouted summat after us but I couldn't be doing with it. I weren't scaredy of going back there behind the bar nor nothing, I just needed a moment to meself first.

No one were in the bog and I were glad of it. I got meself out and let her go. I'd only been going about a minute when I heard one of the crapper doors swing open behind us. My nose filled with the smell of shite. 'Hoy, you, you fuckin' fucker,' says someone.

I turned me head just in time to see it were Jack. I might have guessed that from his turn of phrase there but you never know, do you. He got us by the parka and rammed me swede into the wall. I got me paws out onto the tiles in time and though the blow were far from pleasant it could have been worse. He tried doing it again but I stuck me elbow out behind us and got him one in the kidney. He staggered back into the sink. I turned around, tadger still out and dripping.

''S fuckin' matter with you?' I says, putting it away.

Jack's blade were out before I'd got meself zipped up. He were breathing hard and didn't look too rosy. But Jack hadn't ever looked rosy since Mangel Jail, and it hadn't stopped him killing Frankenstein, had it. 'Fuckin' come here you, you fucker. Steal my credit, would you? I reads the fuckin' papers. Sayin' iss you knifed the fuckin' doorman, they is. *You*, you fucker. You couldn't—'

'Hang about . . .' I says.

'You ain't fuckin' thievin' this one off us.' He pointed the blade at us. 'No fucker's keepin' us out this time.'

'Come on, Jack . . .'

'I can't fuckin' stand it out here. Things has changed too much, Blakey.' His voice were getting softer. The blade were dropping down a bit. 'Ain't like the old days no more, it ain't.'

I hadn't heard Jack say so many words since he'd come out of jail, and it scared us a bit. Weren't going barmy on us, were he? A blade's one thing but a barmy feller's summat else besides.

'Used to have a laugh in them days,' he were going on. 'Did we, Blakey? Sometimes I can't recall nuthin' before goin' inside. I dunno woss what out here, Blakey. I tell you, I fuckin' hates it. There's fuck all for us here. There's nobody. I ain't even got mates, you know. I drinks on me own cos every bastard's scared of us. If I only had a mate, a proper mate. One mate . . .'

His whole body sagged and he let himself fall against the piss wall, sobbing. Mind you, he hadn't dropped the blade yet so I had to be careful.

I moved quick, aiming a boot at his spuds.

But he seen it and stepped away. I couldn't fucking believe it. And him with tears running down his scarred cheeks and all.

Me boot swung past him but I just about kept meself upright. He jumped away from the piss wall and fixed us with them eyes of his. I watched the blade weaving side to side like it were alive. Jack went left with it. I moved the other way. Jack were a fast mover for one so ravaged by the long-term effects of alcohol abuse, and he went to change direction. But there were piss all over the floor and he went arse up.

He landed hard, flat on his back. You could hear the puff going right out of him but he didn't stay down. I backed off, reaching for me monkey wrench. But I couldn't get the fucking zip down enough on me parka. 'Jack,' I were saying, cos he were on his knees now and the blade were still pointed at us. 'Jack, come on, mate . . .'

His whole head were bright red and he didn't look cheerful. He showed us his yellow and black gnashers and says, panting: 'I'm . . . I'm goin' back inside an' no . . . no fucker's . . .'

But it stopped there. His eyes opened wide and I saw the whites of em, though they wasn't really white what with all them red lines and that. His body went stiff and he toppled sideways into the puddle of piss.

I watched him lying there for a bit before I made

a move. He were going more and more purple, making noises like an old door creaking, whole body juddering slow, like he were riding a horse or shagging. He were pawing at his chest trying to get at summat in there. But the twat had forgot to drop his knife, hadn't he. I don't reckon he even noticed the little stabs he gave himself through his shirt. They got slower and slower until the blade dropped out of his hand and he went still.

After a bit I got meself out again and finished off the piss. I thought about things during that piss. I thought about the way it ain't your fault a lot of the time cos there just ain't no accounting for other folks, is there. You can try doing it all but it just don't work – somewhere along the way you're gonna have to call on someone. And that's when things turn to shite. I mean, look at me here – all set to start a new life as Mangel's top minder, I were. But what happens?

Jack is what fucking happens.

I told him, didn't I, down that alley there last night. I fucking told the cunt to leave it alone cos I've got it all sorted. But he don't listen, do he. Never does, the like of him – hears what they wants to hear and fuck the rest. Fucking wanker. I'll show em, I thought to meself as I turned about and pissed on his face.

I were trying to get it right in his ear but I dried up just when I got me aim right. I put meself away and started kicking him until his chest were like a sack of soup and kindling. I stopped when the door opened behind us and someone came in. I don't even know who it were. I ran at him and dropped my head on his nose, splitting it asunder and filling the air with little red drops. He stayed up so I drew me fist back and gave it him on the jaw. He went down this time.

'Hoy, woss goin' on up there?' says Nathan as I opened the fire door. 'That you, Blake? Where'd you get to?'

I fucked off.

16

INFORMER REPORTER BUTCHERED
Robbie Sleeter, Junior Reporter

*Steve Dowie, this newspaper's crime editor, was found
dead at his flat in Shatter Crescent early this morning. A
police pathologist has described the body as 'a right state.
Stabbed forty-seven times he was. Blood all over the carpet. Went right through the floorboards and into the flat
below, where an old lady lives with her cat. I've never
seen so much blood leave a man's body. You ain't either,
have you, Bri?'*

'No,' replied Dr Wimmer.

*The door to Dowie's flat had been kicked down. 'I
heard a racket about two in the morning,' said a neighbour. 'But I didn't think anything of it. You don't, do you.
Noises are normal round here, what with folks coming
home drunk and the like. So no . . . But when I came out
in the morning to get my milk there it were: his door
kicked down and the frame all splintered and broken.
Well, I had a peep inside. You've got to watch out for your
neighbours in this day and age, after all. And there he*

*were on the floor. Blood everywhere . . . except the thing
on the bed there, there were no blood on that. What is it
they call them? Blow-up dolly, is it? You know, the ones
lonely men pleasure themselves with. Mind you, I always
knew he were a bit odd, with his spectacles and his secre-
tive ways.'*

*Police, who suspect foul play, are desperate to speak to
Royston Blake. The former Hoppers doorman is already
sought in connection with the murder of Dean Stone last
night. Members of the public are urged not to approach
him. 'If you see him, just give us a bell,' said a police
spokesman.*

'Woss you doin' here?' she says. 'And woss you
wearin' that daft coat for?'

I found her again and grabbed her wrist. As a barmaid Rache never stood still for very long, and with
me parka done up high like it were I kept losing sight
of her. 'Rache,' I says, putting me snorkel right up
close. ''S me, ennit. Blake.'

'I knows it's you. I ain't stupid, you know. Woss
you doin' here anyhow? Coppers is after you, ain't
they?'

'Coppers?'

'Well, ain't they?'

'Ain't spoke to none yet,' I says, shrugging.

'Why's you got yer face all hid, then?'

'Dunno,' I says. 'You never knows, does you.'

'Never knows when you broke the law?'

'No, you don't. An' I'll tell you what – I might start
wearin' this here coat permanent. New image an'
that. You heared about me new job? No? Guess what
it is.'

'Blake, I—'

'Go on – guess.'

'Oh, alright. Slaughter yard.'

'Fuckin' slaughter yard? Don't be daft. Go on – proper guess. Think o' summat no one could do better than Royston Blake, what with me special skills an' that.'

'Road sweeper?'

'You fuckin' what?'

'I dunno, Blake. Look, there's fellers wants servin' up there . . .'

I tightened me grip. 'You ain't goin' nowhere til you done a proper guess.'

'Blake, let go of us.'

'*Guess.* Tell you what – I can see you ain't that clever so I'll give you a clue, alright? Right, here it is: what motor I got?'

She stopped struggling and started thinking, turning her eyes up and biting her bottom lip. 'Ford,' she says after a bit. 'Let us go now.'

'No. No. I mean aye, I drives a Ford, but . . .'

'Blake, tell us about it later, alright? Please let us go. You're hurtin'—'

'No, right . . . Just listen to us, will yer. What *type* of Ford does I drive? Come *on*, Rache.'

'Please, Blake . . . I—'

'Fuckin' shut it an' answer us, will you? Tell you what . . . tell you what, here's a clue: my motor is the bestest Ford ever to grace the streets. Now *come on*.'

'Blake . . .' she sobbed.

'*Answer*, you fuckin' dozy—'

I stopped there cos someone punched us on the ear. I turned to see who it were and got another one on the same ear. 'Hoy,' I were shouting. 'Hoy, you fuckin' . . .' But I couldn't hardly get nothing out. Each time I turned the bastard sidestepped. The parka were a top disguise and that but it were no good for aggro. I tried getting the zip down but it were jammed again, or I weren't doing it right or summat. And you couldn't blame us for not doing it right cos me swede and bollocks was fielding fist and boot aplenty now, which got us to thinking there was two cunts here and not just the one of em. I gave up with the zip and started swinging paws. That stopped the blows coming down on us but it were fucking knackering, and I weren't connecting anyhow. *You* try zipping your parka right up and getting into a rumble and you'll get the idea. Actually I wouldn't do that if I was you – you'd get a shoeing like as not no matter what you was wearing.

After a bit I were getting dog arse knackered so I stopped. I could hear folks hooting and sniggering around us and I didn't like that. But what could I do? I tried hauling the parka up over me head but the fucker were tight as a johnny on a marrow. Then someone kicked me legs away.

'Hoy,' I shouts again, sitting up. 'Who's that? Fuckin' pack it—'

But I took one right on the chin and me jaw turned to jelly. I rolled over and tried making a ball of meself on the deck, but I never really had made much of a ball, being such a big lad. And all it got us was eight or nine boots up the arse harder than I'd ever got or given. You don't by habit get such an open target as my arse were right then, so whoever the cunts was would be having a right old time of it at my expenditure.

'Don't you worry,' I were yelling now. 'I'll have you. I'll find you an' fuckin . . . Soon as I gets this fuckin' par . . .'

I stopped there cos there's a point where you can't go on and I'd just reached it. I weren't out cold nor nothing, but what the fuck could I do, eh? I just lay flat on me face and tried hard to think of summat else, summat nice, like shagging a bird or eating a nice big plate of saveloy and chips with mushy peas atop em. But it were hard to coax either of them things into the turmoil that were my swede at that moment in time. All I could think about were how these cunts here had broke my jaw and one of me arse cheeks, by the feels of em.

There were a fair bit of merriment being had roundabout, like I were just telling you, but after I'd being laying there a while I noticed another sound coming through the cackles and hoots.

It were our Rache.

'Leave him alone, you fuckin' bastards,' she were saying. Or summat of the like. I can't recall for surely on account of the way my head were right then. 'Can't you see he's helpless?' she says and all. I didn't like that too much but it were Rache and she were on my side, which were a nice thing to know right then. 'Get off him, you fuckin' . . .' she were starting to say again. But then came a nasty slapping sound followed by a sort of yelp from her. Then another couple of slaps and a bit of a wail. Then a lot of sobbing.

They got one of my ankles apiece and started tugging. I knew who it were now, course. And I ought to have known all along and kept me peepers peeled for em. Weren't just cos they'd hit a bird in public that gave em away. I'd seen birds openly slapped now and then, though such a practice is frowned on by and large in Mangel. Course, I'd never done such a thing meself. What do you fucking take us for? And I wouldn't stand by and watch no other fucker do it neither. But sometimes it don't pay to stick your hooter in, depending on who's doing the bird-slapping. And from the way no one were laughing now nor making no other sound, there weren't much doubting it were Nobby and Cosh.

They dragged us out back and kicked the fire door open. When they got us out on the hard stuff I tried to stand another couple of times, but they kept booting us in the kidneys so I stopped. I heard a car boot open and shut and then a jangling like heavy chains. Actually they was heavy chains. One of the two cunts poked summat sharp and shiny at me neck while t'other did his best to feed the chain around us, which weren't easy considering what a big man I am. When I were good and bound from ankle to elbow they tried lifting us.

I could have told em it'd be hard work, mind. What with the weight of the heavy chains and my natural heft I were a bit of a handful. And if they wanted us in that fucking 1.3 Capri they wasn't getting no help from meself.

I reckon you're sitting there scratching your arse and wondering what I were thinking this whole time, and why I hadn't kicked up more of a fuss instead of letting meself get tied down.

Well, fret you fucking well not.

Quiet I might well have been, but it were all going on up in the place where it counts – the place that separates two-bob doormen from top minders. I were planning, see. Thinking ahead. Had it all mapped out, I did. No fucker hits Rache without getting some comeback. So that's what I were doing – working out how I'd teach Nobby and Cosh about hitting our Rache, and how they perhaps oughtn't to do it. That's what kept us preoccupied and let us relax while they tied us up. Cos there were no good struggling, were there. Any wanker could see that. Even you.

So I got in the 1.3.

I were still ironing out the finer points of what they had coming when the motor pulled up some while later. Fuck knew where we was at first cos I hadn't been paying heed and I still had me snorkel up. Mind you, there were a peculiar whiff to the place that marked it out as somewhere I ought to know. It were like when you gets out of town for a bit – not too far, mind – and then when you gets back the pong of Mangel hits you. It were like that here but a bit worse, like this were the bit of Mangel it all came from, the stench and pain and shite and piss and death and strife and general nastiness that makes life what it is by and large.

Aye, it were Norbert Green.

Like I says, me snorkel were up so I couldn't tell specific like where we was in Norbert Green, but there were a brick wall a few yard up the way that I seemed to know.

Neither of the two cunts up front seemed keen on

saying much nor getting out. Nobby were at the wheel looking straight on. Cosh were next to him but turned back to face us, dangling that sharp and shiny thing from his right paw. Like I says, he were facing us but he weren't clocking us. His eyes was off out the back window watching a feller walking up. I could hear the feller's feet crunching stones. And when I heard them stones and looked at the high brick wall again I knew where we was.

Round back of the Bee Hive, for fuck's fucking sake.

'Hoy, you,' says Nobby, looking at us in the rear-view. 'Fuckin' pack that in.'

But I couldn't. I didn't give a toss how many chains were round us. They wanted us in the Bee Hive and I weren't going. I'd bust out of chains if I had to. They'd have to kill us dead before getting us in there.

'Stick him,' says Nobby to Cosh. 'Go on, stick his leg.'

'He can't get out them chains, you know.'

'Rockin' the car, ain't he. Go on, stick him with that before he knacks me suspension.'

'But . . . But Nick says—'

'*Fuck* Nick. Go on, before he gets here.'

Cosh poked the blade at us but it hit the chain. He tried again and got me kneecap, which weren't nice but could have been worser.

'What the fuckin' hell are you doin'?' I could hear Nick Wossname yelling outside. 'Open the door,' he says, banging on the window.

Cosh stopped his stabbing but no one opened no door. 'You what?' shouts Nobby.

'Open the door,' says Nick.

'Can't hear you.'

'Just open the fucking door or you're fired.'

I'd quietened down now cos this looked interesting. You could hear Nobby thinking about it, but after five seconds or so he gave in and pulled the handle.

'Get out,' says Nick. 'Come on, piss off out of it. I ain't fuckin' around. Go inside for a drink or whatever. Go and do Mona if you like. She's in the back room.'

Another few seconds passed and then Nobby did like he'd been told.

Cosh opened his door and all. 'Had to chain him up, didn't we,' he says once outside. 'Bastard got nasty again. Wouldn't come with us for no coaxin'.'

''S right,' says Nobby. 'He were knockin' the bird from Hoppers about an' all when we found him. Wossername . . . Her with the baps.'

'Yeah, yeah,' says Nick. He went round the passenger side and got in, shutting the door behind him. I heard four feet trudging off across the stones.

'I ain't goin' in there,' I says.

'Where?'

'Back there,' I says, jerking my head back at the pub in question.

'I don't want you in there. That's why you're out here. Look, I'm sorry about the chains, man. Why didn't you just go with them?'

'Never asked us, did they. Just laid into us. From behind an' all. Had me snorkel up so I had no hope of—'

'Alright. Look, you know why I brought you here. What the fuck is *this* shit?'

I pointed me snorkel at him.

He were holding up a *Mangel Informer*. As you well knows I don't read that particular journal by choice. But the headline were big and nasty so choice didn't come into it. INFORMER REPORTER BUTCHERED went the big fat words, one atop t'other. And to be fair it weren't them I found nasty. It were the picture next to em that twisted me guts so. A normal picture it were, of a speccy feller in a shirt and tie smiling at you. Looked a bit of a wanker to be fair but that were getting sideways of the point, which were that I knew this feller. I'd seen him recent, like. I mean *fucking* recent.

'Oh,' I says, harking back to the way I'd felt upon waking that morn, all queasy and not so sure of nothing on account of not remembering jack shite about last night. 'Well,' I says from me snorkel. 'That clears that one up, I suppose. Only . . .'

'I knew it. I fucking knew it. You don't even remember it, do you? You were so pissed you don't even remember it. I fuckin' *knew* I shouldn't have let you drink all that beer.'

'Weren't the fuckin' beer,' I snaps. 'Lager don't get us like that. I can drink thirty pints and still be on me game, everyone knows that. No way. It were the . . . er . . .'

'Go on. We're fucked anyway so you might as well spill.'

'You know . . . I took some whisky for the road, like. Anyone would of done same. It were well parky out.'

'You drank a bottle of whisky before seeing him?'

'Hold up, I never says I drank no whole bottle.'

'But did you, though? I mean, come on, man – Royston Blake wouldn't get pissed on *half* a bottle, now, would he?'

'Aye, well . . .'

'Course he fucking wouldn't.'

'Hoy, you, don't you fuckin' curse at us like that. I knows yer me boss in a way but outsiders ain't meant to—'

'Who says I'm an outsider?'

'Eh?'

'Forget that a minute. We're talkin' about you, not me. I asked you to lean on the Dowie bloke a bit and suggest he mind his own business. Do you remember that bit?'

'Aye, aye, but . . .'

I didn't actually.

'So how the fuck did that turn into this?' He tossed the paper at us. I were alright, mind, cos me snorkel were up and protected us from flying newspapers and the like. I were growing fond of that snorkel as it happens. I could hide in there and pretend nothing hairy were going on.

I shrugged a bit. I couldn't shrug for proper on account of the chains holding me shoulders down. 'Turns out like that sometimes, dunnit,' I says.

Cos it did turn out like that sometimes. And if you says it don't you're a fucking liar. I couldn't remember doing none of it, but I could see how it might have happened. 'Woss they said I done this time?'

'Blake, you took a knife from his kitchen and . . . and . . . Oh, Blake, I never wanted none of this. All I wanted was . . . was . . .'

I pointed me snorkel at him again. I hadn't heard him like this before and I didn't much like it. Weak, he sounded, like he'd never before heard of a feller getting carked and he couldn't handle it. He were meant to be my boss, and bosses is meant to be strong, ain't they. Where were the flash outsider now, feller who'd come in and took over half of Mangel?

I reckoned he were all set to start bawling, but instead he pulled himself together and pointed a finger at us. 'You're on your own,' he says. '*You* fucked up, so *you* sort it out.'

'Fuck off,' I says. 'I were only doin' a job for you, weren't I.' Cos I couldn't think what else I might have been doing. 'Ain't my fault a job turns bad. Look at them two cunts Nobby and Cosh. You sends them to get us and every time it turns nasty. What if you'd sent them to see this feller in the paper here? What then, eh?'

'I didn't send them because I knew they'd fuck up. No amount of money can make someone reliable, Blake. That's why I asked you.'

'But why? You knows fuck all about us. Why'd you ask us?'

'Because I *do* know you.'

'But . . .'

'But nothin'. You're on your own. I'll tell Nobby to dump you some place the pigs can find you. Won't take them long to finger you for this. Not after we give them the tip-off, anyway. And if you mention me to the pigs I'll just deny it. They'll never believe you with your record.' He started opening the door.

'Hoy,' I shouts. 'Hold up a min, er . . . Nick.'

He stopped at that so I stopped talking. Whatever

I said here I had to get right. If the coppers got us for this I'd be fucked and no arguing. I'd got off with shite before but that were with Nathan's help, and I'd had summat to pay him for his trouble that time. But I had fuck all for him this time around. And even if I had summat I wouldn't go to him – he might ask us to go through that door behind the bar again.

Look at us, will you: chained up in the back of a 1.3 Capri. Sore all over. Not a penny to me name. No motor. And what mates did I have to call upon? Finney. And he were marked for sausages round Doug's. Plus he were useless anyhow.

So aye, there were a fair bit riding on whatever I said next. That's why I took me time and thought it over.

But he got one in first. 'Actually my name's not Nick,' he says. 'It's Sa—'

'Alright, Nick,' I shouts. Cos I'd thought of summat now. 'Look, think about it a minute. You ain't got nuthin' to gain from dumpin' us for the coppers. Just let us go. Coppers won't work it out if you don't do the workin' out for em. They never does. Come on, Nick. I'll make it up to you.'

He looked at us for a bit then leaned forward and undid the zip on me parka, thereby exposing my head. I were pleased that the zip weren't jammed after all, but I'd been in that snorkel a long time now and being out of it felt a bit odd.

'Fuck me,' he says, eyes roaming around me face. 'What did they do to you?'

I couldn't see what he were seeing but I knew what he meant. There was soreness around the jaw and me right eye were going black by the feels of him. Plus

both ears throbbed and me cheek were hurting.
Them was the main bits. Elsewhere you had the
hooter damage and tooth loss Frankenstein had gave
us, the cosh wound in the side of the swede from last
night, and an ache in the middle of it all from general wear and tear. But I'd known worse. And I'd know
worser still if I went down for this thing here in the
paper. I couldn't go to Mangel Jail. Not after seeing
what Mangel Jail had done to Jack. I'd rather saw me
own swede off than end up like him.

'Tell you what, Blake,' he says. 'You do summat for
me and I'll help you out of this. Fair play?'

'I'll do it. I'll do whatever you says.'

'Whatever?'

'Aye, what fuckin' ever.'

He told us what he had in mind.

'You fuckin' what?' I says. 'Why?'

'Blake,' he says, putting his face right up close.
'Don't you recognise me at all?'

'Course I fuckin' do,' I says, eyes rolling. 'What
d'you take us for? You're Nick Wossname.'

He sat back, shoulders slumping, head shaking.

'Look,' I says, thinking about what I'd said and
how I ought to be keeping him sweet. 'I'm sorry
about the Wossname. But I just can't ever recall what
your proper name is.'

'It don't matter,' he says. 'Just do it. Do it quick. If
you can't prove he's dead by midnight tonight I'm
dropping you in it.'

'Now hang on, that ain't hardly enough—'

'Midnight, Blake.' He had his fingers on the door
handle. 'Run it by us again, Blake. Cos this time I
want no fuck-ups. Who do I want dead?'

'Midnight's too s—'

'*Shut up*, Blake. Who you gonna kill?'

'Alright, alright,' I says. 'Doug. Doug the bastard shopkeeper.'

He nodded and opened the door. Norbert Green air filled my lungs.

'Hold up,' I says as he touched gravel. 'There's one other thing.'

'What?' he says, not turning but not ignoring us neither.

'Can you sub us a fifty?'

17

DRUGS AND CRIME: THE CHIEF SPEAKS
Robbie Sleeter, Junior Reporter

In a press conference today Police Chief Robert Cadwallader outlined the two main challenges facing Mangel today: drugs and crime.

'When you think about it they're both the same thing. I mean, it's obvious really. You've got drugs springing up here out of nowhere in the past few weeks, and you've got crime spiralling out of all reckoning at the same time. Aye, I've had a talk with the lads and we've decided that them two things is tied up together, like.'

The chief had a word of warning for the perpetrators: 'We're taking a tough stance. We've never been shy on punishment on this force but now we're upping it, switching her up a gear, like. You get caught for drugs or crime, you'll be looking at the inside of Mangel Jail for a long one. And we'll get you, don't you worry about that. We got officers staking out all known druggy places and anyone they catch will be put away. No appeal.'

Asked about Royston Blake – prime suspect for the

murders of Steve Dowie and Dean Stone – the chief sighed and said: 'We said before that no one should approach him. Well, that's just standard procedure for us to say that when your suspect has done summat violent. But in this case you can probably get away with it. Far as I know Royston Blake is all belly these days, and all that pop drinking has done his coordination no favours. To be honest I don't reckon he were ever that hard anyhow. And he's always been soft up top, as everyone knows by now. All mouth and no trousers, I'd call him. So aye, you're probably alright to approach him.'

Frankly I were a bit put out when Nobby and Cosh dropped us in Frotfield Way. They'd took the chains off first but I were still put out. Wouldn't have been so bad if they'd stopped the motor before shoving us out, but they didn't, so there you go. To be fair I were glad of it in a way. There's no better way of patching up differences with a feller than stopping your motor before letting him out. And I didn't want mine with them patched up. Like I says just now, I had plans for em.

Mind you, soon as I picked meself up and brushed my arse down and got the ten notes out I felt a lot better. I know fifty sheets is hardly what you'd call a fortune these days, but it were alright for my requirements. Sooner I knocked off Doug the better, but I had to be careful about how I done it. Doug were a wily old cunt and one duff step might see him extending his sausage special another week. So I had some headwork to do. And empty guts is no good for headwork.

I were thinking all this as I stood across the

way from the arky. There were summat different about the place, to see it from outside on that day. Knackered and old, it looked. I crossed the road for a closer gander, zipping me snorkel up so Fat Sandra wouldn't recognise us and chuck us out for being banned. I were thinking about a game of pinball, which I reckon is the best way of working out plans. Not that I'd played much pinball of late, being banned from the arky and Mangel not having no other tables besides the ones in there. But as a lad I always used to flip the steel ball when I had a problem to overcome. A superior swede like mine requires limbering up if you wants him performing.

I saw what were up with the place once I stepped inside. No one were in it. Not one punter. Not even the one or two old fellers you always gets in there. Fruities was bleeping and flashing but no one were there to feed em. Only Fat Sandra, sat there in her kiosk. I made sure me snorkel were tight then strolled up, walking funny to disguise meself a bit more.

'Hiya, Blake,' she says, barely looking up.

'Alright, San. How'd you know I . . . Ah, forget it.'

I slipped a bluey under the mesh. Straight away I wished I hadn't. I should have waited to see if she wanted us out first. But I were fretting without cause as it turned out. She took the fiver and doled us out some change with nary a word.

'Er, San,' I says, trying to pick it up. 'Where the fuck is everyone?'

She smiled. First time I'd ever seen her smile for proper, that were, the grumpy old bitch. 'Always had trouble pickin' coins up, you did. Even back when you was a youngun you had fat fingers.'

'Fat fingers?' I says, looking at em. 'Fuck off. Muscle it is.'

She shrugged. Shrugging weren't like her.

In a minute or two I got all the coins up and headed for the pinball. 'They'm gone,' she says, as I stepped away.

'Who is?'

'Everyone. You asked where everyone is. Gone, ain't they. Thass all I knows.'

I looked at her. The kiosk were full of fag smoke as usual and you couldn't see much, but I could see enough. Knackered and old I'd say she looked. And fat. 'Why's that, then?' I says.

She looked up at us like I'd just flicked shite on the glass partition. 'You takin' the piss?' she says. 'Don't you read no fuckin' papers?'

I shook me head slow and looked at the sun coming in through the doors, wishing I'd never come in. 'Just fuckin' tell us, why don't you.'

'Don't you get arsey with us,' she says, spraying spit all over the glass. 'You'm banned, remember? Only reason I'm lettin' you in here is no one else is in.'

'Alright,' I says. Cos I'd fucking well had enough of Fat Sandra and her knackered old arcade. 'Alright, Fat Sandra . . .' And then there were them arcade monkeys doing Hoppers over the other day, which I'd forgot about until just now what with one thing and another. 'Alright, Fat fuckin' Sandra . . .' And then there was the years I'd spent not playing pinball thanks to the life ban she'd doled us back then, when it weren't even me who bust the pinball machine and honked on the floor – it were Legs and Finney, wernit. 'Alright, F—'

'Gonna say summat or what?' she shouts. 'You blinkin' useless old tosspot . . . It were your fault, all this. If you'd of done what Doug telled you from straight off we'd all be alright.'

'Eh?' I says, wishing more than ever I'd not come in.

'Eh?' she says, meaning to mock us, I suppose. 'Eh? Eh? That all you can say, is it? Sort out woss-name, Doug telled you. Woss so hard about that? But you couldn't even do that, could you. You had to fuck about and bottle it and turn the whole thing to shit. Now hark woss happened – we ain't got no punters here cos of you. An' no punters means no arky. Why couldn't you do it, you stupid old sod? If you'd of done it everyone would of gone back to normal an' there'd of been no muck spread about the arky in the paper.'

'Muck?' I says. 'About the arky?'

'Pull yer fuckin' head out yer arse, Royston Blake. Open yer eyes for once and clock what a thick, fat wazzock you are. Everyone laughs at you, behind yer back. There's many who does it to your face now an' all, so I hears. And why not? Look at you. You couldn't even keep door at Hoppers proper. I heared you got punched out by a youngun. Head Doorman? Biggest fuckin' joke this town has ever seen more like.'

'Right,' I says, clenching me paw. I swung it at the kiosk, shutting me eyes on impact. Didn't want bits of glass in em, did I.

But fuck all happened. The glass wobbled a bit but me paw just pinged back off of it, hurting. I swung again. Cos I weren't having Fat Sandra telling folks how Royston Blake couldn't punch a hole through a window.

Me fist bounced off again, hurting quite a bit more now. Meanwhile Fat San were bent double in the kiosk, laughing and calling us more names. I went round and tried the kiosk door but it were locked. I shouldered it but the fucker weren't giving. I went to smack the glass again but couldn't go through with it, not the way me knuckles was throbbing.

'Ah ha ha ha, you stupid cunt,' says Fat Sandra. 'Come on, do it again. Ah ha ha hee . . .'

But I were staying in control. Don't you fucking fret about that, mate. If you're waiting on me losing it you'll be waiting a long time. Royston Blake don't lose it. He stays calm and focused. It's every other fucker who loses it.

See, I'm clever.

If I couldn't get into her kiosk I'd get to her another way.

I went over to the nearest fruitie and put shoulder to it. 'Raaagh,' I yells. Cos when you're working the weights you've got to let off steam, else give yourself a hernia. 'Raagh.'

'Ha ha, cunt,' says San.

'Ragh,' I says. But it were no use. The fucker must have been nailed down cos I couldn't budge him. I tried another un. 'Raaaagh.'

'Hee hee hee,' she were saying now.

'Raaagh.'

'COME OUT, ROYSTON BLAKE.'

'Ragh,' I says, though me heart weren't really in it no more. 'Fuck were that?' I says to Fat San. But she were leaning back in her swivel chair, cackling harder'n ever.

'COME OUT, BLAKE,' comes that big blaring boom once again. Came from everywhere it seemed to, from all sides and overhead at once. 'THE PLACE IS SURROUNDED. POLICE HERE, ENNIT. YOU AIN'T GOT A CHANCE, MATE.'

'Hoy,' I shouts at San, me face right up against the funny glass what wouldn't break and didn't feel much like glass now I came to think about it. 'This a fuckin' joke, is it? Where's that—'

'COME ON, BLAKE,' says the big boom. 'DO YERSELF A FUCKIN' FAVOUR AND COME OUT HERE, FUCK SAKE. WE AIN'T GOT ALL DAY.'

I couldn't handle it no more. There was secret speakers wired up round the walls or summat, just waiting for old Blake to roll in.

Well, I weren't having none of it.

I were off out of it. Had better things to do anyhow, though I couldn't recall what they was at that moment. I knew it'd come to us with a bit of fresh air and a smoke, mind.

'Gotcha,' says PC Plim, cuffing us as I went out the door.

'Have this,' says PC Jonah, ramming his truncheon in me guts.

Don't you worry about me.

I'd been in Mangel pig station many a time before and I'll be there again like as not. Me and that place has a special relationship whereby I'm took there now and then and let out a short while thereafter.

Keeps the coppers happy and reminds us that I ought to be careful, like. I've never made the trip on to Mangel Jail and I never would. This town needs Royston Blake, and the coppers knows it. Place'd turn to shite without meself around to keep her stoked.

So don't you worry about me, mate.

Besides, soon as they put us in a cell I knew I'd be alright. Cells is alright here. Four walls, one floor, a ceiling and an iron door. Plus a mattress. And a pan in the corner there. What more can a feller ask for, eh? A telly'd be alright, but if a man can't sit tight for a bit with his own thoughts he ain't a proper man in my book. And if you looks at it a certain way a cell were the best place for us right then. I had thinking to do, didn't I. I had to work out how to do Doug the shopkeeper. It were plain as spilt beer that I wouldn't get no headwork done in town, what with folks going on at us everywhere. So a short spell in a cell were best for everyone.

Except they hadn't put us in a cell yet. Not yet, anyhow. Soon as they finished hitting my belly with a truncheon they'd sort a cell out for us. Aye.

To be fair on em they weren't truly hitting us for proper. Not like I hits folks, or Frankenstein hit us back there. Fellers like Plim and Jonah just ain't made for hitting. (Unless you means hitting them, in which case they was born to it.) Try all they liked, they couldn't hurt us. Not even with them big old truncheons they had what they couldn't hardly lift, and meself strapped to the chair like I were. Guts of rock, me. You could crash an airplane into my guts and I wouldn't so much as flinch. And, being coppers, my guts was all they was bothered with. Couldn't leave no nasty cuts and bruises, could they. Mind you, could be they was scaredy of hitting us in the chops. You hit a feller in the guts it's like slapping him on the back. Hit em in the mug and you're asking for comeback. Which is what I'd done to Jonah in the ozzy a couple of days ago according to him, though I couldn't recall it meself. His bottom lip were all swelled and stitched up, mind, so someone had had a good go at him. And if it were meself then fair's fair – flap away with your truncheon.

But you ain't hurting us.

I didn't let on about that, mind. I groaned and retched like the best of em. Let em enjoy emselves for once, I says. No skin off my teeth. And if Plim were right and I had made a public cunt of him over a parking offence in Frotfield Way the other day, I can't say I blamed him.

Mind you, I weren't so happy-go-lucky when he landed one in me knackers. 'Hoy, you cunt,' I says. 'Fuckin' watch it.'

They looked at each other, then started taking turns ramming their sticks in me knackers while I tried to keep em hid between me thighs. They couldn't hurt us, mind. Not for proper, anyhow. Didn't I tell you?

Knackers of steel, me.

I heard the door open.

The light came on. I closed me lids against the harshness of it all. I'd been lying here in darkness for going on fours hours or so now and I were just getting used to it. I'd even stopped fretting over me plums quite so much. They ached like Billy still but least I could feel em. And like I says, made of steel they was.

The puff went out of us as Plim and Jonah lifted us and set us back in the chair. They tightened the straps then went and stood arms folded either side of the door, which were a bit open.

'Alright, lads?' I says to em. Cos in a way we was like pals, despite everything. They was doormen and I were a doorman, though I were a minder now if you're being technical. Mind you, they was coppers. And you can't never be pals with no copper.

They looked back and didn't answer.

'Got a fag?' I says.

Nothing from that neither, straight off. But after a bit Plim nodded at Jonah, who stepped forward and planted a Benny between me teeth.

'Got a light?' I had to say and all, him just stood there all grim and statue-like. He lit us up and went back to his spot. 'Fuckin' hell,' I says, puffing. ''S matter with you two? Vow o' silence, is it?'

Halfway down the fag someone comes through the door and shuts it behind him. It were an older feller wearing a shirt with stripes on the shoulder and holding a big red folder. He were twice as big as your typical feller in every way. Except his height, which were about same. And his mouth, which would be too little even for a feller half as big. And I can't speak for the bits of him kept hid in his trolleys. He sat across the table from us and waggled a finger in his massive right ear.

It were Big Bob Cadwallader.

You know, the police chief.

Well, I certainly fucking knew him, anyhow. And he knew us. Had a couple of run-ins with him in me time, hadn't I. We had an understanding, like. He knew I were a bit of a lad and I knew he weren't so thick as the other coppers.

'Alright, Bob,' I says.

'Shut up, you cunt,' he says, not even clocking us.

'Heh heh,' I says. 'Still a charmer, eh?'

'I says shut up, you.' He waved Jonah over. 'PC Jones? Do the honours.'

Jonah reached us in two strides and slapped us hard across the cheek. Fucking coppers.

I were all set to say 'Summat on yer mind?' but Big Bob got in first. 'Royston Roger Blake?' he says, opening his big red folder.

I sucked on the Benny and says: 'But . . .'

'You Royston Roger Blake or not?'

'Aye, but—'

'Dear oh dear,' he says, shaking his swede and turning to the last few pages. 'Dear oh dear oh dear. This lot here ain't good.'

'Wossit say?' I says, leaning forward an inch. I couldn't read the writing but I clocked one or two photos here and there. I couldn't make much of them out neither. Except a lot of red.

'Never you mind. It says what it says and it ain't good. Door broken down . . . telephone pulled out o' the wall . . . preliminary blows to the head . . . kitchen knife . . . stabbed forty-seven times . . .'

'Woss that, then?' I says.

Big Bob closed the book. On the front of it were a dirty white label saying 'ROYSTON ROGER BLAKE' in big faded letters. He looked at us for the first time since coming in. 'What this means, Royston Roger Blake,' he says, 'what this means is we got you.' He opened the folder again and started flicking from the middle backwards. 'No, I can't see how you can get around it this time,' he says, slamming it shut again. 'How many lives a cat got, eh?'

'Dunno,' I says.

'Not you. PC Jones, how many lives he got?'

Jonah unfolded his arms and rubbed his face and says: 'Wha? Who?'

'Cat. How many lives he got?'

'What cat?'

Big Bob didn't seem happy. He looked up and started turning his head.

'Nine, chief,' says Plim. He didn't even have to rub his face.

'Thank you, PC Palmer,' says Big Bob, relaxing a bit. 'What were I sayin'?'

'You can't see how he can get around it this time, chief.'

'How many lives you got?'

I looked at Plim and waited.

'Hoy,' shouts Big Bob at us. 'I'm talkin' to you.'

'Oh, right,' I says. 'Well, less have a look here . . . How many'd the cat have?'

'Nine,' says Plim.

'Nine, eh?' I says, rubbing me chin, which were getting right beardy. 'Nine, eh . . .' I says again. But it weren't like a question this time. It were me thinking aloud. I'd always hated grillings with the coppers and this here were typical of one of em. Always asking hard questions, they was. Why couldn't they start easy for once? 'How's that, then?' I says.

Jonah looked at Plim. You could hear him think-ing, *Aye, how's that, then, PC Clever Bollocks?* I could see trouble between them two later on, down the pig club.

'I'll answer that,' says Big Bob, making Plim and Jonah and meself jump. 'Cat's got nine lives cos he's lucky. You been lucky and all, Blake. You been *this* lucky,' he says, showing how thick the folder were. 'But that's that. No more luck. What happens when a cat lost his nine lives, eh?'

Jonah looked at everyone else then goes: 'Dies, don' he?'

'No.'

Jonah went red faced and an inch shorter. Plim smirked at him. Big Bob leaned forward on the table, making it creak. 'He goes to Mangel Jail,' he says. 'And he stays there.'

I dunno what I did then but them two by the door came over and held us down. All I knew were the inside of my head, which were just then showing us the Deblin Hills at sundown and the view south from the crest of the East Bloater Road. Then you got a view of Hoppers on a good night, punters laughing and drinking and that. Last of all you had Hurk Wood clocked from overhead like you was a bird. I'd never been partial to Hurk Wood as you well knows, but the thought of never seeing her again were too much for us. It were Big Bob who slapped us this time.

'Hoy,' he says. 'We'll have less o' that. Where's yer pride, eh? Call yerself a man?' He went back round the table and sat on his chair, making it groan. The hills and the wood and the Hoppers and the East

Bloater Road faded into grey fog. Then lines drew emselves up and down the fog until it were a big stone wall going up and along and backways and frontways for ever and ever amen.

Goodbye, Royston Blake, says Mangel.

'Goodbye, Mangel,' I says back.

'Wossat?' says Big Bob. 'Anyhow, as I were sayin' there it's Mangel Jail fer you, and let that be an end to it.' He got up and winked at us and pissed off out the door. The light were off when I opened me eyes. I closed em again.

I dunno how long but some while later I noticed the light were on, except different this time – less harsh and more shadowy like. I went to flex me arms and found I could lift em. I stretched me legs and all and they went straight out in front of us. In fact no bit of us was strapped down now. So I got up.

There were summat on the table, summat that hadn't been there before. Or perhaps it had been there and I'd not been paying heed. It were a length of rope, wound up tightish.

I picked him up and shook him loose. About four or five yards he were, clean and sort of white and never used by the looks of him. Not a bad bit of rope all in all. I got hold a bit in each hand and yanked. Strong and all. Tow a motor if you wanted it to. And if I'd found it out there on the street I'd have took it home with just such a usage in mind. But I weren't out on the street. I were in here.

And I were headed jailward.

I sank to me knees, the thought of it all coming down on us like a bag of rubbish chucked off a roof.

But I didn't stay there long. Crying only makes matters worse, and ain't right for a feller to do anyhow. I blinked the tears back and held my head high.

And noticed the hook in the ceiling.

Heavy-duty one it were. Iron. Half-inch thick and curled right the way round. I could have swore it weren't there before. Fuck knows how they could have put it there short notice, mind. I could see how they might have dumped a rope on the table but not put a hook up there and plaster around it. I looked down at the rope, which were still in my hands. I looked at the hook again three foot overhead. I stood on the chair and pulled down on the hook with me thumb. It were firm alright. Then I got started on the rope.

Five minutes later and I had a noose hanging off the hook. If I tippy-toed on the chair I could get me swede through it. And that's what I done.

Don't you shed no tears, mind. Not over me anyhow. It's Finney you ought to cry for.

'Soz, Fin,' I says, tightening the rope.

Who'd save him from Doug now? Even if Doug let him go he'd be fucked. With me gone there were no one to look out for him. But I couldn't let that stop us. He'd be fucked anyhow, what with me going to jail.

'We had some laughs, eh?' I says, trying and failing to think of some of the laughs we'd had. I wished I could recall some, mind. I wanted to end it all on a laugh. You dies laughing, you dies happy. I ain't never heard no one say that before but it sounds alright, don't it?

'Heh heh,' I says. 'Heh.'
I kicked the chair from under us.
I hanged.
'Gggggnh,' I says.

18

THE OUTSIDER WITHIN
Steve Dowie, Crime Editor

[This article was found on Steve's desk after we heard the sad news of his passing on. We're putting it here as a tribute to the man and his work. So here's to Steve Dowie, the crime editor who fell foul of the thing he loved writing and editing and going on about most.]
Malcolm Pigg, Chief Editor

Someone answers the telephone at Hoppers but it is not Nick Nopoly. At least he says it is not him. He will not say who he is. All he says is 'He ain't in.'

So Nick Nopoly will not speak to me. Nor will he return my calls. That does not leave much for me to write about.

Being an outsider, little is known of his background. Rumours abound. Some say he is a gangster in hiding, like his predecessor James Fenton. Others say he is a deserting soldier, an escaped lunatic, the messiah . . . a combination of the above. What he did before slipping into Mangel only he can know. What he has done since arriving here we can try to piece together.

For write about Nick Nopoly I must. The trail leads to him and goes no farther. And since he will not tell me about himself, I can only write what I have found out.

Early sightings of him date back five or six months. He was first noticed hanging around the Forager's Arms, alone at first but soon never without Nigel Oberon and Roderick Slee, both residents of Norbert Green and better known respectively as 'Nobby' and 'Cosh'. (Oberon and Slee have appeared on these pages several times in the past in connection with violent and sexual offences. They escaped conviction for the most serious of these, which involved the disappearance of a young girl fourteen years ago.) It is at the Forager's Arms – a pub notorious for its indulgence of under-age drinking – that Nopoly sowed the first seeds of 'Joey'.

With his intimidating new retinue Nopoly gained unhindered access to Mangel's roughest corners, including the amusement arcade. Here he established a network of dealers who took the drug and sold it wherever young people could be found, including schools. It was not long before Joey achieved the saturation it enjoys today.

Where Hoppers fits into all of this remains a mystery. Drugs can be sold anywhere in Mangel, and already are. Turning a pub into a drug den is equivalent to turning a profitable business into a loss-making one on paper, since the main interest is no longer legal beer but illicit drugs. But Hoppers is no ordinary pub. Unsavoury as its history is, Hoppers is the natural hub of Mangel social life. Swapping its sturdy, mature, beer-drinking clientele for youthful yet moribund addicts seems a move calculated to destroy the very fabric of Mangel society.

'Fffffh fffng,' I says.

Come on, I were thinking. *Fucking hurry up, will*

you. But it were getting hard to think now. The rope were squeezing the life out of us but it weren't half taking its time about it.

Then it all ended.

It were like summat snapped inside of us and I were thrown out into the sky. I flew through the clouds like a plane or a bird going very high. Then I landed hard on summat, which I took to be the place where deadfolk goes. It weren't a bad place so far as I could see, but the floor were hard and I smacked my head on it. And it were cloudy all about so I couldn't see nothing anyhow. Someone were lobbing rocks at us and all, one of em hitting my head and a big un landing on me poor hand.

I'd changed my mind now and decided it weren't such a nice place after all. And to be frank with you I wished I'd held on for a bit and gave Mangel Jail a look. Specially when I heared summat coming.

I were thinking it must be the rock-lobbing feller. Or perhaps it weren't a feller at all but a monster or summat. Whatever it were I didn't like the sound of him, shouting and bawling like that. I crawled off the other way and hoped for the best. I could hear more than one of em now, grunting and roaring. I felt about for me monkey wrench. But I were wearing some other feller's clothes now and it weren't there. A big hand got hold of my ankle.

Then the other one.

I screamed. I know screaming's for birds but I weren't in Mangel now, were I. I were in fucking Deadfolkland or summat and normal rules weren't applying. 'Aaaargh,' I says, wondering when they'd chop me legs off. I knew they would. Getting us back, them monsters was, for all the bad things I'd done in life. It were useless to fight. I couldn't beat monsters, could I. And there were nowhere to run.

I lay still and tried shutting it all out.

That's a trick I'd learned as a youngun. You goes right back into your swede and tells yourself them arms and legs ain't you, that gut ain't yours and the arse back there is just a cushion or summat. Works a treat when you gets it just right, no matter how hard your old man's pinging you. Stay like it for hours, you can, even blocking out all the verbal if you goes back far enough into your swede. That's what I done, blocked out all the roaring and rough handling them two monsters was giving us. Weren't til one of em put a fag in me gob and lit it that I came out for a peep.

Big Bob, wernit.

And the other two.

'Woss you doin' here?' I says. Then I worked it out for meself:

I weren't in Deadfolkland no more. Were I.

Big Bob looked at us like I'd just pissed in his mam's kitchen sink. Plim and Jonah was looking up at the ceiling. I did and all. There were a big hole up there and a big dark empty space beyond it.

'Fucking hell,' I says to meself, realising what must have come to pass. A fucking miracle it were. 'Well, lads,' I says puffing on the smoke and rubbing me sore neck where I'd hanged meself dead just now. 'Ta for that.'

Jonah put a cup o' tea in front of us and got a broom from by the door. Plim were already picking up big bits of plaster.

'Right, then,' says Big Bob, sweeping some dust

and crap off the table with his big hand and putting another folder atop it. This un were black. 'JOEY' it says on the front in big letters not faded at all. 'Remember that cat we was on about?'

'No,' I says.

He didn't like that. His little gob tightened up like a belly button. I hadn't meant to piss him off, mind. I just couldn't think what cat he were on about.

'I'll spell him blunt for you, shall I. You been saved. Rescued. Brung back from the dead.'

I looked up at the hole in the ceiling, shaking me swede, and says: 'I know.'

'You don't know,' he says, rubbing his face. 'You dunno the half of it. Seems you've got friends in high—'

'I does,' I says, coughing a bit cos Jonah were just then kicking up a lot of dust around us with his broom. 'I does know I been brung back from the dead. I were in Deadfolkland, right, an' you an' the lads reached in an' hoiked us out through that hole up there, savin' us from them monsters an'—'

'Shut up and listen for once,' he yells, banging his big fists down.

'You ain't in the clear, you know.'

I tapped him on the shoulder and says: 'Fag.'

He flinched, the motor swerving.

'Hoy, watch yer steerin',' says Plim to him.

'I says "fag",' I says, tapping him on the shoulder again.

Jonah turned his head sideways. 'Fuckin' get off us.'

'Hoy,' Plim says again. 'Pack in flobbin' on us, will yer.'

'I never flobbed on yer.' Jonah turned into the Wall Road and put his foot down.

Plim wiped the flob off his face. 'You bloody did.'

'Fuckin' never.' Jonah glared in the rear-view at us. '*He* shoved us.'

'I fuckin' never,' I says.

'Fuckin' did.'

'Giz a fuckin' fag.' I dangled me paw over his shoulder.

After a bit of nothing Plim says: 'Give him a bloody fag, will yer.'

'You give him a fag,' he says, brushing us off his shoulder.

'You bloody knows I don't smoke,' says Plim. 'Give him his bl—'

'*Alright.* Fuck sake.' He rummaged around and lobbed one back at us. I squinted at it in the light spilling in from the street lamps. It were quiet out. My watch says half midnight. The fag were a Benny. Every fucker were smoking Bennies these days. 'Fuckin' Bennies,' I says.

'You complainin'? Giz him back, then. Come on.'

'I ain't complainin'. I'm just sayin', ain't I. Giz a fuckin' light, eh.'

'Woss you sayin'?' He lobbed the lighter hard over his shoulder, just missing us. It pinged off the back window.

I found it on the back ledge atop an old woolly jumper. 'I'm just sayin' "fuckin' Bennies". Crime, is it, sayin' "fuckin' Bennies"?'

'You cheeky fuckin'—'

'Bloody shut it, the both of yer.' You could tell Plim were losing it a bit, wringing his hands and rubbing his fat thighs like that. Never could handle folks rowing, him. 'Blake . . .' He craned back to face us, wafting fag smoke away from his fat head. 'You knows what to do, right? We drops you on the corner an' you goes round back. Sure you don't want us to get you inside?'

'I told you – I works alone.'

'"I works alone".' Jonah taking the piss there.

'Aye, I fuckin' does work alone. I don't need no bumboy mate like you does.'

Jonah braked hard, throwing Plim out of his seat and smacking his face on the screen.

'You bloody twat,' says Plim to him. He were still losing it but not so bad now. You could tell the knock had done him good. He stopped rubbing his face and turned it to me. 'Alright, woss you do once inside?'

I shrugged. 'Go for a piss.'

'Come *on*, Blake.'

'Alright, alright.' I couldn't help it. Plim and Jonah was a couple of pissy-arse fuckers from school. Me and the lads used to walk all over em. I couldn't believe how low I'd sunk to be working with em on a job.

A fucking police job.

'I goes inside and hides,' I says. 'No lights cos we're takin' em by surprise, like. When he comes in I does him. I does Nobby an' Cosh an' all.'

'You don't have to do Nobby an' Cosh.'

'Aye, but Big Bob says it don't matter, right? Says the town'd be better off without them two.'

'You gets Nopoly first, though, alright?' Jonah was staring at us in the rear-view. 'Make sure you gets Nopoly *first*.'

'Why? Who cares who I does first if I gets your one?'

Plim were confused and all. 'Aye, PC Jones. Why?'

'Cos . . . Cos fuckin' . . . You know, cos no matter what happens after you fires that shot, you've done the job. Right? You get one o' them others first an' they might get you.'

I were clocking him in the mirror now. 'My job though, ennit. An' I does it my way. Alright? I'm the pro here.' Cos it were true. How many folks had they topped?

'Just get Nopoly first. I'm tellin' you . . .'

'Alright, PC Jones,' says Plim in a nice soothing voice. He says to me a bit gruffer: 'Then what?'

'Dunno,' I says. 'I fucks off home, I suppose.'

'Wrong. You comes down Strake Hill and meets us in the car park, bringin' the weapons in that holdall. Right?'

'Aye, alright.'

Jonah says: 'An' you stay away from that bar.'

'Woss you sayin'? Sayin' I can't do a job proper?'

'I'm sayin' don't get pissed while yer waitin'.'

'Who says I'm gonna?'

'Just stay away from the fuckin' bar.'

'Yeah, fuck off.' I hated Jonah. You're meant to feel sorry for tossers like him who can't help emselves but I fucking hated the cunt. I don't reckon he liked us neither.

'Right,' says Plim, rubbing his fat little paws. 'Here

we are, then. Blake? Good luck.' He stuck a chubby paw out to us.

I ignored it and says: 'Where's the fuckin' hardware, then?'

He frowned and reached down to the floor. A bit of grunting and groaning later he comes up with a holdall. 'Be careful with this now,' he says. 'It's a powerful weapon.'

'How would you know?' Jonah says, sneering. 'You ain't fired it.'

'I knows cos Big . . . er, Chief Cadwallader telled us.'

'He ain't fired it neither.'

'How'd you know?'

I took the holdall while they was rowing and had a gander inside. It were there alright. Nice holdall and all. Reckon I'd hang on to that after.

'Just remember,' says Jonah. 'Nopoly first. An' don't miss him.'

'Just remember,' I says. 'Fuck off. An' giz yer fags first.' Me reaching a paw out.

He shook his head but I knew I had him. Had to give us everything I needed to get the job done, didn't they. And that meant smokes. He got em out and tossed em back to us.

'Nice one.' I got out, leaving him searching himself for the lighter I had here in me pocket.

I knew how to get into Hoppers. Course I fucking knew. No one had spent more time there than I had over the years. I knew every crook and nanny of that place. I'd had to learn em, hadn't I. You'd not believe some of the shite I'd been involved in down there. So

I won't bother telling you. I'll just get on with this bit here, me standing round the side alley having a go at the window to Nick Wossname's office.

Only it weren't opening this time, were it. He'd changed the fucking latch or summat cos I'd been there for three fags and I hadn't got it budging.

I shook me swede and leaned on the wall, wondering what to do for the best, still feeling like the minder I'd always known meself to be in my heart. Except I were more than a minder now, weren't I, when you looked at it a bit. I had a gun. Minder never had no gun. He had a Ford Capri and his mitts and that were all a minder needed. But I needed a bit extra now, and I had it here in me holdall. So I weren't no minder really.

I were a fucking Clint Eastwood.

And do you know what, soon as I realised it I knew I were doing the right thing. I know the coppers had pushed us into it, but it were like they'd been led to it. Clint had shown em the way so they could show me the way. I just knew that's how it had happened.

I felt it in me bollocks.

I knew that this were it and all. A proper showdown just like what Clint has with bandits all the time. You never saw him nor the bandits walking away with cuts and bruises. You walked away a harder man. Or you squirmed in the sand til the blood ran out of you.

Well, come on then.

Cos I weren't afraid.

I got the gun out. It were a big un alright. I stuck it down the inside of me leather, which the coppers had been kind enough to give us back. It clinked and jangled next to the monkey wrench. I liked that sound. Made us feel like a pro. You needs your wrench for looking after yourself, but you needs summat more for the special job I had to do. I were standing there clinking and jangling and thinking how to get in when I heard summat out back.

I crouched low against the wall, knees cracking, head aching, guts whining from not having no scran for so long. I reached for the pistol but it were tangled and jangled up with the monkey wrench and weren't budging. I got it out finally but only after ripping the fucking coat lining. Have to get a shoulder holster or summat later, although I couldn't think of no shoulder holster shops in Mangel. Maybe Sal could make one for us. She could make us a nice poncho and all. And a hat.

The noise again, right down the back of the car park in the scrub between it and the Wall Road. Twigs cracking. Dry leaves crunching.

I crept on, keeping low and tight to the wall, feeling proper hard with the cold metal in me paws. I flicked the safety off. I ain't thick, you know. A little tree down there were waving about a bit when it oughtn't to be, the wind being low. I crossed to the other side and crept down that wall then tippy-toed down the back, eyes on the tree, gun out front, gut sucked in. A motor revved behind us.

I spun and near fell over. Long lights pointing at the alley entrance. Headlights. A motor turning just now.

I run across the alley and hid behind them big tin bins in the corner. Stinks down there but I'd smelt worse. Furry bastards scuttling away as I settle down on me haunches. I fucking hates rats but I hates the

idea of Mangel Jail worse. Long lights pointed up the
car park now, getting brighter. Motor comes in,
parks herself slap bang centre, turns herself off. 1.3
Capri. Lawnmower engine ticking. Door opens. Bird
comes out.

No fucking kit on.

Leg in plaster.

Fuck me, I'm thinking. Bit skinny, ain't she.

You'd not have known it were Mona from looking
at her face. Like a mask on her it were, blank and
dozy and hiding summat under it. She stands there
blocking the motor's open shotgun door. A foot
comes out and finds her arse, spilling her on the hard
stuff. She looks sideways, face all twisted up and not
happy with her grazed knees and tits and bust leg
and that. But then it's back to blank and dozy and
hiding summat under it.

Boots touching gravel. Feller stands up: Cosh.

Then Nick Wossname comes out the same door.

Nobby getting out driver side.

Nick stands next to the fallen Mona, looking her
over and shaking his head. He's wearing a long
leather coat now that brushes the ground. It don't
suit him. But then no togs ever did suit Nick
Wossname. 'Get her up,' he says, moving on, not
happy. 'Fuck sake get her inside.' He goes to the back
door, lets himself in.

Nobby runs after, catching the door before it
swings to. He holds it open for Cosh, who's picked
her up, holding her to him face to face like he's doing
her. Only he can't be cos his knob ain't out. One
grimy paw reaches round her back. The other's
squeezing her arse cheek. He goes in.

The door starts creaking shut behind him, warning us that this is it, this is your last chance else it's Mangel Jail for you, mate. I get up and spring meself from behind the bins, not even clattering one of em. The Hoppers door is creaking and squeaking, warning. I'm quick over twenty yard so I get there no problem, this being only ten or so. I slot me boot in nice and soft.

I stay like so for a bit – not moving, hardly breathing. Let em get in and settled, pour a drink and spark up and that. I'm a pro, me. I'm Clint and I got bandits in me sights.

Watch and learn.

'. . . ninety-eight, ninety-nine, hundred,' I says under me puff. I open the door ever so quiet. Creaky fucker it is but I ain't having none of it. I peers in. Light comes on in the main bit showing the wood floor and a few chairs and that. I'm hearing grunting and banging. Grunt-bang-grunt-bang-grunt, like. I step in, gun up high.

I let the door swing to nice and slow, then have a thought and reach into me leather.

Monkey wrench out.

But not for twocking heads this time. I bend me knees and set it down quiet in the doorway, stopping the door shutting for proper. The push-down bar is bust as I recalls, and I might wanna get out sharpish.

See? Clint were in us. I fucking swear he were.

It's Nobby doing the grunting-banging-shagging. I knows it cos it can't be Nick. Don't ask us why but I just knows it ain't Nick Wossname shagging Mona out there in the main bit. Just ain't got it in him, has he. And I knows it ain't Cosh cos here he is now walking across the floor in the main bit, turning his head to us slow motion.

'Hoy,' he says, clocking us and stopping dead. 'Hoy, you f—'

But he shuts up there. I shuts him up. I shuts him up dead with a bullet in his head. And I don't even know about it til it's done. The trigger's pulled and the bullet's off and so's his head. I mean it's gone, not on him no more, like. He's stood swedeless, paws still reaching for his cosh, splatter spraying out behind him like a bucket of slops tossed out the back yard. Legs and arms is going jelly but he pulls out his cosh and lobs it a couple o' yards on the wood floor. He goes down then.

'Fuckin' hell,' I says, looking at the gun. Plim said it were powerful, but for fuck sake.

No more grunting-banging now. Only foot-sliding and whimpering. That's Mona with the whimpering, and it's muffled like a bar towel's in her gob or summat. She's trying to scream but it ain't happening for her. That's Nobby with the foot-sliding, trying to get hid before I gets him and all. But he ain't going nowhere. I got my gun and it's a powerful one. I stride into Hoppers, big and hard with a big hard gun.

Having a laugh, ain't I.

Too late, mate, I'm thinking as I clocks his socked ankle slying off behind the bar. The bird's staying put, face down on the raised drinking area with her legs hanging off it and arse in the air, arms tied to a table with a pair of jeans. 'Yer alright, love,' I says, winking at her. But she don't clock us, gagged and shagged and fuck knows what else like she is.

I gets to the one end of the bar now and looks down behind it.

And there he is, curled up tight with no strides nor trolleys, hands over head like that's gonna help him. But it ain't. Nothing's gonna help the ginger-haired cunt now. 'Here's for makin' us ride in a 1.3,' I says. 'An' slappin' our Rache.'

I shoots him in the head.

Only there ain't no bullet coming out this time.

'Hang on a sec,' I says, pulling the trigger again and again. Clickety-click it's going but no bang. 'Cunt,' I'm saying, thinking of Jonah's narky eyes in the rear-view. *Make sure you gets Nick Wossname first time.*

Nobby's hands is coming off his head now. He's eyeing us up and working it out. I'm clicking and clicking while he gets back on his feet, smirk turning his chops up at the corners, showing a line of gappy gnashers like a big bruised banana. He's wearing a footie top and white socks with a blue stripe round the top and fuck all besides. But he ain't bothered by it. The smirk turns into summat not so agreeable. To be honest it weren't so pleasant beforehand but this is worser, lairyer. He's still eyeing us as he picks an optic off the side and smashes it on the bar. Pernod, I reckon, by the whiff.

Just like our Sal used to like when she were on one.

I were saying just now he had a lairy look on his face. But it's summat else now. Can't make up his mind, he can't. His eyes is glistening and his gob turned down like he's trying hard not to blubber. 'You fuckin' killed Cosh,' he says all quiet, holding the jagged Pernod bottle high.

'Aye,' I says.

Him coming closer.

Me clicking the trigger.

No bullet coming out.

'Aye, but . . .'

He goes to vault over the bar. I don't reckon he can do it but he does, not even dropping his bottle. I turn and peg it. I ain't scaredy of him but that bottle don't look friendly. I've seen enough glassings to know how that goes and I ain't having none o' that. So I'm off into the main bit, picking up a chair and lobbing it at him.

It misses but it's alright cos there's plenty more. In the corner of me eye I clocks Nick coming out to check the commotion. He's saying summat but me and Nob ain't listening. Me and Nob got a little game going and no one else can play. Nobby stood there six yard off, glass jaggedy in front of him, legs bent, shifting side to side. I toss another chair but he dodges easy. I'm still holding the gun so I lobs that and all. It gets to him quicker but he still dodges it. I reach pocketward for me monkey. But it ain't there.

Holding the back door open, ennit.

He's closer now, looking lairy and a bit sad. But mostly lairy what with that bottle-end in his paw. I gets another chair and holds it out like he's a lion and I don't wanna get ate. But them chairs is getting heavy and me arms is getting knackered.

I lobs the chair and climbs up onstage.

He moves in sharpish and takes a stab at me poor leg. 'Aaargh,' I says. Cos he's got us a good un there. To be honest things ain't looking too rosy for us. I find a few more chairs onstage and start chucking em at him. Cos I gotta do summat, ain't I. None of em hit him but they hold him off for a bit. Mona's lying still between us, but I ain't bothered about her.

Only two chairs left now and I'm slowing down, arms going jelly. I go to pick the one up but summat hits us hard. A fucking chair. Nobby's lobbed a chair of his own and gets us straight off, the jammy fucker. That ain't fair, I'm thinking, falling over.

He's onstage himself now, me on the deck knackered with a table atop us like a big shield. Then the shield's off as he kicks it aside. He's stood over us with his jaggedy Pernod and his lairy frown.

I sit on my arse, gob agape, paws palm out to him.

He throws himself on us and pins me arms down.

I'm thinking about Finney tied up in Doug's shop.

'Sausages,' I says.

Nobby frowns a bit more, says: 'You what?'

'Bang,' some other feller says.

But it ain't a feller at all. Proper bang, ennit, like a gun. Nobby coughs up some blood and drops the Pernod. Then he carks it.

I shoves him off us and looks down at him. There's a hole between his shoulders like a horse pissed for half-hour in the snow.

'Fuck,' says Nick Wossname down there holding the gun. Long and pointy cowboy one from t'other day by the looks of him.

'Fuckin' fuck.'

19

MANGEL'S WAYWARD SON
Malcolm Pigg, Chief Editor

Years ago, when I was but a fresh-faced reporter with snot running out of his nose and gumming up in his bum-fluff moustache, we on the local news desk got wind of a young lad in trouble with the coppers for something or other. Come to think of it I wasn't so young at the time. But I did have a cold, so I'm not wrong about the snot.

Turns out the lad wasn't in trouble after all. His old man, pissed, fell down the stairs and knocked himself dead, leaving the lad an orphan. I wrote it up and went down the pub. As I sat there fondling my glass I thought about that call coming in back there, and why my first thought had been of trouble. Cynical I might well be, but I don't suspect foul play every time an accident crops up. So why did I this time? I'll tell you why: it were the lad's name. Summat about his name told us it couldn't be anything but foul play.

Royston Blake.

Of course, if you've been a reader of this here paper

any length of time you'll know that name well. Royston this, Blake that . . . Anything bad happens in Mangel, he's right there with his name all over it.

There's the time Hoppers burned down, taking the life of a young woman with it. Whose wife was it? Royston Blake's. Who got arrested for it? Royston Blake. Who got off on a technical?

You guessed him.

Then there's the goings-on with the Munton brothers a couple of year back. Folks dying left, right and middle, there was, including Blake's cohort Tyrone Finney (multiple chainsaw injuries). Blake was in the frame around that time too, and I'll admit that this newspaper used up a lot of ink telling you about it. But what happened? He got off again. Munton brothers got the blame for it, along with Blake's other cohort Nigel Leghorne – the lot of them believed to have absconded into the world beyond.

Alright, perhaps I'm being a mite unfair on the man. Nothing ever sticks to him, so on paper he hasn't done much wrong. But whenever something bad happens . . . rest assured the name Royston Blake will be all over it.

And now this, the murders of a young doorman barely out of school, and our very own dearly departed fellow Mangel Informant, Steve Dowie. That's right – something bad is happening again, right under our noses. And whose name is all over it, yet again?

'You what?' I says. Not cos I didn't hear it. Cos I couldn't understand it. The whole situation here, like.

Nick Wossname started to say summat but it weren't coming out right. So he shook his head and says: 'Never mind. Come down here.'

I came down careful. He had a gun and I were here to kill him, weren't I. But I knew he wouldn't shoot us. I just knew.

'You alright?' he says, shuffling the stupid leather coat off his weedy shoulders. He sat on a stool and put the gun on the bar. He had a little blue bag and all that he put next to it. Bit like my new holdall it were, but blue and little. He looked over at Mona. She were bent over the stage still. Nick didn't look too happy about it.

I still couldn't understand. I didn't reckon I ever would. I sat meself on a stool two up from him. 'Aye,' I says, ignoring all the cuts and bruises and ruptures and slashes and everything else giving us grief just then. 'I'm alright, ain't I.'

'Look, I'm sorry about that earlier on. Me threatenin' you and that.'

I shrugged.

He clocked us close and says: 'You know, don't you.'

'Know what?'

'Come on, man . . .'

I were clocking him now. 'What the fuck is you on about?'

'You serious?' He got a fag out and offered us one.

I took it and says: 'Ta.'

We smoked.

'You know who I am. You must do.'

'Telled you already,' I says. 'I never remembers yer last name. Can't help it.' Cos you just don't call folks by their last name, does you. You don't go round shouting 'Hoy, Davis' or what have you. More like 'Hoy, Keith'. Mind you, there's always exceptions.

There's meself, for one. But Royston's a hard name for some folks to say, so I gets called Blake. Then there's Finney . . .

'Fuck my last name. It's a bollocks name anyway. Who the hell calls himself Nopoly? My real name is . . . I can trust you, can't I, Blake? Not like these two bastards here, Nobby and Cosh. Fuckin' losers. I sort of hoped they'd end up like this and when I saw you here tonight doin' it I thought, *Yeah, Blake's the man*. I don't blame you for a second, Blake. I know how they provoked you.'

'Aye,' I says. But I weren't really listening now. I were thinking of Finney. I slied a gander at me watch. Quarter past one. 'Fuck,' I says under me breath, feeling the sap seeping south.

'I'm no outsider, Blake,' he says. 'I'm Mangel like you, through and through. I may not like it but I am. Aye, took us a long time to hide me Mangel accent it did, in that there big city.'

I couldn't fucking believe it. Hour and a bit late I were. I ought to have sorted this bollocks out and sprung Fin days ago, not an hour and a quarter late.

'Blake, listen. Doug's corner shop, years and years ago. Five thievin' tykes lookin' to rob sweets. Doug comes in and grabs one of em. Everyone scarpers but that one boy. Remember now?'

But Doug'd be alright about it, wouldn't he? He wouldn't put Fin through the sausage maker right away, would he? Nah, course he wouldn't. He'd get up early and do it first thing like as not. Don't want to wake no neighbours up.

'Sammy Johnson,' he says. 'That's my real name. That's who you knew me as. I thought you'd recognise me, outside here the other night. I couldn't believe it when you didn't. But I suppose it has been a long time . . .'

Mind you, what if Doug did turn Fin into bangers? What if I'd fucked it all up and Fin were getting ground up right now? I shook my head hard. No, I didn't believe it. I couldn't.

'You don't believe us?' he says. 'How about this: your dad used to shave yer head once a week on Sunday nights to stop you gettin' fleas. You never knew your mum and no one knew what had happened to her, not even you. There were five of us that day in the corner shop: you, me, Johnny Fuidge, George Bundage, and . . . er . . .'

Weighing it all up I reckoned I had a good chance. If I got it all sorted now and went round Doug's within the hour I had a good chance of being alright. I could give Doug what he wanted and get Fin back.

'Finney, that's him. Hey, I heard about him. What a shame, eh? Chainsaw, wasn't it? What a way to die. You must have been gutted.'

Poor old Fin. I had to get him out. Your mates is all you got, ain't they.

'You probably don't know what happened to me. My mum and dad moved away after the . . . you know, in the corner shop. It was hard for them. This is hard for me now. I never told no one before. Doug . . . Fuck, this is so hard to say. Doug . . . did stuff to us. And do you know what? Do you know what the worst of it is? No one did a thing about it. Not even my mum and dad. They believed me, even after the police said I was lyin'. But they wouldn't do nuthin' about it. Dad wouldn't go and slay the dragon in the corner shop.'

Like I says before, the pistol were a long and pointy one like what Clint has. I'd been eyeing it up all the while, sat there all suggestive like it were.

'That's what it needs, Blake. It's taken me twenty-four years to work it out. Nuthin's gonna get better until the dragon is slain.'

I started moving me paw along the bartop. Nick were still going on about summat or other and he weren't looking.

'That's why I came back here, Blake. To settle the score. I tried gettin' him back the same way, fuckin' up his precious little girl over there. Look at her. Fuckin' pathetic, ennit, fucked up on drugs, doin' whatever for a fix. And I mean *whatever*, Blake. You wouldn't believe . . . What the fuck are you doin'?'

It were a good weight in my hand and I preferred it to the one I'd shot Cosh's head off with just now. There were no safety wossname on it like on the other one. So I pulled back the curly thing on the top and it made a nice clicking sound like you gets on them old cap guns. I pointed him at Nick Wossname's head. 'Soz, mate,' I says.

'Wha . . . What are you doin'? I thought we . . .'

'Aye, but I gotta do this, so . . .'

'What? Why?'

I shrugged. 'Someone asked us to.' I didn't have no grudge against this feller. Didn't even know him, did I. So I wanted him to see why I were doing it. 'I gotta do it, mate. No hard feelin's,' I says by way of explanation.

'Hold up . . . Who put you up to this?'

'Don't matter, mate. Best shut yer eyes . . .'

'No, wait. Blake, we can sort this out. You're bein' paid for this and you want the money. I can understand that.' He were talking a bit fast and I were only getting bits of it. 'But listen, we can go away. Look at all this . . .' He opened up the little leather bag. Full of other little bags it were, placcy uns full up of sweets like them others I'd seen before, except there was blue uns and yeller uns here as well as the white uns. 'There's more where this lot came from. I'm a fuckin' factory, Blake. I churn em out by the lorry-load. We can make a fuckin' fortune in the big city. We can go there, Blake, you and me. You don't wanna stay in this dump.'

'Big city, eh?' I says.

'Yeah. That's where all this started. I used to make em for some guys there but you . . . Me and you, Blake, we could clean up. Come *on*, Blake. Whaddya say?'

I had a little think. The big city, fuck sake. Me in the big city. I knows Mangel folk can't leave Mangel and that but I'd be leaving with an outsider. That's got to work different, ennit? What do you reckon?

And what the fuck were there to keep us in Mangel? I weren't even on the door at Hoppers no more. And as for Fin . . .

Well, he'd be meat by now. Wouldn't he.

'Alright, then,' I says. I meant it and all. Big city here we come, straight down the East Bloater Road in Sammy's flash outsider motor. 'Alright, then,' I says again. 'Less fuckin' go.'

He had time for a quick smile. We smiled at each other for about a second altogether. It were a nice time all in all, that second or so. I trusted him and he trusted us and we both knew about it. We was the answer to each other's worries, though it had took us a fair bit o' shilly-shallying to come by that knowledge. Aye, it were a sweet moment. But then his left eye popped out.

Fucking horrible it were. Just sort of went bang, flying out and squirting lardy stuff on us. He went down. Dead, by the looks of him.

I still had the big city in my head as I lobbed meself over the bartop. I were doing it by reflex, like Clint does when there's shite flying. Cos eyes don't just pop out like that for no good cause. Normally you've got summat pushing em from behind. Like a bullet or summat. Specially when there's a bang.

I squatted low for a bit, then poked me swede up between the beer pumps. A feller were stood there holding a gun.

Dave.

Back from the fucking dead.

Only just, mind. Looked a right state he did, and if he weren't stood up you'd have thought him a month past burying. Filthy he were, covered in muck and dried blood and fuck knows what else. One of the sleeves on his donkey jacket were ripped right off. Both shoes was missing. He'd strapped bits of old truck tyre to his feet with rags instead. His glasses was still on but they was shattered to fuck. Looked like a pair of milk bottle tops strung together with twigs.

'I told you,' he were screaming, waving the little pistol around. It were the one I'd clocked him with in Hurk Wood back then. He came closer, looking down at the dead Nick Wossname. 'I blinkin' told you not to push us, Blake. But you didn't listen, did yer. None of em listened.'

I covered me ears as he shot Nick a couple more times.

'Well, no one pushes us no more. You hear? No blinkin' bastard's pushin' us never again. Thought you could kill us, eh? Eh, Blake?' Couple more gun pops. 'Who's laughin' now?'

He started laughing. 'Who's blinkin' laughin' now, eh? Who—'

Another bang.

And a thud.

'Well, fuck me,' I says, peeping over the bartop at Dave down there, half his guts out. 'Well, just fuck me,' I says, clocking PC Plim over there by the back door, dropping his gun and honking all over the hard stuff.

20

DOWIE KILLER CAUGHT
Robbie Sleeter, Junior Reporter

A man has been arrested for the double murders of Informer *reporter Stephen Dowie and* Hoppers *doorman Dean Stone. Dave, of Fosbert Street, Mangel, has also been charged with the triple murders of Nick Nopoly, Nigel 'Nobby' Oberon, and Roderick 'Cosh' Slee, all three taking place at* Hoppers *last night (see SHOOTOUT AT HOPPERS, page 7, paragraph 11). Dave, who went on to kill himself, is being held at Mangel police station.*

Investigating officers believe Dave went mad after crashing his car north of Mangel several days ago. A police psychologist had this to say: 'The impact of the crash could have dislodged something in his brain, turning a mild-mannered, law-abiding citizen into a bloodthirsty mass murderer. There's no other explanation, is there, Bri?'

'No,' replied Dr Wimmer.

'I can't believe it,' said Tracey Flagel of Margaret Hurge Twentieth Century Hair Design, where Dave was

employed as a hair-sweep. 'Mind you, I always said he'd come to no good. Always the quiet ones you has to watch out for. Ain't that right, Marge?'

'Did you hear what they found in his bedsit?' said Marge. 'Guns. Hundreds of them. Bullets and all. No one knows where he got them from. Nor why he had them. What would someone like him want with guns?'

'Marge, I don't know.'

'Exactly.'

In a statement released this morning Police Chief Bob Cadwallader said: 'It is always a shame when it comes to this. Truly I think it is. That said, we've got to look on the bright side. Justice has been served and this town has been delivered from a vicious madman. So really you can't complain, can you.'

Asked about Royston Blake – hitherto the main suspect for Dowie's murder – the chief said: 'What of him? I told you we've got the murderer, didn't I? You want to know about Royston Blake, go ask him. I've got nothing to say about him.'

OTHER NEWS: The body of a man was found on a bench in Vomage Park early this morning. Jack Jones, an unemployed panel beater and former convict from Piecemeal Road in the Muckfield district, leaves five illegitimate children. 'Going by the damage in his chest area,' said a police pathologist, 'I'd say he had a massive heart attack, brought on by prolonged alcohol abuse. You could tell he was an alcoholic just by looking at him. And he stank of urine, which just confirms it. I mean, come on – tattoos all over him, stinks of piss, sleeps on park benches. Ain't hard to work out the kind of man he were. Is it, Bri?'

'Yes,' replied Dr Wimmer.

'Well?' he says.

'I done it,' I says. 'Can I have our Fin back now?'

He looked us up and down, his eyes the only bit of him moving. Then they went behind us. 'Where is she, then?'

I were looking behind him and all. The shop were dark but I could see the shelves had hardly nothing on em now. Couldn't see nothing else in there neither. 'In the motor,' I says. 'In that motor there.' I pointed to the 1.3 Capri a few cars up.

'And the feller who led her astray?'

I shrugged. 'Woss you want us to do? Bring you his head? He's dead, ain't he. Read it in the paper.'

Doug looked at us for a bit, chewing his lip. 'Well, bring her up, then.'

'But she ain't—'

'I says bring her.'

I went back to the 1.3. She were sat shotgun and hadn't moved. Looking straight on, she were, eyes half open, head tilted roadside a bit. I'd told him she were in the motor, but to be honest there were only about half a person here.

'Come on, love,' I says, opening the door.

She didn't move. I might have known I'd have to lug her. I don't mind carrying birds on most days. Specially ones not wearing nothing besides my leather. But I just didn't fancy this un here. Weren't just the plastered leg neither. She seemed a bit mucky, like. And not in the good way. I bent down to get me arms under her.

'I knows how to make it, you know,' she says as I slipped a paw under her thighs.

I stepped back. I'd reckoned her out of it, and her

turning out to be in it after all threw us just a mite. 'You what?'

'Joey. I knows how to make it. I watched him do it tons of times. It's easy when you knows how. Just a matter of gettin' the balance right.'

I looked at her close up. Eyes still wasn't focusing and her face were sweating a bit. She were sick and fucked in the head, in short, which is why she were talking shite. I mean, who the fuck is Joey?

She got up and started hobbling. I were grateful for that. I took her arm to stop her falling over.

'Where's her clothin'?' says Doug back at his shop door. 'And what happened to her leg?'

I shrugged. 'Found her like it, didn't I.'

I could see he wanted to say summat else about that but the words just wouldn't come for him. He got her by the arm and yanked her in.

'Er . . .' I says as he went off into the darkness. 'I wants me leather back, you know.'

He disappeared into the back room but I knew he'd be back cos he'd left the door open. I lit one of Jonah's fags but I weren't enjoying it so I stubbed it. Me lungs was telling us they wanted real air for a change, even if it always stank of shite in Mangel. I whiled away the time counting me cuts and bruises instead. Couple of minutes later I heard a squeaking sound.

'Here,' says Doug, wheeling the chair out. Piled up on it were some tinnies. About four hundred of em, I reckoned. On top o' them were two trade-size cartons of bennies. My leather were hanging off one of the handles. 'That's us square,' he says, still stood there. He were waiting for us to come back at him like as not. Then he plonked summat else atop the lager and fags and slammed the door.

I picked up the thing Doug had plonked and turned it over. A paper bag it were with summat stodgy and heavy inside. I sniffed it and put it back on the fags.

No mistaking the whiff of sausages.

I were pushing Finney's cripple chair back over the road when I noticed the light on upstairs in my house. That's a bit odd, I thought. But it didn't rattle us too much. Weren't like a copper car were parked out front. And no one else were after us right then, so far as I knew. Nobby and Cosh must have left the light on t'other night when they'd been touching the place up like as not.

Mind you, there were a strange Viva estate parked out front. Pissy yellow it were. I'd fucking had it with shite motors, and if she were still there when I got up the morrer I'd shift her meself.

I let meself in the front door.

I'd been wrong about the light upstairs. Weren't Nobby and Cosh left it on. Some fucker were in here. I could hear him up there with the Hoover.

I didn't know what to make of that. Nor the hall and kitchen, as I walked through em pushing Finney's chair. Been cleaned good and proper they had. It were hard to be lairy when someone's broke in your house to clean it. I opened the fridge. Clean in there and all. Milk, butter, cheese, bottle of sparkling, eggs, bacon . . .

A bottle of fucking sparkling?

I cracked open one of Doug's tins and sucked on it. Didn't taste right. Drinkable just about but slightly off. I poured him down the sink and tried another from off the bottom.

Same.

I went to the bottom of the stair. That Hoover were still going. I knew what it were now. Coppers had sent someone round to clean up as their way of saying ta for all the work I'd put in for em just now. I'd fucked off with Mona before none of em could tell it to me face. Aye, that's it.

I wandered into the front room.

It were all arse about. None of Fin's things was there, just a couple of armchairs and the telly from Sal's flat on a little table in the corner. I put the bangers atop the telly and flopped into one of the chairs.

'Bye, Fin, mate,' I says, looking at the sausages. 'I tried.'

I fucking did and all, didn't I.

It were a smell what woke us. A nice smell. And a sound. Sizzling. Back there in the kitchen.

'Well?' says someone. A bird. 'What d'you think?'

I turned. 'Alright, Sal,' I says. Cos she were stood by the door, hands on hips, smile on chops, apron round that big belly of hers. 'Woss I think to what?'

'Here,' she says, coming over and parking herself on me knee. 'The house. Done it nice, ain't I? Only took us a day an' all. Mind you, this room here were the hardest. I bagged all that rubbish from in here and dumped it, Blakey. You don't mind, do you. Only it were your dead mate's stuff and he's . . . You know, he don't need it where he is.'

She were stroking my cheek. Her hand stank of

bleach. She had her arm round us, pulling me face to her tits.

Her apron smelt of sausages.

'Nuthin' worth keepin' anyhow,' she says. 'And besides, we needs the room now.'

I looked at the telly. Them bangers weren't there no more. Gone and cooked em, hadn't she.

She'd gone and cooked our Fin.

'Blake,' she says, pushing my head back so she could see it. 'We've been rowin' a bit of late. You knows it and I knows it. But I forgives you. I knows you didn't mean it and I don't care no more anyhow. We got to put all that behind us, Blake. Things is gonna be different now. I'm . . .'

Her eyes was wet. A little tear rolled from her eye and settled in the deep red furrow across her cheek.

'I tried to tell you before, Blake. I'm . . .'

She'd had her stitches out but not even half an inch of slap could hide the damage.

'We're havin' a babby.'

She flung her arms round us and started sobbing.

After a bit she got up, saying: 'Oh, don't look at us. Let me fix me face first. You go an' get that bubbly from the fridge, eh? Ain't it marvellous, though. A babby. *Our* babby . . .' She went up the stair.

I got up. Soon as I opened the cellar door I knew from the smell that she hadn't been down there. Never had been down there she hadn't. Scaredy of it, weren't she. I turned the light on, went in and bolted the door behind us.

'Oh, feller phoned for you about your car,' she says. Her upstairs and me in the cellar and still I could hear her. 'Says he wants some money for fixin'

it. I . . . Blake? I hope you don't mind. I sold it,
Blakey. Part-exchanged it for summat more sensi-
bler. See it out front, did you? Nice one, ennit. We'll
be needin' that now, with the babby an' all.'

I got the placcy bags out. Ten of em there were,
stuffed down the lining of me leather. I poured the
sweets out onto the wooden box I used to put me
feet on. White uns and blue uns and yeller uns.
Couple o' pink uns and all. I knew what they was
now. Them sweets we used to get in Doug's shop
when we was younguns, weren't they.

What the fuck had Nick Wossname been doing
with em?

'Oh, and Blakey? That other man rang for you. You
know – wossname from that little pub you goes to.
Nathaniel, is it? He says don't worry about settlin'
yer debt to him just now but he may call it in later.
That about a bar tab is it, Blakey? You'll have to stop
all that now, what with the babby. I dunno . . . You're
such a naughty boy, you. An' you knows what I does
to naughty boys . . . Blakey? Blakey?'

I got up and put summat on the vid. When I sat
down again Clint were riding his horse and I
couldn't hear Sal no more, which were alright. I took
a handful of them sweets and put em in me gob.

I started chewing.